Rejex

A Dystopian Novel

Ashley Jude Collie

Pulp Hero Press
The Most Dangerous Books on Earth
www.PulpHeroPress.com

Editor: Bob McLain
Layout: Artisanal Text

ISBN 978-1-68390-184-6
Printed in the United States of America

Pulp Hero Press | **www.PulpHeroPress.com**
Address queries to bob@pulpheropress.com

CONTENTS

PART TWO

Mainlandia Calls

PART THREE

And Everything Under the Sun

Comes the Darkness

"Imagine if you will, looking at act one, scene one, of a living nightmare!"

So says One-10, a late-20s scientist, a cheeky geek in a dull gray windbreaker, who sits in a spiffy, motorized power chair muttering into his headset. In the far distance to his left, he gawks at dancing fires that reflect in his eyes. The fires are controlled by firefighters, but the flames devour everything in their immediate path—green grass, lush foliage, and innocent creatures. The sap from giant trees bleeds red rivers onto the ground. And the hungry fires leave nothing but destruction. One-10 thinks he also sees a charred human hand colored with a splash of blue, and pitifully reaching up from out of the charred ash.

"And he's off..." replies a droll voice over his headset.

"A bloody, living nightmare!"

"Again with the drama, One-10."

"Fix your camera, One-9, because you ain't eyeballing our growing wasteland up here!"

"And always with the smartass comments!"

"Well, as Confucius said, 'Never give a sword to a man who can't dance, eh?'"

"There you go again!"

"Hey, someone's got to be a pain in big bully's butt!"

Away from the fires, One-10 leads a small research team of scientists and engineers. He hears an irritating *bing* and looks down to swipe an annoying pop-up off his handheld: "Conformity is a warm blanket of bliss." Another *bing* also goes off on the wearable computer on his wrist. To which he mutters with a crooked smirk, "Yeah, PISS off!"

"What'd you say, One-10?"

"Oh, just thinking out loud of how damn freakin' happy we all are," he lies.

His power chair idles near a shimmering domed structure away from which stretches the scavenged, bone-dry Basin of Mainlandia. This flat man-made desert lies between a mountain range way to its west and a lush green forest way to its east. On the Basin's northernmost fringe, where the controlled fires burn, a black and ugly open pit is being dug to extract oil from the sand below the surface. And day-by-day, the lush forest is either burned or chopped away. The ever-retreating green vainly tries to battle back against the murderous attack of burning flames, chainsaws, shovels, and crushers. But all that's left in the wake of this assault are bleeding trees, smushed plants, and more charred bones.

There's no sweet birdsong this early morn, as they all seem to have skedaddled the hell out of here. And, even though the big bashing machines are still asleep, dawn shyly peeks out, almost afraid to see what new horrors have been seared and hacked into the landscape.

While One-10 works near the dome, the rest of his team of pale young adults, dressed in similarly grubby windbreakers, surveys the construction and destruction on the Basin. One of them, who lags behind, is consumed by his ultra-slim e-device. A pop-up promo flashes, "Be careful, be clever. Don't act like a Rejex and you won't get expelled to Geto, like never."

The message is clear—conform or be cast out!

With a DNA strand symbol on the right breast of his windbreaker, and wearing headphones, this lagging scientist is so focused on the graphs and stats on his device, he's totally clueless to something going on just ahead of him—several ancient but vicious weapons that hiss and hurl through the air not fifty yards away. The primitive projectiles rain down upon the Basin's arid land. *Sharp, zing, zang!* The spears and arrows soon arrive at the feet of his fellow researchers. *Zing, zang!* The group stops dead still, finally sensing something's not quite right. Wakey, wakey, people!

They're scared frozen in their tracks. Their mouths become as dry as the ravaged land. And their eyes truly bug-open wide when they see who's throwing the spears—a couple of savage-looking, almost naked but magnificent creatures covered in blue paint. The pale scientists are so shocked, they try to scream but nothing comes out. They finally back up, then churn their legs to stumble and run. Not used to running, they awkwardly fall over each other as they head back toward their oblivious co-worker.

Mainlandians aren't much into touching each other, but needs must, so they grab hands as their hearts pound and their legs pump with a sound something like *tap-tap-terap.*

Also oblivious, One-10 doesn't hear or see what's happening to his fellow researchers, so he closes off a "Don't forget, Thirty days and counting..." pop-up on his wristband, rebelliously cursing under his breath. "And, screw the freakin' countdown!" He finally looks up ahead to the Basin, blinks to clear his eyes, then is totally alarmed to see his buddies scrambling toward him. He shouts into his headset. "Aiyaa! I think we're in some deep do-do, One-9!"

"Okay, what've you done, now?" comes the reply.

"Freakin' nothing, I swear. But this is soooo not looking good!"

The stumbling, bumbling group grabs the lagging man and yanks him along. The projectiles continue to rain down on the rock-hard Basin as the research team screams bloody murder for HELP and desperately runs toward One-10 and the dome behind him.

Humming and shimmering like an oasis of escape, the dome entity casts a shadow over One-10, who now screams back to his escaping colleagues. "Run! Run faster!"

The scientist spins his power chair around to the dome and commands, "Open, open, open!" But the voice recognition system doesn't work as he hears gears grinding. "Hey, it's scientist One-10 up here!" He shifts position, hoping that will help communication. "Hello, can you hear me now?!" But still nothing. "Anyone, hello? We got to get out of here!"

The voice of his associate shouts back over his headset, "Keep trying, One-10!"

"One of those old magic wand thingamajigs would help right now!"

"No time for bad jokes, One-10, do it manually. Pronto!"

One-10 places his trembling hand at a certain spot, and a small section of the dome's wall slowly appears to break down into individual molecules. "Anytime now would be good! Hello! Please open up!" the rebel with a cause now pleads as he glances over his shoulder at the horrifying picture—a group of scared shitless and weak-kneed geeks with laser pencils in their pockets being chased by fearsome blue warriors.

But after more gritty grinds, and a torrent of cuss words by One-10, the portal finally swooshes open. The research team stumbles straight toward the section as one spear hungrily finds its mark, burying itself into one man's shoulder. But somehow they all manage to bumble and stumble through the portal into complete blackness.

"One-10? One-10, are you safe?" says the voice on the headset.

There are some deathly silent moments. Then, "Sure thing, Dar, but can someone, down where you are, turn on the lights? You know how I just hate being in the dark!"

Outside, the dome's portal shifts back to shimmering solidity, as more spears and arrows clatter harmlessly against its outer shell. Clank, clank, clank!

And, somewhere else, in a hushed, dimmed suite buried deep below the Basin in the Underground City, a 3-D hologram displays a close up image of a blue-faced, long-haired savage hurling a spear against the dome's shell. Someone who looks like a hooded holy man is intently watching as he says over and over, "Fake, fake, fake! This whole setup is fake!" He then falls to his knees in front of the holographic battle of high-tech against wooden spears. "Please forgive the blue brutes, for they know not what they do!"

With what looks like a speckled band wrapped serpent-like around his left wrist, he then prays, "Thirty days and counting—comes the great Darkness. Thirty days and counting..."

But way over in the West, on a sort of low-tech, island nirvana called Geto...

PART ONE

Geto's Paradise of Perils
Mainlandia Rules
Occulo Help Us

CHAPTER ONE

Aiya's Hope

Last night, I dreamed I almost escaped paradise.

But then something awful happened. And, somehow I feel we got to get out of here!

I'm Aiya, and with my handmade goggles on to keep out dawn's early light, I'm laying half-asleep outside on a cozy bed of springy new grass, under my favorite leafy pal—a massive, gnarly tree that they say is as old as passing time itself. I've climbed it, swung from it, and fallen from it, scraping my flesh and scraping away my childhood with every tumble. And over time, this big leafy bud has become a friend, providing an umbrella of protection from nighttime cold in the past, and from the chills of coming change.

Even with my goggles on, I keep my eyes purposely closed—I mean who really likes to wake up from a snug sleep or, worse still, wake up to a nightmare. I hear birds shrieking out like a wake-up alarm. But I'm not ready to get up, so I settle back in to figure out some things that are bugging me.

We live on an island called Geto in a steampunk-driven village. It's way rustic. We have few metals, no plastics, and no leather. And everything, from our clothes to paper and fuel, is mostly made of natural stuff like hemp and resins. Our village homes are constructed of rattan and bamboo, of anything we can happily cobble together, a kind of grab-what-you-can tech.

Our village life is much like that of the counter-culture communes I've heard about. In fact, I look kind of like a post-modern, hippie-punk, as many in my exiled tribe do. However, it's said that all of my tribe, each one of us, are supposedly called "Rejex"—outsiders who somehow don't match up to normal. It's true, we're all oddballs. Some are artists, some alchemists, some are left-handed, some are gay, some have afflictions like Tourette's like my mentor Alkima. But we're basically misfits with attitude, living in our really green but low-tech, oceanside paradise. Oh, did I say that we've been banished by a bunch of bullies on Mainlandia? Hello, and that so pisses me off! And like any outside-the-box-thinker, as all we Rejexes are, I have so many questions. Burning questions, like, why am I a Rejex? I'd do anything to find out.

But be careful what you wish for, eh? Because last night, I remember from deep in my sleep that I found myself alone in pitch darkness. Cold and alone without my tribe, I felt disconnected. So I shouted out, "Where am I? What's going on? Anyone there?!"—but no answers echoed back. Bravely, I asked, "Did I tell you I hate the darkness?"

Seconds dragged into minutes. I shivered in my aloneness.

Then I heard someone clear his throat. I asked, "Is anyone there?" Nothing came back. Until one candle was sparked up, revealing a man in a hooded cloak high above me. With his head bowed, he had his hands clasped like he was praying. Was he some holy man? I wondered. Then I asked, "So, like, who are you?"

"You've come all the way here, little one, and that's all you've got—where am I, who are you, what's going on? But, what do you really want to ask, Aiya, my child?" he whispered in a guru-like tone. Even though I couldn't see his face, there was a fluorescent glow from under his hood, which was totally weird and scary.

And somehow he knew my name. So maybe I was tapping into something in my dreams, some mystic who could answer my most personal questions, so I let fly: "Okay, so why am I called Rejex? Who gets to decide who's IN and who's OUT? And, why? What's beyond our island? And, oh yeah, who's my father?"

"Better. But for now, all I'll tell you is, thirty days and count-ing—comes the Darkness. So, all praise to the Darkness... because out of dark night comes new light!"

Could he have been more vague? Thirty days and counting? And, what darkness? Anyway, the candle blew out and the "holy man" crept away into the back regions of my mind. Yeah, just stay there! I mean, who needs some spooky guru in your dreams! Like, whatever! Except, there was something else. Why did I feel some icky connection to him?

Anyhoo, as my dream shifted to something way cooler, I heard something else, the brave hurtling of feet.

> *Tap-tap-terap!* Four hooves, that percussive pound.
> *Tap-tap-terap!* Edging closer, cracking the ground
> Eating up the miles between us
> *Tap-tap-terap!*
> Hidden here in the shadows, I see you first
> Sparking brighter, wisps of flame, a magnificent mane
> Heart throbbing, you crash through
> the membrane that separates us.
> Appearing inside my defenses
> All rearing power and grace, all wild-eyed and untamed
> As dark as I am pale, as fierce as I am afraid.
> But, yet you slow, and I fix my magick gaze
> Now you stop, and then I think I have you!
> My partner, my steed, my awesome Red...my fire horse!

Just as quickly, my "fiery" creature thundered off. He had first galloped into my dreams when I was just knee-high to a late summer cricket. To imitate him I used to scoot about on all fours like a small pony, as soon as I was able. Then, when I could walk, I went almost straight to running, stumbling at first but trying so hard to gallop like a horse. It was funny to watch and made my mother, Ma-Tu, smile.

Now my fantastical fire horse is happily coming more often into my teenaged dreams. Maybe it has to do with the arrival of spring, with the beginning of new life in our whispering fields of flowers and in the trilling trees. It may also have to do with the stirrings inside my own body and soul. Ma-Tu says, "Little one, if we don't change, we don't grow. If we don't grow, we aren't really living."

Or maybe he's coming for some other reason. He now teases me with the hope of escape. But always before I can grab him, he goes thundering off by himself into the night, free to explore where I know I can't yet go. And the more times that he comes to me in my dreams, the more I want to grab his mane, jump onto him, hold on real tight and finally get to see what's beyond my island paradise of Geto.

As memories of last night's dreams ebb and flow in the shallows between sleeping and waking, my fire horse teasingly reappears again and for the first time, like ever, he kneels to accept me. Me, a Rejex. I'm tickled with excitement. But then I want to scream when I hear the savage slash of rope, and see that the holy man is whipping it through the air.

Now, I try to shout "Run!" but nothing comes out of my mouth. And then the rope strikes, circling my fire horse's proud neck, and I hear a winch yank the rope back hard and tight. His sensitive eyes bulge wide in shock, as the tight rope almost strangles him. Oh, no! The scene reminds me of a mythical story, of another poor thing. Some dude named Prometheus, a brave but chained creature who had his liver pecked out every day in punishment for helping people by bringing them fire. But their gods put out that fire. And then darkness ruled.

Now, deep in my mind, everything also fades back to black. And all I can hear is my horse's awful cries, the frightened neighs of my downed friend fading into the recesses of my mind. His cries jerk me completely out of my sleepy fantasy turned full-blown nightmare. What people would want to tie down such a beauty, and put out its fire? Only scared, little-minded people, bullies who praise the darkness like that "holy man"!

It takes me a few seconds to orient myself. I open my eyes slowly, fearing the worst. But all's cool, I'm in the light and there's no darkness. I'm now fully awake but sheltered under my gnarly friend, safe and protected from above and around. I remove my goggles and pull back my long black hair from my face with my tattooed hands. They both still have awesome henna designs inked on them, designs that snake up my wrists, hiding the youthful scars of my "tomboy" exuberance. People say I'm pretty, that my almond-shaped eyes are hypnotic. That the tiny folds that cover the inner corner of both eyes give me an exotic look. But when I check my reflection deep in waters, I don't see it. My two front teeth are a little too big. My nose is not perfectly straight. I was a little chubby as a kid. It goes on. But that's okay, I'm just me...Aiya, an outsider, a Rejex, a little tilted, and sometimes a bit of a goon, but someone with a fiery dream and an instinct about things.

I push away the hemp-woven blanket covering me on the grass, sit up while throwing out my arms: "Bonjour, everyone!" I shout to the sky overhead and to no one in particular, just glad to be alive. As I look back down, I glimpse a small black shadow creep away with a "meow..." Like, was the kitty watching me? Whatever, he's now gone.

Then I reach out to pick up and pocket several magick charms, like mandrake roots, that I'd left circled around me for added protection as I slept. You just gotta know that even paradise has its perils. 'Cause I've seen them, up close and personal. And, pyew, they stink!

I then shade my eyes and track down the hillside half a mile to our bamboo home below, as smoke puffs up from the chimney. I can see Ma-Tu in our steam-driven kitchen, so I cup my hands around my mouth and shout in a sort of patois, "Bon matin! Morning, Ma-Tu!" The sun-kissed woman smiles and waves back, at peace with the fact her daughter has safely slept out under the stars. I feel her breath and blood in me, pumping strong.

Ma-Tu says she was a victim of an anonymous sexual assault when she was just my age. Not long after, she was banished and then I was born. While there's a lot of unanswered questions, we've done all right, she and me.

Just then I get a PIM, a personal instant message, a telepathic text message in my head. Now this person I do know. The message says, "Let's Bonko, don't forget...L-8-ter!" It's from my "trans" pal Ayuna who like most teens is often looking to make a love connection. Except, Ayuna was born a guy on Mainlandia and also banished...for dressing up as a girl. Now recently arrived on Geto, she's my best new gal pal.

As I wash my face with water from a skin, it seems to also wash away my bad dreams, and my unanswered questions, for now. Then something else gets my attention. Ma-Tu shouts "Aiya!" and wags her finger like a metronomic timepiece. I get her meaning—tick, tock, there are errands to run and things to do.

"Sure thing, Ma-Tu, je suis totally on it!"

I then pull out an old, dog-eared, handwritten book from a pocket and read the good word for the day. Aloud, I say,

"Wherever you go, go with all your heart." Then add, "Yeah, you got that right, Mr. Confucius!" Haha!

Wearing soft-soled flats, leggings, and a punkishly ripped shirt, which I cinch at my waist, I put away my little book, jump up and tie my long hair. I recite Ma-Tu's words, "Do your practice and all is coming." So, I perform the art of yoga practiced by our ancients. I stretch and pull my limber body, breathing deeply. I finish my routine by doing a bouncy set of back walkovers and flips. And for fun, I shout, "Aiyaaaaaa!" as I show off some martial arts punches that my mentor has taught me.

I'm also glad there's no school today. "Yippee!" I take in all the sounds starting up around me—plants with trumpet-like flowers trill, cane shoots percussively beat against each other in the spring breezes, and birds-on-the-fly are sending up a chorus of chirps, honks, and hoots. There is no official school on Geto, no morning alarms to wake up to, which, trust me, is muchly appreciated by all us young peeps. When it's time to learn a skill, us kids are brought together and get the skinny from an expert. It's kind of like homeschool but way cooler and more fun. Anyway, today there are no lessons to be taught. Or, so I think.

Anyways, I shout out, "Feel good, be good, and do good." And, it does feel good as I look up to the sky and take in our sun's healing rays for a few moments. Then I look down, put on my handmade aviator beanie. I put my goggles on again— while they do keep flying bugs out when I'm scrounging around, they're mostly just to look cool. But now for some weird reason, someone in my head keeps jibber jabbering, "Run, run faster!"

CHAPTER TWO

On the Run

Galloping on like a spring filly, I sprint into a nearby forest that vibrates and sings with more trembling trees. The spring flora gone wild explodes with different scents and aromas. I pause, lift my head and tilt my delicate nostrils slightly into the wind, and focus in on one telltale scent. Haha, found it. "Wow, cho, co! There you are!" I say in that patois we sometimes speak on Geto.

But a pond covered in big lily pads lies between me and a straight path to the source of that smell. I know the pond is deep so I lean over, giggle at my reflection—my nose *is* crooked—and I test the lily pads with my now bare toes. I think if I "run" really fast—those words again—they'll be strong enough to hold my weight. I gaze deeper into the water, and gather my courage because I know neon beady eyes await, staring up from the water's depths. "Ech!"

But a girl's got to do what a girl's got to do. I back off, remove my shoes, adjust my goggles, take a running start, and yell out loud to focus my effort. And then I sprint superfast and barefoot across the lily pads, lightly touching on them. As I do, underwater jaws, tiny but sharp, snap at my flitting feet as the water froths and rolls. Dem bebettes—them lil' critters! They say never look back or down, so I keep moving fast and forward, churning my legs like my fire horse on the run. So fast, I feel as if I'm skimming across the water like a skipping stone.

But halfway across, one of my feet slips on an oily pad. "Whoops!" But without thinking, just using my instincts, I use my tumbling skills to do a front flip and land on two other pads. Barely. But one foot slides again, this time into the water and I feel a slash of sharpness above my ankle. Ouch!

The teeth keep nipping, but I don't hang around and keep scooting across the pads, arriving safely on the other side of the pond. Phew! Immediately, without even looking at my ankle, I glance at the vegetation around me. My keen eyes pick it out, a bush of lime-green leaves and white flowers protected by multi-pronged thorns. More ouch! But, I carefully reach in and manage to collect a couple of the "blanchflowers" as I flop to the ground, then rub the juice of the flowers on the gash. Owww! Immediately, the juice's antiseptic stings and I jerk back. But I can still smile as I look at the pond as the frothing waters subside, and the surface calmness returns. After treating myself, I put on my flats, and jump up to start running again, glancing back to yell, "Missed me, you lil' monsters. Better luck, next time!"

Haha! Prickly, pintsized perils in paradise.

But I can't even imagine what monsters lie beyond our island.

Out of nowhere, I crack up laughing as something else pings around inside my head. My extra-sensory powers are going a little bonkers. Ayuna, my newly arrived Rejex pal, sends me another PIM—via that extra-sensory social network we've been developing.

"Hey, guess who says he likes U, beb?"

"My eye, never! That cute boy with a purple mohawk?" I reply to her as I hook my backpack over my shoulders, still laughing.

"Um-huh, he was asking after U, again, girlfriend!"

"Ga lee, really?!"

"I'm not kidding, says his name's Abana. And, says it'd be cool if U pass by 2 cheer on his Bonko team."

"Even more reasons not to be tar-dee 4 the game!"

"You're a bad, bad, girl, Aiya Hope."

"Yeah, I know, but someone's got to do it, right?!"

Just then, I get yet another PIM, this time from my mentor, Alkima: "Forget Bonko 4 now, U R wanted, kiddo. Up on Solsbury Hill, so run!" That's my Alkima, the prince of paradox, who always seems to know what I'm planning. I dig him, but I dig him not—a genius and a wizard of sorts. But such a pill, sometimes, if you get what I mean.

Ahead of her, on the small hilltop, mystical Alkima practices a combination of yoga and martial arts moves—similar to what Aiya had been practicing. He transitions smoothly from deep stretching to deflecting and striking movements. Wiry and strong, he finishes by breaking several thick dead logs with his bare hands and with deadly force.

After he finishes his routine, he stares out to the sea and horizon, his long hair sweeping back. While his face is calm, he sucks in the incoming air—salty, damp, cool, and something else. He bites his lip for a second. Then he pirouettes out of his contemplation and walks by the nearby teepee, his home, rising high on the promontory.

The alchemist returns to sit yoga-like on the ground, wearing a comfortable and loose-fitting long shirt and leggings, all in camouflage colors. He laughingly puts on his quilt-patch sorcerer's hat for fun and leans over a natural tabletop—a dead old tree trunk cut flat for the purpose. Alkima watches with glee as his steam-powered gadgets churn and hiss, while resin and clay bowls full of liquids sizzle and broil over small flames. Suddenly, his face involuntarily shakes—his Tourette's temporarily overtaking him—and he shouts, "FIRE BURN... and cauldron bubble!"

In a minute or so, his face relaxes from the Tourette's tension then beams like a young child working at his first chemistry set. He picks up various powders, smells and rubs them in his fingers, then drops samples into the cups that bubble even more. He's genuinely pleased with his efforts, as he focuses on a "scrying" bowl full of still liquid. He touches the liquid with the tip of a finger to send out tiny ripples then stares into his bowl, as if he can actually look into some incoming future. But a worried frown crosses his face.

A few moments later, way down below him, his keen ears hear my happy, young voice chirping to myself. That lifts him. So he picks up another cup and grandly throws a big handful of powder onto the ground, from where a puff of gorgeous purple haze rises up and engulfs him, making him seem to disappear.

Running toward my summons, I scramble up a steep path winding up Solsbury that's bathed in an outrageous combo of colors, more trembling trees and bamboo stalks that tap their own tune, like they're in their own music band. Off the path, I spy some plump white mushrooms in the shade of a big overhanging cave and I'm about to head straight toward them when I stop suddenly. "Oopsie!" It's too late. I temporarily forget that the mushrooms are often found near watery mires, and I feel myself slowly being sucked into the quicksand-like guck. Okay, really not good!

My natural reaction is to make two fists, punch and struggle like mad and refuse to go down without a fearsome fight, the way I've fought all my life since being born premature. But an even higher survival instinct takes over. I immediately relax, throw aside my hemp backpack, and instead of fighting it, I let my body weight spread out. Slowly, my legs lift up, and I begin to float on top of the muck. Glancing up to the sky, I'm momentarily distracted by the ridiculous deep blue above. Ma-Tu always tells me to take the time to look up and not down. I sigh, "Ahhhhhhhhh!" Until a mean-looking rodent's skull, with dead meat still on it, plops up beside me in the guck. Eeek!

So, I get back to it, gently easing myself backward with my arms and elbows. Bit by bit. Inch by inch. Finally, safe on solid ground, I wipe off the muck with water from a nearby puddle. Then, not to be denied, I find a long stick and cautiously move around the mire and forward again toward the mushroom patch, remembering exactly where I step. I try to quickly pick the mushrooms, recalling that the caves on the hill hide scurrying, furball critters. But not quick enough, as I catch a glimpse of some scuttling furballs heading toward me in the undergrowth with claws and bad intent. So I stash the mushrooms in my backpack and purposely scoot toward the mire, retracing my steps. I hear the scuttling getting closer—the critters are incredibly fast. But I'm smart. I close in on the mire and jump, stretching as far as I can. I time it just right, leaping maybe forty feet and landing on solid ground beyond the mire. I keep running, not looking behind but hearing the squeals of the rodents as they struggle and sink into the unforgiving bog.

There are hazards for them, too, living in our low-tech heaven.

As I jog, I excitedly pick up my pace and easily ascend the hilltop without breathing too heavily. I remove my hat and goggles. I feel so alive and suck the incoming salty air.

"Alkima!" The name echoes over the promontory to the horizon. "Alkima! Alkima!"

I first check in his open teepee. It's jam-packed with fancy gourds filled high with powders, hanging dream catchers, animal claws, and gorgeous feathers. But everything seems to be arranged in some chaotic order. In a central spot on the inside wall is a handwritten chart of alchemic symbols, Alkima's personal vocabulary. There's also another diagram, the Wu Xing, the five element or phases chart—an ancient system that Alkima tells me helps explain all sorts of phenomena, from cosmic cycles to the workings of medicinal drugs and acupuncture treatments.

I carefully pick up a handwritten book of medicine called the *Neijing*—he'd told me that it argued that you "get sick when the yin and yang of your body are out of balance."

The book and diagrams are cool, colorful, and kind of magical, but—yeah, whatever —it's all a little beyond me.

But there's also strange, awesome machinery—like small devices that whirr and tick. And also one with well-oiled fulcrums, pendulums, and what look like natural magnets. I see a small crystal ball sitting close to it and a note: "Use at your own risk." Yeah, right. I can't help myself, as the note is an invitation. I pick up the ball and place it on a smooth track, and as it begins to roll, the whole device goes into action. What have I started—some kind of perpetual motion gizmo? Haha, I giggle as the ball smoothly keeps going round and round, perhaps never to stop. Alrighty, then!

Until I hear a loud crash...

Jumping back outside the teepee, hoping I didn't cause it, I see a bowl has smashed over. I look around the hilltop but still see no one except for the tree-trunk tabletop, and the other steaming cups full of liquids, and a mortar and pestle. I look more closely and on the far side of the trunk I spy Alkima's pal, Mystikat, that kitty who always seems to be skulking about, following me. Mystikat's intently staring at all the bubbling liquids. Up here on the windy outcrop, his fur looks as smooth and rich as dark brown-black velvet. His eyes seem aflame, as sparks reflect in his pupils.

"My, you do get around, sha," I whisper to the kitty who flashes a Cheshire grin and turns back to standing guard over the liquids.

As for Alkima, he's nowhere to be seen. So I close my eyes, and send him a PIM: "Alkima, where R U hiding? Got some of those special shrooms."

But there's still no answer as I approach the tabletop. I cheekily peek around again, then reach for and empty some of the mortar's purple contents into my hands. Rubbing and crushing the powder, I bring their scent to my nose. It's dangerously intoxicating.

I whisper his name again. But still no Alkima. I use some water from a bowl to wash the remaining muck off me. Drying off, I now spot and grab a handful of white powder. I taste and recognize its sweetness. Then I glide a few steps forward and peer over the promontory's edge to the crashing sea and rocks below. I toss a handful of "white" high out over the edge and it morphs into a spectacular fracture of rainbow dust. I can't help but enjoy my creation. Then, unafraid of falling, I let my gaze, like an inquisitive finger, track from the rocks down below to the horizon in the distance. Suddenly, I feel strange freesôns, chills, on the back of my neck. "Whoaaa!" Something strange this way comes, but I can't pinpoint it. And just like that, the sensation is gone. Poof!

Then, for some reason, I think about my fire horse, free and not roped: "All rearing power and grace, all wild eyed and untamed..."

A PIM pings me back, completing my thought: "Horses have always been a real and magical symbol of free will, of freedom without restraint..."

I whirl to look behind and around me. But all I see are the bubbling cups, some battling seabirds squawking overhead and the waters slashing the rocks below. That's all. About to lose it a little, I try to still my thoughts and being—breathing in deeply, and sensing the remnants of that purple powder that still lingers in my nostrils. And then it's as if a curtain is raised from in front of my eyes to reveal the show. Greetings!

There sits the alchemist next to where the kitty was sitting before, Cheshire cat grinning to himself with his hat on.

"Where were you?"

"You're INSANE!" he mutters because of his Tourette's. He wiggles his body, shaking his affliction's temporary control over him. "Sorry, I was right here, next to Mystikat. You observed but did not see, little lady."

"No way, you did some of your conjuring?!"

"Look closer..."

I screw up my face to think harder. I go over to the tabletop and pick up the mortar again and smell it. I look to him as he beckons me to go ahead. Once again, I breathe in the exotic scent of the mortar's purple contents.

"Aiya, you are beginning to smell and taste in a whole new way, but you also need to observe in every way."

That does it. Bingo. Illumination. As I see it, he nods, and I ask, "Cho, co-wow! This stuff, it can cloud someone's mind, right?"

"When used in just the right amount, sha..."

"So, it can create a sort of invisible cloak, right?"

"Always handy if you're coming in late and don't want your Ma-Tu to flip," he teases.

He ain't kidding. But now impatient like any teenager, I put the mortar down. "Okay, I got your PIM. Cool, now wassup?" I giggle. "'Cause I know that you know that I already know, that I got places to go..."

"And places to be seen," he winks, as I blush at his embarrassingly spot-on observation.

CHAPTER THREE

Why Are We Called Rejexes?

Suddenly, Alkima blurts out the words, "Holy CRAP." Maybe his affliction, again?

"Hello, ground to Alkima!"

"Sorry, I've been hearing these voices in my head."

"Funny, me too! But, hey, you asked me up here!"

Bringing himself back, he gestures to the horizon and asks, "Right, so what do you think is up, Aiya?"

I sometimes can't stand his little tests. But I tramp barefoot back to the edge and look back to him, a little impatient.

He starts to say, "Breathe deep. Silence is a true friend..." and I finish it, adding, "...who never betrays." Then I face the horizon. Close my eyes, breathe deeply then listen and feel hard. Soon enough, the hair again rises on the back of my neck. "Oooo, I feel freesôns...maybe some trouble."

"When you own your breath, nobody can steal your peace. What else?"

Keeping my eyes closed, I slowly breathe in the incoming sea air again and remember that strange holy man's words. I say, "Something in thirty days...maybe darkness." I don't catch Alkima looking a little alarmed at my reference.

I hear him say, "Calm the mind, avoid worrying about worldly cares..." I continue deeply sucking in the sea air, all my enhanced senses alert, feeling the various vibrations of the earth, sea, and sky.

I again hear "Run!" and whirl to face him. He's shifted again. But this time I sense his move and nab him out of the corner of my eye. He stands there with his head cocked.

"Why'd you say 'run,' Alkima? Because that's what I heard in my head this morning. Someone shouting 'run,' and that's what I've been doing all morning!"

"I'm not sure. But something is coming. Thing is, we can't always control the things that come to us, but we sure can control how we react to them, right?" Changing topic, he eyes my bag.

"Shrooms, the magic ones you like," I enthuse as I proudly present a couple of really big juicy ones and plop them on the tabletop.

He considers me, watching me move. He's told me he sees me as some sparkling butterfly chrysalis, about to go through some unusual transformation into something better than my normal self. Transformation seems cool, I guess, if you're a bug.

"As your Ma-Tu says, change is unavoidable. On the other hand, growing up, well, that's optional," he quips.

Alkima sits down cross-legged at the table and adjusts his hat so it's just fashionably crooked. He invites me to also sit, and pours some liquid into a cup. "Tea?"

"Why, what's in it, oh wise one, or shouldn't I ask?"

"A dash of this, a bit of that. And a dose of courage thrown in!"

We both sip the tea. I like it. "Mmmmmmmm."

Then he picks up one shroom and smells it. "Just what I needed." He oversees his wares. "We need to prepare some more salves for your village apothecary." I give him my questioning look. "For what we both sense is coming." Yeah, okay, I guess. "So start crushing those multi-colored seeds. Then mix the powder with those dried leaves." I take to it, easily. But he senses I have more questions. "Go ahead, ask away."

"I heard kids from the south side say we are all Rejexes here or the children of Rejexes, right. So, why exactly were our people banished? Who dumped us here like some flotsam on the beach? Why are we designated Rejexes? Hello, and who gets to judge? And, why?"

"That's five, but who's counting. How much time do you have?"

Scrunch. I crush the seeds with glee. "Why, you got a date or something?" I quip back. His eyes crinkle with true laughter. He also has a great hunger for life.

"Well, first thing—raise your hand and point a finger at me." I do that and he continues. "When you point a finger at someone else, you're pointing three back at yourself."

"So those who judge, should be ready to be judged themselves?"

"HERESY...freakin'...smeresy!" I see him pause then shake his head, as if he doesn't quite know where that rebellious thought came from. "Uh, just keep grinding, sha."

I continue grinding. He talks about my increasing instinctual and physical skills, but always preaches patience to me. "It doesn't matter how slowly you go as long as you don't stop." Oh, great, more lessons. Really?! Then he adds like he's reading my mind, "A gem can't be polished without friction, nor man perfected without trials." Way more lessons. He continues, "You know how you're expanding your perception and are now able to mentally communicate with friends here."

I interrupt him. "Yeah, sign me up, already. Because you said, we're becoming like super teens, right?"

He slides over my interruption. "Guess what? I've been getting messages from Mainlandia." He wonders again who exactly is thinking "heresy" on Mainlandia.

"What? You are? You have friends there? Who? Where?" I stumble, hardly containing myself.

"I wouldn't call them close friends, but we share the same source."

"Hello, what, there are Rejexes like us on Mainlandia?"

I sense him thinking—how could anyone call someone, as shimmering and alive as us young people on Geto, a name like Rejex? Then he says, "Those who judge are just playing with fire. And fire always burns the hands of those who play with it."

"Okay, but I need more."

"You always do. Didn't Ma-Tu explain this?"

"I might've skipped lessons that day." He chuckles at my joke.

"Mainlandians are created in test tubes from ten main genetic sources, resulting in ten different types of workers. From the scientist and engineer, to enforcement and general workers, ten groups in all. For the programmers there, artificial selection and everything in order is the height of progress."

"Everyone the same, that sounds boring. So, you don't agree, right?"

He raises a stylish eyebrow and the cock of his head expresses exactly what he thinks. "They actually believe that natural and artificial selection are two sides of the same coin—that they'll both get to the same point. However, they just feel doing it artificially is quicker and more efficient." He passes some other ingredients to me. "I was engineered there on Mainlandia. Created in a test tube and deposited into a surrogate birther's womb. But something didn't go according to their genetic plans—it happens less than five percent of the time. As a young teen, I started developing dormant traits that were outside of their well-defined box for a student scientist."

I can't help myself. "You started messing around with all this, this, what do you call it?"

"Alchemy."

"Yeah, this transformation thingee, right?"

"Exactly. Plus, I laughed too much. They so didn't like that."

"They sound way bor-rring!"

"So I was designated a Rejex, banished, and washed up here like some flotsam on Geto. Just like Ma-Tu."

"But being different and not the boring same-old should be cool, right, and more fun?"

"You would think..." He looks up with a smile, "So, you're wondering, 'What really is this alchemy thingee?' Well, you called it. Because alchemy really is about transformation." I keep grinding, while listening, kind of intrigued. "The ancients said alchemy was about transmuting, changing things like base metals such as lead into a precious metal like gold. Or, it was about creating a potion for long life. Or, about the creation of cures for diseases."

"Kinda like what we're doing here?" He smiles. "So, it's for real?"

"Well, I don't see the need for changing base metal into a precious metal. But an elixir for rejuvenating life or a cure-all for disease, that's helpful, for sure."

"But, what?" I ask, as I finish my grinding. He pours more kernels into my bowl to mash up.

"Well, I've come to see modern alchemy also as a spiritual practice, a way to self-transform the practitioner. Or, to transform a negative belief, attitude, or behavior into something positive. For example, say you fear something. Well, turn it around and do the thing you fear and beat it. And that way you transform yourself."

"So, it's like a modern not old application of alchemy?"

He nods. "So meditate on that. And there'll be a test next week!" My face drops, but he cracks up. "I'm kidding!" He whips out a tiny little book with a handwritten title, *My Philosopher's Stone.* "But I do have this cute book I wrote about alchemy, if you're interested."

I open it and read a few notes. But then like a mad, brilliant scientist, I see a look of satisfaction spread on his face as he pours, sifts, and mixes up his strange brew of liquids and extracts. He shows me how to do it and we continue working without speaking for a bit. Until he says, "I may be different than other Mainlandian scientists, but we share the same gene pool. And now my senses are allowing me to read their thoughts—and while they may not know it, we're still connected." He takes a pause. "I keep getting a gut feeling some of them are finally seeing that their type of engineered, short-cut evolution may be more like devolution. That unconstrained scientific progress without humanity has its downsides."

"You know, I've always felt some connection beyond here." I watch in glee as my own jars froth up and change into layers of kaleidoscopic colors. "This is très cool. But, like, I'm not the same type of Rejex as you, right, Alkima?"

"You're like second generation because you weren't created in a test tube like me. We didn't know if it could still work, that two test-tube people could reproduce and have kids, but you were conceived and then born here in the very old way. Truth is, natural breeding creates mysteries. And you are a miracle, Aiya, a true mystery in so many ways!"

"Cool, so, what about my father, again?" I sneakily ask.

Suddenly, we both feel the jolt of a single, deep tremor. We spring up in a flash. He runs to the cliff's edge and peers over. But some of the cliffside gives way, and Alkima disappears over the edge, leaving his hat behind, as he shouts, "Help!"

CHAPTER FOUR

Up for an Adventure?

I drop to my knees, my fearful breath caught in my lungs, as I frantically look over the edge. The scary tremor has stopped, but the soft earth gives way too easily. So once again I spread out my weight. "Alkima!" I can't see him. Looking down to the jagged rocks, I scan the area and I'm relieved to see no blood or his smashed body. "Alkima!"

The only thing that answers me back are the once-squabbling sea birds overhead who are now looking out to the horizon, raising a different squawk.

My head spins and my throat is dry from the fear of losing him. This cannot be happening! Geto is a real paradise of many hazards but Alkima, of all people, knows what dangers lay under our island's "happy smile" surface. So this cannot be over. Please, not now. And then I go into action. I grab some vine-like thingees that crawl over the edge, and I lower myself down.

From deep inside a burrowed out hole in the cliff face, something with beady glowing eyes secretly peers out at me as I let myself down on the vine. I don't initially see it, having never descended this cliff face before. But I sure can smell it, as I screw up my nose. "Poo-yee!" Then, just as I catch a glimpse of Alkima's body face down on a hidden ledge below me, this hidden creature tries to stab its spikey appendage at me from inside the burrow. I luckily dodge at the last moment and watch its needle just miss my eye. But its stink almost chokes me. Using my inborn agility and speed, I duck a second attack and swing over to another vine. But my eyes are now wide open when I see another group of burrows and just manage to slip yet another spikey attack.

"Later, little critters, 'cause I got to bounce!"

I twirl down the vine to the ledge below where Alkima sits up rubbing a bloody head wound.

"Just a flesh wound, m'petite, nothing broken!" He slowly lifts himself up.

"We shouldn't go back up the way I came down. Those creepy crawlies are mean, they're possédé!"

"True dat, their venom is called three-step—you get stung, you're dead after three steps!"

"Now you tell me!" We both look down to the jagged rocks below.

"Then going down it is!"

"So, like, you've done free climbing before, right, Alkima?"

"No, but I heard about it in a story!"

He reaches out to grab a hand and foothold, then, very carefully, he starts our tricky descent. I follow right after. We are doing well until both of his footholds break away and he's desperately left hanging on by the fingertips of just one hand.

I immediately act, letting one of my own handholds go to grab his free hand, and there we hang, as even the seabirds overhead shut up to watch our dangerous little drama play out. We hang there for awhile with no apparent move to make.

"What should we do?" Pain shoots through my body.

"I've lived a good life, let go, Aiya! Save yourself."

"Yeah, as if!" I hate losing at anything. So while I grit my teeth to focus all my physical strength, I also try to calm my racing mind and not notice the pain.

"My life, it don matta, sha!"

"My eye! Never!" I scream in fear and pain. Then, illumination sparks all over me again. "Gar ici, look, I'm going to swing you over to that crevice!"

"Let me go!"

"Shush, I can save you!" He does shut up, and I claw in as deep as I can into my one handhold and two footholds. Digging deep into a well of strength and super resolve I never knew I had, I brace myself. Then with one arm only, I swing his body back and forth, almost feeling like my shoulder is going to pop out. But I manage to swing him toward the crevice where he finally gets both a foot- and a hand-hold.

"Okay, I'm good!" he says, while I think, *Wow, who knew I was that strong?!* He reads my mind, casually saying, "Well, I did...sort of." Of course he did, and that so bugs me!

A few minutes later, we have descended to the small beach below which lies at the bottom of a well-beaten animal path. Alkima rubs some oil deep into my shoulder and my pain magically fades. Mystikat is there waiting for us with a mildly pissed look on his face. But when the alchemist chuckles, he jumps up onto Alkima's shoulder, purring away.

"Why are you laughing? You almost died!"

"Aiya, I am so grateful, trust me. But you cannot be risking yourself. Your time really is coming and you must learn to make choices," he says as he points to both my heart and head. "From both these places...promise?!"

Yeah, sure, I nod. I guess.

Awhile later, back up on the outcrop, we discover the tremor hasn't destroyed anything. We pack up the liquids in small vials, and the powders in pouches.

I lead the way off the hilltop. But glancing at Mystikat on his shoulder, Alkima winks conspiratorially while the kitty meows back. I catch their play. "Hold on, hold on!" I consider them, rocking on my toes. "Was that all some test or something?"

"Why? And, who wants to know?" he tries to innocently ask. "Hello?!"

"Okay, just for argument's sake, let's say it was a test." Mystikat meows again. "Well, you just passed!"

"You cannot be serious?!"

"With fugitive colors!"

I turn on my heels, pissed, and swoosh off. But, as they follow me, their young protégé, like a small mystical entourage, Alkima mischievously throws something else out there. "So what do you think, time for a journey, Aiya?"

Without looking back and still steaming. "What, more rock climbing?"

"No. But GAG me!" His Tourette's again. "Sorry." Collects himself. "Would you be up for an adventure to, you know, Mainlandia?!"

"What the...?" I whip my head around again, my pounding heart on fire. This time maybe I'm not dreaming.

"Although Ma-Tu will fight me on this because there are worse monsters on Mainlandia, ones you've never dreamed of, even in your worst nightmares."

Sheesh, does he know of my recent dreams and that holy man? I keep it zipped, as his serious face transforms. "Oh, and on a more fun note," he teases as I can hardly contain myself.

"What, afterwards...THEN we do rock climbing, again?"

"No, funny girl," he playfully winks, "We Rejexes don't actually live on an island!"

CHAPTER FIVE

Let's Bonko!

A sturdy foot in hemp sandals steps into some soggy poop, causing the strapping young lad to moan, "Oh, shit!"

To which another lad replies, "No worries, bro, it's good luck for Bonko today!"

Nearby in our kitchen, Ma-Tu expertly twirls a deadly obsidian cutting tool as if it was just a stick, not something that could take your fingers off. She stops and listens hard, then throws the cutting tool into a board where it shivers. Then she steps outside for a moment. She checks out a steam-driven system of exposed pipes that carry fresh water into the home and kitchen. Everything's working fine.

Then, instinctually, she looks to her left up a path, as if waiting for something to happen. A minute later, the group of strapping young lads, all wearing punked-out hats and canvas vests exposing their muscled arms, are yukking it up as they roll by. Each has a pair of goggles around his neck and carries a short Bonko stick with a flattened, curved, scooped-out end. One lad is still trying to scrape the poop off his shoe.

Ma-Tu's eyes size them up. She likes the boys and knows some of them personally. But she always tells Aiya that young testosterone is always a little unstable, like young estrogen, of course. But boys will always be boys. They have more muscle and maybe less sense. Two of them, who have dazzling screaming eagle tattoos on their shoulders, playfully elbow each other. Then one taps the other on the head with his Bonko stick. The other reciprocates, hitting the first guy, only harder, on the head. And that draws a trickle of blood.

"Hey, bro!" growls the injured lad as his whole body tenses up for action. Other annoyed words start to rise up.

The group then suddenly sees Ma-Tu watching and they all stop in mid-sentence, as the heat cools. The one who had struck the other tries to explain innocently, "Tete dure—he's got a hard head. Look!" He gently taps his "bonked" pal with his knuckles. And they all try to laugh it off, including the injured one. But for Ma-Tu this is new behavior. She twitches. It's a little unsettling.

A ball drops from the group and slowly rolls down toward Ma-Tu in the hushed silence. She allows it to roll onto her foot, niftily kicks it up to her hand, and spins it around in her fingers and palm. Considering them, she suddenly whips it with some skill back at the group. A handsome lad with a purple mohawk snaps his hand out to catch it, just as niftily. "Respect, m'ame, my name is Abana from the Southside," he says as he cracks a pearly white grin and bows low to his elder. She accepts his gesture. The situation defused, the birds overhead fire up their song, again. Then the boys all wave and walk off, slapping each other while laughing out loud.

In spite of the seeming restored peace, Ma-Tu shouts after them, "Maybe later, I'll come watch you guys and the game." The lads slip into the forest, and Abana glances back.

Just then, Alkima and I appear with me sensing something. "What's up, Ma-Tu, what did I miss?" She smiles and shrugs, so I hand Alkima my bag, telling him, "I gotta clean up and bounce."

Awhile later, I appear all scrubbed up with a yellow slash of paint around one eye. I have new goggles around my neck for show, punk leggings, comfy moccasin boots, and a loose sleeveless top that has an asymmetrical hem. I see them both watching me. "What? I gotta see a boy about a horse," I joke.

"A bon homme called Abana?"

"Why, who wants to know?"

"My lips are sealed," he winks.

I smile and wonder if he knows that I know that he hides things? Does he know that I also hide things from him? Because adults always seem to know this stuff. They don't ever admit it, but they're way better at deception than we young ones are.

"Hold on, m'petite. Always be sure to wear some flowers in your hair," says Ma-Tu as she puts a tiny garland of spring daisies in my hair, then strokes my cheek and my silky hair. The last strands of my hair flow through her hand as I scoot off with nearby chimes and bells ringing all round me.

I barely hear Alkima tell Ma-Tu, "We have to talk...and you may not like it, sha."

Faster than a falling star, I reach the clearing behind the village. In my head, I laugh at a new PIM I surprisingly get from my new secret admirer: "Make sure U cheer 4 us at the game. Just get ready 2 duck!"

Duck? How exciting! I'd never really seen a full-out game of Bonko. I can't wait, so I take a shortcut. I crouch down and push through a hedgerow as the sounds of slamming bodies, shouts, and raucous laughter deliriously cover me. I poke my head through some branches to see...a bunch of teenaged, sweating males stripped down to their short shorts. With safety goggles on, each holds a short stick with a flattened, curved, scooped out end. They catch and whack a ball around in the air as they powerfully slam their bodies together. Hard and fast. Wow, it explodes into mesmerizing madness!

The visiting south-side islanders have brought the competitive spirit out in both sides. They bash and yell and joust, but all in a friendly way. The players are so alive in their joy of the game. And that joy of life is picked up by the appreciative spectators all wearing cool hats and including a rainbow mix of different people: two men who sit arm in arm and in love together; a group of adults and teenagers with blue eyes who are happy as punch to just cheer on the players; and a couple of attentive albinos who shade themselves from the beating down sun. They keep official score of the game, using a scoreboard contraption that sends up spurts of cool, colored steam when one or the other side scores.

Without ever having met him, I glom onto Abana, the one with the mohawk. He's got darker skin, and he isn't the tallest, the biggest, or the loudest of the players. But he's so smooth and goes about his game with quiet glee. When he gets elbowed in the mouth, he concedes, "Good one!" to his opponent and then gives as good as he gets.

I scurry over to settle comfortably under a glitter tree, next to my always-playful friend Ayuna, saying, "I like him, I mean, I like it, the game. Bonko!" We giggle.

She's dressed in a sexy corset over a blouse with billowing sleeves and a spiffy top hat. Like I said, Ayuna was born a male on Mainlandia but when he/she started displaying female tendencies, she was bullied. She tried to fight back, but it didn't help, she says, and so she was banished here to Geto. Lucky for us and for me as Ayuna was the first of my pals to start reading my mind. We two new besties bump fists and giggle more.

Then she stops and gathers herself. Suddenly, she opens up her heart to me. "The hooded ones used to shame me and make me cry. When I tried to fight back with clever words, they hurt me. And then they banished me." She wipes a tear from her eye but sucks it up. "But I love the fact that on Geto, we can be who we are, not who someone else says we are. Thanks, Aiya, for letting me be who I am—a girl inside a boy's body. I mean I don't fully know my identity—I think it's still developing. But thanks for having my back."

"Always, you're my BFF!"

We hug, then Ayuna shifts back to her playful side, winking at me as she gestures to Abana. "See, I was right, he is totally cute!" He sure is.

The cut and action of the game is just awesome, and we find ourselves cheering the players on, coming up with our own chants. "There's only one Ah-bana. Only one Ah-bana. Only one Ahhh-bannnna. Only one Ah-bana!"

There is a moment when two opposing players, two of the bigger ones, square up against each other. They look like they're about to throw some serious punches. I note that they both have a similar tattoo on their right shoulder—a screaming eagle. But the fact they're even considering fighting is way weird for Geto. They smack their foreheads together with a deep thud, and menacingly growl. Wow!

I later find out they are the same two that Ma-Tu had seen square off outside our home. And a lot of surprised stares now watch them, as the ball lies at their feet. They drop their sticks and grab each other's arms. Their ripped muscles reflect the momentary tension in the air. Then out of nowhere,

Abana swiftly nips in, scoops up the loose ball, and shouts, "Brothers...game on. Let's Bonko!" Abana takes off running and that breaks the tension. The muscled players grunt and blend back into the flow of the game.

When a player scores, both sides shout, "Bonko!" The colored steam explodes up. So much fun! And, boy, that Abana dude has some moves. He can slip into spaces with a drop of his shoulder or a shimmy of his hips. On one play, Abana, almost faster than you can see, streaks down the flank waiting for the ball to be passed his way. Sure enough, he catches it in full stride and is about to shoot for goal when he's tripped and goes flying into the air. I can tell he also doesn't like to lose as he still tries to fire the ball toward the goal as he sails through the air. But it goes off at right angles and speeds instead toward us two girls. It strikes the glitter tree trunk just above our heads and ricochets off my goggles. Lucky me!

"Oooops!" apologizes Abana.

The whole trunk trembles, as shivers travel up the tree's body to its branches, loosening the silvery tinkling blossoms. As they fall, it truly does look like a cascade of glitter...with sound. Ayuna and I look splendid in our coat of glitter as the players pause their game and howl their pleasure.

Abana's handsome face breaks into a lopsided grin, as he momentarily removes his goggles to flash kind but mischievous eyes. "Sorry, I'm Abana," he officially introduces himself. Then he shrugs his powerful shoulders, re-sets his goggles, and sheepishly goes back to the game. We shout after him, "Abana, Bonko!" My heart is on fire. Okay, I know that's a little quick. But, hey, what're you going to do?

Back at the village, Alkima and Ma-Tu hug silently with open spirits. It's easy to see they have an intimate knowledge of each other. It's as if they have a shorthand between them—a look here, a tilt of the head there, and they can communicate easily without words. He shakes his bag of goodies then opens it and starts revealing the various vials and pouches. "Extra medicine...salve for any cuts...relief for swelling...balm for one's spirit..." Then he produces a skin full of some liquid. "And something fun to drink."

"Extra medicinal supplies? But why? For who? And when?"
"Your daughter really has learned the art of multiple questioning from you." He gestures with a tip of his head. "But it's for what's coming."
She quickly glances to the horizon with understanding. "Mother Nature always has her way of keeping us humble."
Alkima sits, picks up a bushy brush and hands it to her. She knows what he wants and she begins to brush out his magnificent head of hair. Another example of their unspoken intimacy.
"Remember the secret texts we snuck a peek at when we were young?" asks Alkima.
"*The Book of Myths*. It's the final reason you got banished, for showing them to me."
"Way worth it," he winks. "But, there was talk of a prophecy."
"About the coming of another catalyst, like the Zephyrian Crystals had been when they first brought fire to our planet Occulo."
"And gave us the way and the light out of the shadow of cold and darkness our ancestors had been living in." He sips from the skin as he enjoys her brushing his hair. "For all of their scientific progress since then, I believe some Mainlandians are finally realizing they're entering another dark period."
She stops brushing his hair. "You've been getting messages from them!" His lack of an immediate response nevertheless answers her. "So, you sense they're ready?"
"It could be just a tiny pebble in the sea, just a ripple now. But some may be willing to be free from the shackles of the science and intolerance that ties them down."
"Those governing bullies have had it coming for a long, long time. But, Alkima, returning to Mainlandia after all these years could be suicidal."
"Fortune favors the brave, no? Besides, she keeps asking about her father."
"Is this where you're going to upset me?"
He sees her slowly close her eyes, but he continues. "Well, yes, I am looking for a volunteer or two to come with me." He looks up mischievously into her surprised face with an innocent cock of his head. But she's not buying it!

CHAPTER SIX

Min and Gang Jun

My gal-pal Ayuna tugs on my shirt, again. "You've got to ask him straight up about his ex. Come on, your Ma-Tu is a counselor, that's what she'd tell you to do." She's right. I nod as she continues. "No one knows what happened to his girl, if she died or just got lost. Permanently. You can't let it slide, Aiya. You got to get ahead of any problems. You got it, girl?" When I nod again, Ayuna goes off to flirt with one of the other spectators, twirling her hair around her finger. The girl has some bag of tricks.

After washing himself off—the lad's got muscles on muscles—Abana slides on over and settles in beside me. We sit silent for a while, shyly not looking directly at each other, while taking in each other's natural scents and vibrations. Like two creatures in nature, doing a silent dance of observation. I breathe in his scent. I like how he smells. I can hear my little big heart go pit-a-pat.

Still without looking directly at me, he grins at the glitter still layering my hair. I smile back, playing a game all girls know. I simply ask, "So, Bonko?"

He respectfully replies, "They say it comes from the ancient game of lacrosse, that it must be played hard with power, grace, and joy, but without anger and without revenge. That you must play in a way that shows respect to your opponent and what he brings to the game. You also play for the people who are watching here, and also for those who have played and passed on. They say it's a reflection of life, the good, the bad, and the ugly. So, yes, Bonko, it's the game of life!"

"Wow," I whisper, but keep my head shyly down. Then I'm drawn to peek at the screaming eagle tattoo on his shoulder, just like those other combatants have. He guesses my question.

"I am Abana, the child of a soldier Rejex, just like my two big brothers out there. You're right, there don't seem to be many soldier Rejexes on our island. I guess a soldier is a soldier is a soldier. All muscle and aggro—pretty basic."

He catches me checking him out as I ask, "Yeah, but your Pa-Tu, your father, must've had something going on that didn't fit into being a regular soldier, or they wouldn't have dumped him here, right?"

"True dat, smart girl!"

I laugh, but try not to show my big-ish teeth too much, now feeling self-conscious of them, as a few more glitter blossoms feather down onto my face. It makes me feel pretty.

"You're right, there may be more to me. Haven't quite figured that out, but...hey, did you ever hear of the Middle Kingdom legend of Min and his adversary Gang Jun?" I shake my head, and he jumps up. "I don't know how much of it is true or myth, but it's still a cool story, and also like a blueprint for fighting against a superior enemy or even a bully."

The whole concept of bullying makes me want to puke, not that we see it here on Geto. Anyway, I sense this guy knows stuff as my eyes open wide with intrigue. "Can you show me?"

Hell, yeah, his mischievous look says, as he holds out his hand to help lift me to my feet. Then he stands me under another nearby fruit tree looking at the sun behind him. He pulls out a well-used slingshot and stretches it out. "The sling was one of the earliest projectile weapons, simple but deadly. The sling-bullet could be made of lead ore, like this one I'm going to use, or it could even be spiked with fast-acting poison that would instantly knock out the victim when they were hit."

"Cho! Co! Wow!" I exclaim, all ears. Hold on, do my ears stick out too much?

Abana points up to the tree above me and readies his sling. "Catch!" He unleashes the projectile and it strikes a piece of fruit that plops toward me. I try not to be so good at it and purposely fumble the fruit, with a laugh. "You are good!"

"I'm better than good," he says, with an irresistible laugh I could get really used to.

He backs off a ways. "Instead of using and wasting great armies, the Middle Kingdom legend tells of another way that disagreeing people settled their differences. One-on-one combat as a solution to a disagreement. Or, for all the booty, or even for a fair princess like you." I giggle. "Anyway, this one story tells of the tribe of Timur that politely asked for a trade route through the lands of Kaz. But, they couldn't agree terms, so it came down to Kaz's warrior king, Gang Jun, taking on Timur's knight-prince, Min. Gang Jun was a massive warrior with these huge guns." Abana flexes his own muscled arms for me. "You know, biceps. Anyway, Gang Jun could snap an opponent's neck with his bare hands. Min sensed he couldn't overcome his opponent's strength, so he relied on guerilla tactics using surprise, stealth, and smarts."

"You mean, like super senses and skills?"

"Right on, exactly!" Abana shifts his position and theat-rically acts out his story for me. "Min would fly his personal emblem of a fighting cock with spurs on its feet. Bold. His army members were all dressed in brilliant lily white—with a blanchflower, a beautiful but deadly white flower, embroi-dered into their clothing. Min and his blanchflower army were adept tacticians. In combat, they would cleverly take advantage of the elements around them. They'd attack from downwind against opponents that had a superior sense of smell. They'd change to camouflage colors when needed for opponents with superior vision. But against Gang Jun, Min used his agile feet to keep away from the giant warrior's sword. He was a constantly moving target that couldn't be taken down by Gang Jun's vicious sword—a weapon so sharp it could slice a wild predator in two. So, Min feinted, he dodged, he weaved, all the while looking for one specific moment when Gang Jun lifted his head and exposed his throat. Strategically using the falling sun behind him to temporarily blind Gang Jun, Min let fly with his sling and his dead-eye shot hit home, taking down Gang Jun who collapsed like he was a falling tree trunk."

"Timberrrrr! I think Min is my new hero, because he helped Timur find a new trade route without a bloody battle, right?"

"Hahaha, you got it! There are similar underdog myths. Like in the land of Londinium where the army of Tottenham, led by a knight called Gazza, defeated the marauding interlopers called the Arsenal. Then there's David versus Goliath. They all have the same message." He then motions for me to put the fresh fruit on my head. I do without pausing. "Trust me?"

"Sure, I guess, but what're you going to do?" I pretend to be a little scared.

He loads up his sling, takes careful aim and then even closes his eyes. But I don't flinch, such is my surprising new-found trust in this frisky bold creature called Abana. He swings his sling and it strikes the fruit, knocking it off my head. Bonko, sort of!

Some of the gamers and spectators have seen this play out and slap their chests to recognize Abana's effort. He takes a bow and approaches me. "Your turn!"

"Quoi? What? No, not me!" I pretend again. But I'm so stoked to try and prove myself.

He shows me how to use the sling. He doesn't give me a sling-bullet, but something less deadly. He picks up another fruit from the ground and steps back away from me. "Just don't close your eyes," he jokes as he holds the fruit in his open hand. I take aim, keep my eyes focused, and shoot the projectile. It misses the fruit and nicks his wrist. A red welt begins to appear, but he doesn't show any pain. Is he showing off, or is he just really tough?

"Go again!" He tosses me another projectile. I arm my weapon. "Just, relax, focus, and then let it go."

I do just that and knock the fruit out of his hand. Wow, who knew!

"You are a quick study!" The spectators cheer again. I like the attention. Tres cool!

When the spectators go back to watching the game, Abana demonstrates to me how to make other ancient but simple weapons, like a blowgun out of a reed or big green leaf. When he shows me how to use them, I really do feel very natural. Maybe I could become a super-soldier one day. Time ticks and shadows grow longer, more glitter falls, and I'm enthralled by every second of it. And so we continued to "vay-yay," and talk to blend our spirits together.

Later, we go to find some more fruit for our friends. I admire his six-pack stomach. So, I provocatively threw off my top— causing Abana to catch his breath—only to reveal a skin-tight undergarment. His eyes open wide. He likes what he sees. But I don't stick around. Being an ace climber, I quickly shimmy up a tree and look back to him. "What's keeping you, Abana?" Not to be outdone, he springs up, not as smoothly as me, but we're soon grabbing up all sorts of berries and edibles. We collect a bounty, descend, and then wash and lay it out for the players and spectators to snack on.

"This is so fun!" he yells.

"Bonko!" continues to be shouted out.

"Way fun!" I giggle.

Then we settle back under the glitter tree and let the blooms fall down, as we share in silence, doing that non-verbal dance, a syncing up of two tuning forks.

Nearby, Alkima and Ma-Tu appear arm in arm, with Mystikat in tow. They are only in their late 20s—my mother had me very young. Both are very sprite in spirit and appearance, but they are among the oldest of Geto's Rejexes. The couple check out the game of Bonko and talk secretly about it and other things. Ma-Tu gestures to the lads with the screaming eagle tattoos, and tells him her story about them almost coming to blows. Alkima looks up to their sun and I read his lips. "Perhaps something is out of whack, out of balance, not only on Mainlandia but also here." Ma-Tu gently takes his arm.

I finally break the shimmering quiet between Abana and me, remembering what Ayuna said I have to do. "So, have you ever been in love, Abana?"

He nervously laughs. "You don't mess around. Zing zang to the heart of the point?!" He checks me out directly for a second.

"Isn't that what you do when you fire your weapons?"

I have him. "All right, yes, I have been in love." Our shoulders are touching ever so lightly. I feel him take a slow deep inhale then an equally slow exhale as he looks off. "Her name was Azi. I thought she'd be my first and only love." He glances at me, but he can sense I want him to finish his tale. "We were like two of those mourning doves that are now passé."

"The ones who mated for life?" He nods, and I add, "I think I remember the last time I heard one of them crying. I was little and I'd hear them every morning until one day

I heard them cry no more. Just a whisper of emptiness in the sounds around."

"I think I've had the same experience. Anyhoo...she and several fishermen, who harvested kelp, were lost off the northern shore. They found no sign of their boat. They just disappeared. Vanished. There'd been heavy winds out there. But I never even got a chance to say 'so long' because we would never say goodbye to each other. We'd always say, 'See you, a la prochaine.' You know, next time."

I let the silence drop its heavy curtain again. I lift it only to ask. "Are you still in love?"

"Some man called John Lennon once sang, 'love is all you need,'" says a calming woman's voice.

Ma-Tu and Alkima have wandered over, bringing a heavier shawl for me. "For the cool air coming, m'petite."

I make the introductions, and Abana jumps up to offer his respect to both of them. "Alkima, sir, your magick and conjure is talked about all over, even with us on the south side!" Abana bows dramatically out of respect. Turning, he looks to my mother, realizing he'd met her earlier in the day. "And Ma-Tu, Aiya's spectacular beauty springs from you." He presents both of them with a clutch of fruit, and more cherry-berries. Ma-Tu giggles like me. I see in their eyes that they approve of my new handsome, cool friend. Alkima whispers in my ear, "I think he's a keeper!"

But the couple doesn't linger and walk on, without interfering, deep in their own discussion. They pause not too far off, and glance back from behind some trees—Alkima with an optimistic view, Ma-Tu with a more cautious, maternal view.

We spy them and think alike. "They are a special pair!"

Poetically, he observes, "Like two mourning doves...but who's this dude called John Lennon?"

CHAPTER SEVEN

Run Faster

Our radiant Occulo sun sets and the evening descends with a rainbow of stunning reds, oranges, and purples as if some painter has decided to blow any observer's mind by throwing great splashes of color onto the sky's canvas.

We mosey along a beach. Just off in the treeline is a steam-driven desalinization system.

We still don't touch, except perhaps when brushing up against each other—maybe purposely or by accident. And when we do that, the feeling is, well, kind of magnetic. We both feel little jolts that make the hairs on our arms rise to attention. Playfully, he etches one word, like graffiti, in the sand: "Rejex." Then I add another word to make it: "I, Rejex." We laugh and brush up against each other again. Then I stop, my heightened senses making me look out to the horizon.

"What?"

"I don't know, but I got freesôns!"

"Goosebumps? Me, too!"

Yes, he feels it, too. Then it goes as the lapping sea waters wash away the words we'd made in the sand. For a second, I think of us Rejexes being dumped here on Geto by those who wished that we'd just wash away. But we weren't going anywhere.

I come back to the moment because something else is going on. I sense that something deeper has a chance of building between us. I turn to try to say more, but stop myself when I feel some well-hidden defenses rise up against my welling attraction. That curtain of silence descends again between us.

The first evening stars are poking out, glittering in the colorful ever-shifting mural around them. I crane my neck to catch them, my smiling eyes catching their light. Abana looks up, too, pointing at the astral bodies. He doesn't nab me as I pull out some powdered dust from a pocket.

"I wonder about the life out there, looking at the other planetary bodies like ours and maybe other people wondering about the same thing," he says.

"My friend Alkima says they can't see our planet, that we're hidden from view because of magnetic streams that act like a kind of camouflage."

Abana is still looking up. "That is so weird and so sweet, that we can see them but they can't see us. Kind of like that Middle Kingdom tale." He turns his glance back down and looks around but can't locate me. "Aiya?" He opens his eyes wider. Still nothing. "Aiya, where are you?"

"Over here!" I playfully say.

Without moving his body, he turns his face slightly to his right. And there I am just standing there. "Wow, so you do know about camouflage!"

"Alkima calls it hiding in plain sight."

"That's an amazing trick, p'tite."

I like that he called me by my nickname, little one. I show him the purple haze dust. "You just throw some around and it disorients the person who breathes it in."

"And in the wrong hands, it could be one darkness of a weapon."

I haven't thought about it that way. But he is so right. I quickly put the remaining dust back in my pocket. We stroll on along the shore. His hand traces the arc of some shooting stars that explode into a band of silvery streaks.

I steal a glance at his dark but bright face, full of curiosity. I struggle to keep control, but I open my heart. "I know people talk about what's out there. But I'd also like to know what's beyond our island down here. What're they hiding from us Rejexes on Mainlandia?" I feel provocative again. "And what is love, anyway?"

Before he can reply, I feel an underground vibration rumble toward us under the sand, and my balance is thrown off a little. Then I see something strange. The waters at the shore's edge start to rapidly recede. I know about tides, but this is something very different. "Is that really weird or what?"

"Ga lee!"

"What do you think?"

"Let's see if it passes by."

He braces himself. I do likewise. We both stare far out to the horizon. There are strange cloud formations puffing up in the remnants of the once-vivid hues. "We need to run. Like fast."

"To where?"

"Higher ground!"

He breathes in a huge gulp of air then cups his hands around his mouth and exhales an alarm cry with amazing power. "People, run!" He does it again. But louder. "Run!" It vibrates through the evening air.

I follow his lead, and we send out the alarm cry together. Then we run. I keep pace with him as we scoot uphill, crying to the islanders around us. "People, run. Run faster!"

Some sort of quake or high-energy natural event must be happening way down in the sea. The waters receded then soon came back smashing into Geto's shore.

Because of Abana's early call, our island's residents have responded and are quickly reaching higher ground. We're aware of such natural events and are always somewhat prepared. So, as the winds and storm come, young and old alike gather on the higher ground. Abana and I continue to bark out instructions.

"Get down low and lash yourselves to each other and then to the mlap trees!" he shouts.

"Do it now, people!"

"The mlaps are strong and bendable. They won't break in the winds. Trust them, they may creak, but they will bend with the flow!" So our fellow islanders tie themselves with hemp rope to the trees in groups and hunker down low to the ground.

"Don't be scared, be strong like the mlaps," commands Abana.

I add, "We can ride this out!" as he and I direct people, and get our fellow teens and Bonko players to help out.

"We'll be alright, just don't let go and hang in there!" I shout.

Nearby Alkima and Ma-Tu also shout, "Listen to them, and stay calm!" They note how us two teens are becoming leaders right before their eyes, showing others how to stay both calm and strong.

Then the winds arrive—screaming, whipping banshees that scare aside everything in their path, carrying great waves of water. And the cold crashing rain soaks everything. The wild creatures, even the stinky dangerous ones, bury deep into their burrows trying to stay as far removed from the storm as possible. More howling winds thunder in. Rolling clouds unfurl. Then the skies darken to stark and fiery black and blue. The air cracks with electrical strikes that pound and bash the island in an incredible light show. It's all shock and awe. It would be wondrous if it wasn't so terrifying.

As the elements slam down, we hold on tight with strong hands and true grit—each tied to another and being our brother and sister's keeper.

I am roped next to Abana. We both shout more encouragement to our fellow islanders.

"We are one, don't surrender!"

"Hold on, hold on tight!"

"We will survive, if we all hold together as a team!"

Other teens, including the Bonko players and fans, echo our inspiring words—a tribe of banished misfits and outsiders and their kids shouting encouragement down the line to the next Rejex. "Hold together!"

I feel Abana's power next to me and know for sure that we will survive this. Besides, I still have to work on him and get past his emotional defenses. But that's for later. We now stare into each other's eyes.

"I'm good, you?" I shout through the surrounding chaos.

"Better with you around, Aiya!"

My inner smile turns into a snarl against the encroaching turmoil, as I now face the winds. My hair sweeps back. My eyes are fiercely aglow. Abana turns his face, too. The two of us seem on fire with determination, so alive in the face of possible doom and disaster. With a rebellious collective smile, we all courageously face Nature's ferocity together.

Nearby, Alkima holds his arm around Ma-Tu as they look on proudly. Even more so when Abana and I grab each other and embrace.

Mystikat sits alone on a grassy rock, seemingly untouched by the ferocity of the storm and the change wrapped up in its wrath. But his claws dig in deep. His fur brushes back in black waves tinged with fiery red at the tips. He is either totally unafraid or totally accepting of come what may. He, too, gazes out to the chaos on the horizon, and its uncertain future, as birds fly over squawking hurriedly toward Mainlandia.

Screech, squawk, screech...

PART ONE

Geto's Paradise of Perils
Mainlandia Rules
Occulo Help Us

CHAPTER EIGHT

Heresy, Freakin' Smeresy

Buried deep down in the Underground City below the wasted Mainlandian Basin, One-9, the colleague of that sarcastic scientist One-10, also wears an off-white lab coat as he zooms along in a spiffy motorized power chair, geekily gazing down at some work on his own handheld. He motors down a long, drab, gray, metallic corridor, consciously choosing not to use the moving sidewalk but motoring alongside it. So rebellious! He doesn't look up to anything around him, such as the digital news crawl on the walls that flashes out inspirational messages like, "Chill, the three-day work week is coming," and "Relax, conformity is cool and comfortable," and again, "Just don't act like a Rejex."

But he does glance up at an image that appears, showing very similar looking, ordinary babies lined up with their arms reaching out together: "Good—a new generation is being birthed as we speak." He taps his own shoulder, smiling proudly. "Well done, One-9...even if no one else says so!"

He peers back down at his handheld. There are "wi-fi" hot spots throughout the Underground City, marked by a painted stencil of a stick figure holding an antenna aloft—someone's attempt at humor, in a place where laughs are as rare as sunshine. But the spray-on hot spots are a brilliant, cute creation by one of Mainlandia's upcoming young female scientists, One-6.

Unfortunately, easy access to the web also means more opportunities for pushy pop-up affirmations and messages from "Big Bad Brudder" as his colleague One-10 calls the authorities. One-9's handheld beeps and he opens the personal message that also comes with a binging pop-up that reads: "Remember, we can all excel...if we all pull together as a team, right?!" It comes with a smily face. He dismisses this pop-up and looks at the personal message he's received, all the while without gazing ahead, as his vehicle moves on autopilot. His oblivious head leans forward, and he's so consumed by the new message that he steams straight into a closed laboratory door—*boing*—bumping his head.

As he looks up and rubs his throbbing skull, from the other side of the door he hears his scientist pal One-10 chuckling. "You don't always have to use your head, One-9! You could've used, you know, the voice recognition system."

The embarrassed scientist backs up, then pushes the door open with his fist instead. He wheels in, grumbling at his now throbbing knuckles. "Yeah, well, call me old-fashioned, but that brand new voice recognition system almost got you killed topside, One-10!" As his associate shrugs playfully, One-9 quips, "Besides, I prefer the old, old system. Using your noggin!"

Inside, One-9 looks across the room to his science partner who also sits in his power chair. One-10, the heroic scientist from topside, is now looking through two-way glass at several individual test rooms. He gazes at one room full of test tubes separated into ten different colored groups. Each group is being gently shaken not stirred by high-tech motorized arms. Hissing cool air keeps the test tubes cooled. Very chill.

Without looking back, One-10 says, "You know, your new test-tube vibrating system is just humming along, One-9. And I like the system's name, Good Vibrations. Well done!"

"Nah-ah, I ain't biting!" One-9 doesn't take the distracting bait and compliment. Instead, he smacks his e-device, referring to the personal message he's just received from his associate. "You should be careful, One-10, because what you're suggesting here about your test primate could be seen as heresy," says One-9, who also has stylized bushy eyebrows under a worried brow. Like some smarty-pants orangutan with sideburns, his head nods with scholarly intent. One-9 motors across the observation room to the two-way window. The two scientists both now stare into another adjacent room, a test room where a sturdy worker drone sits at a table working hard at pushing buttons on some memory tests, right next to a young chimpanzee that waits for its turn, kicking back with its arms impatiently folded behind its head. Super cool!

Both scientists wear identical lab coats, each with a shiny golden disc symbol on the left breast and a DNA strand symbol on the right breast. They look similar—with those bushy eyebrows and sideburns. But their slight differences—One-9's too tightly buttoned collar and matching footwear, versus One-10's loose collar while wearing one gray and one black shoe—gives insight into how each deals with Mainlandia's code of conformity.

"Heresy, freakin' smeresy, One-9! Because, why? Because it's been proven that our ancestors had much keener senses than we do, like our sense of smell. Even you once noted that about half of our olfactory receptors are now inactive. It's highly probable our ancestors, who didn't have complex language and writing skills let alone the capability to boodoogle absolutely any information on their handhelds, had superior memory abilities," One-10 says as he flips his handheld up in the air to show off, but then almost fumbles it. "Crap! And way better motor skills."

One-9 points. "So what are you saying about Bozo here?"

"He's not a bozo! Please, his name is Bonzo. And as a prime example of our evolutionary cousins, he has more acute eyesight than our test subject. He can smell and taste better than him. And these new tests prove he's dramatically better at remembering strings of numbers. How do you like them bananas?" He taps on the window, and when an assistant gives the chimp a treat, the ape finally goes to work on his test module.

"Yeah, but we're comparing Bonzo against a drone. So what?"

One-10 raises a bushy eyebrow. "I did the test on myself."

"And?"

"The chimp beat me on the numbers test, too!"

"That is embarrassing!"

"You're telling me!"

"So what exactly are you implying?"

One-10 sneakily looks around as if to see if anyone is spying on them then says, "As a result of our evolution, all our scientific advancements, all our antibiotics and vaccines, and all our technocratic progress, we may have a longer, more comfortable life..."

"Like our new proposed three-day work week!"

"And, we may well be eliminating genetic variances."

"By banishing anyone who doesn't fit in!"

"Exactly. But overall, I fear we're becoming dumber and more physically limited."

"Fair enough, One-10, but try explaining that to the General Council members who've given the go-ahead to build our super-duper genetic engineering labs." He catches more wrinkled worry on One-10's face. "What, it gets worse?"

"It always does!" He sucks in a deep breath. "Call me paranoid, but something else is up."

"Okay, Dr. Paranoid, are you talking about what happened up-top with you?"

"No, I'm talking about the pounding I keep getting in my own head," he says, rubbing his temples.

Just then Bonzo the chimp finishes punching some keys on his test module, and all sorts of lights and gizmos light up and go jingle-jangle-jingle. The chimp looks at his competitor and starts to cackle. He bends over and farts in the direction of the drone.

In the observation booth, trying to stifle a laugh, One-10 glances to his fellow scientist. "You can take the chimp out of the jungle, eh?"

"Okay, okay, but you do get my concern, right?!" One-9 harrumphs in a scholarly way.

"Fortune favors the brave, right?!" Both scientists see the clever chimp do a sort of victory jig then playfully salute and finally stick out its own tongue at them with a look of 'na-nana-nah!'

"Smart chimp, eh, One-9? What were you were saying about heresy?!"

One-9 worriedly runs his hand through his hair, whispering, "Oh, brother!"

Awhile later, the two slightly oddball scientists motor down a corridor. They're now all dressed up with somewhere to go. Starched, new lab coattails and pristine white gloves. Freshly pressed, stiff pants. But One-10 still has two differently colored shoes—one black and one shiny black. Packed items spill out of their satchels behind their seats. One-10 has brought a special guest along—Bonzo the smartass chimp, who sits in a snazzy cart being pulled along behind his motorized vehicle. The chimp is having the time of his life, wearing a toothy smile, a mini lab coat, and lab goggles, while his head hair is done up in an Einstein do. He's styling and he seems to know it!

They reach a door and One-10 playfully coughs over his shoulder to his trailing colleague then faces the closed elevator door. "Open, sesame!"

The voice recognition system works this time. The elevator swooshes open. "Ta-da!" Grinning, One-10 and Bonzo zoom in, his colleague follows, whispering under his breath, "Heresy by any other name, One-10, is still a dangerous game."

"A poet and you don't even know it." The three disappear into the elevator, as One-10 commands, "Darwin Hall, please!" and the door swooshes closed.

The two scientists' entrance and disappearance is being tracked on a large TV monitor in subdued private quarters. That mysterious monk-like figure watches it, with that speckled band wrapped around his left wrist. He commands, "Repeat entrance sequence...and volume up." The monitor automatically tracks back to the point where the two scientists approached the elevator. An almost perfectly statuesque, off-white coated woman with a shaved head huddles beside the monk-like figure as they watch the replay.

"They ARE playing a dangerous game, One-6," says the mysterious holy man.

"Hello! So what, we should start rounding up more suspects..."

"We could add chubby kids to the list," he quips.

"Enough! What's next, banishing adults as well, X-3?" She senses the "chubby" thing is a personal thing with him. "Besides, didn't you once say that we should allow our beloved fellow citizens their illusions—give them a safety valve, like their video games, to blow off steam? As you like to say, 'take a chill pill, X-3!'"

"You're right, One-6, we in the know understand that free will is just an illusion. It's all fake. One of the basic premises of biochemistry is that biological systems are nothing more than a test tube of chemicals that obey physical and chemical laws. Present company excluded, of course."

"Then logic dictates we should continue to allow them their little fantasies."

"Like that video game, GOH-3?"

"Exactly. To help keep them…"

"Under control!"

"I was going to say happy, Commander!"

"Happy, smappy, same thing, blah, blah." The hooded one raises his open right hand, fitted with a fine leather glove, in a gesture of, "Okay, okay, I'll give you that!"

He closes then opens his hand again. Almost magically, three coins appear in his hand. He pauses as if he's thinking, maybe of a question. Then he throws the coins on his table. When they stop, he bends over them. He says, "Haha!"

"Really, you're practicing some divination now?"

"I find consulting the *I Ching* backs up what our studies indicate. It's just a bit of fun, and weren't you just telling me to chill, One-6?" He pockets the coins without any further explanation. "Now, if you want my support in your bid to head up the General Council, let's talk about my own new title—I do like the sound of 'Commander'—and about my grand plan for topside. Oh, and let's not forget to praise the Darkness, right?!"

CHAPTER NINE

Big Bully Brother

Unlike other desert cities in the galaxy, where concrete, metal, glass and grids of power reach up to the sky, Mainlandia's capital city burrows deep into the sands. Over time, the denizens have stripped bare the once very lush green basin of many of its topside resources like the ancient peoples who had similarly laid waste to once glorious cities like Teotihuacan on the "Blue Planet."

Once Mainlandia's Basin was razed, "Big Bully Brother" decided to tear down their surface structures and rebuild them down below, closer to their remaining underground fossil fuels and minerals. The new Underground City lies under the surface of the central part of the Basin. Great shafts of metal and concrete now dive deep below the surface, where a controlled hive of activity lives and breathes. But the general populous is mostly unaware or maybe comfortably indifferent to the shenanigans ongoing topside...

Meanwhile, below and outside the great Darwin auditorium, young students wearing ten different colors of jumpsuits shuffle disinterestedly along like most teens do, heading into a new semester, with new synthetic backpacks and clothes. Some give the appearance of being excited. Others are bored stiff already. There are geeks, studs, cool girls and the so-called artists. All have brown eyes and seem well fed although their sunless skin is as pale as death. Except for the worker drones who labor topside.

On this the first day of the Spring semester, many students are all a twitter about something else—the promo trailer for GOH-3, the escapist videogame. "Get Outta Here" is a multiplayer game with its objective of getting out alive from the perilous Mainlandian jungle to make it back to the welcoming protection—although some might say, the mind-numbing security—of the Underground City. With a removable but sticky electrode patch on their foreheads, some students are already using a brain-computer interface (BCI) device to access the beta version of the new game.

Suddenly, they all shut up when they see a group of hooded monk-like students slither into view. Faces hidden, this sinister group creepily chants in unison, "Praise the Darkness!" and "For out of Darkness, comes new Light!"

The other students immediately avert their glances or bow their heads. When the long shadow of the hooded bullies passes into the auditorium, one girl who is designated 451 by the patch on her shoulder and who has frizzy long hair and a rainbow colored jumpsuit, murmurs, "I so hate the Darkness!" Then she cheekily hands out flyers. "Come see 'Devo: A Dance of Algorithms,' an approved performance art show. Previews start tonight!" A few students take her flyers and quickly stuff them in their pockets, while others scurry past, afraid to do so. When she persists with, "Come, support us—art can set you free. And it's a ton of fun!" Without looking up, the last hooded one, with X-33 on his shoulder, chuckles at her "fun" comment as he glides by. He threateningly darts his hooded head close to her, causing her to gasp and step back, but he doesn't do anything, except audibly chuckling again under his breath. And then he glides off.

Soon, all of the students stream into the auditorium and sit quietly in their colored designated areas. Many continue to check out the GOH trailer, heads bowed. But some of the Artist cluster whisper secretly to each other. 451 joins them and her message—"More shenanigans, topside!"—is passed onto her group, from art student to another. They share a conspiratorial and maybe dangerous interaction between themselves.

Then. Swoosh. The sound of frictionless, motorized wheels swirls into the hall. The two scientists, One-9 and One-10, wheel onto a stage. But the new semester students are still busy looking down at their various handhelds. As part of their introduction to the new semester, the two scientists zig-zag back and forth across a stage but with absolutely no effect on the young crowd.

Suddenly, little laser lights and fireworks explode from their hi-tech motorized chairs, as the two scientists do wheelies and whoop it up. Well, at least, trying to break the general monotony of Underground City schooling. The "lightshow" gets the new students' attention, sort of. They all look up, and the ones with the BCI devices remove their sticky patches and pay attention.

As governed by the formulas, numbers, lab results and chemical reactions that their lives are about, One-9 and One-10 have a surprisingly playful side to them that's tolerated by the Council of Scientists. Mostly because they're as brilliant as predicted by their gene sources, and their test tube bioengineering. One-9 has been recently tasked to develop a barcoding system for people. Meanwhile, One-10 has been assigned to develop a system that can transmit digital communications, complete with pop-ups, right to a person's retinas. "Easy-peasy! Just lean back and relax, we'll do all the work for you, as Big Brudder would say," as One-10 puts it.

The two have been bio-engineered, lab-conceived and then birthed by separate surrogate female drones almost to the same minute. Actually, they are part of a threesome but the less said of the banished and former One-11, the better.

On this stage in the Darwin auditorium, their job is to welcome the new students in their brand new, color-coded jumpsuits. Ten colors in all. So the new students sit clustered together by their color-coding. On the right breast of their jumpsuits they each have a symbol of one of ten designated Clusters: Scientist, Engineer, Adjudicator, Care-giver/Teacher, Administrator, Systems Technician, Enforcement, Artist, General Worker (which includes everything from birther and home-maker to construction worker), and finally the Cluster-X symbol for the hooded Cluster-10.

Population control is key, and the young students have all been engineered to happily conform to one of these 10 groups. Until they graduate, the left breast of their jumpsuits doesn't yet sport the shiny gold disc that the wise scientists onstage proudly wear on their now gleaming white dress coats.

Cluster-X students wear dark jumpsuits and hoods that cover their faces. The right breast of their jumpsuits simply displays that X. These bullies are noted for their brooding darkness and general silence, broken only by ominous chanting.

"Welcome, dreamers," One-10 enthuses, although, he knows how ridiculously ironic that is.

One-9 chimes in, "Right, welcome to your great adventure. Once we lived like our topside, distant cousins, the Thalandians. But then came the first 'gifts' from our orbiting Collector space station. Later there were more unexpected gifts and then radio and digital signals from outer space. Soon our present and future was changed forever." Then he toes the party line falsely suggesting, "Today, our ten schools of discipline have brought us unparalleled stability. And it proves that artificial selection, not the chaos of natural selection, does bring out the very best in us." He tries to get his audience going with a lame "let's hear it for our ten schools" cheer. But no one responds. "Okidoke, then!"

One-10 bites his tongue and lowers his head a little embarrassed, knowing what his colleague is being forced to mouth really is 'crap.' That Mainlandia's artificial selection program is just a means to highlight and target specific traits for the various groups, like strength and aggressiveness for the enforcement Cluster. All that, plus a way to isolate unwanted traits and behaviors, then boot out any latent misfits! Intolerance taken to its scientific extreme.

One-9 senses One-10's discomfort and cuts short his speech.

So, One-10 jumps right in. "Which reminds me of a joke. A neutrino walks into a synthohol bar. The bartender says, 'We don't serve your kind here.' The neutrino replies, 'I'm just passing through.' Or, for you creative arts students. Two performance artists were sitting on the floor—one fell off!"

There's only a smattering of snickers, mostly from the Artist cluster that seems to get it, twittering to each other, but keeping their response muted.

"Tough crowd, One-10!"

"Well, let's see how this grabs you, sprogs!" First, One-10 signals stage left, and Bonzo appears, shuffling in with his lab coat and goggles. Bonzo jumps up onto One-10's lap. The scientists can hear the stifled surprise, and some muffled giggles.

"Okay, my little friend, why don't you get things really started," says One-10 as he nods to the balcony. Smart Bonzo gets his meaning and points dramatically up to the balcony with a cackle. The auditorium lights dim. A hush descends. Giant speakers up there sizzle and crackle to life. Ta-dah!

Then the opening bars to a piece of music called "Johnny B. Goode" begins to rock the auditorium. For the next two minutes or so, the audience is fascinated by these never-before-heard sounds. Now this is exciting to the students, as their eyes light up, although they don't know quite how to react. But on stage, Bonzo takes the lead, dancing and flailing his arms to the music. The little dude has some sick moves. And some of the Artist cluster goofily shake their heads from side to side.

But after the glorious tune fades out, most of the students still effectively sit on their hands even though some are still tapping their feet. Then 451 in her Artist's rainbow colored jumpsuit starts silently clapping with one hand to show her appreciation. The mock gesture spreads to her fellow Cluster students and most of the crowd is soon silently clapping with one hand. Someone shouts, "Go Johnny, go!" as Bonzo also throws in some chimp cackles.

One-9 has to give it up to his compatriot, One-10, who then speaks to the audience. "So study hard, my sprogs, and maybe some day," he points to his gold disc. "You'll be 'good' enough to earn one of these gold discs."

One-10 scans over the audience, focuses in on 451, and gives a smiling thumbs up at her. But X-33, the hooded bully way in the back, makes a dark gesture towards One-10. The tall, menacing figure uses two fingers to point below his hood to his unseen eyes then points one finger back at One-10. The message is silent and threateningly explicit: "We have our eyes on you!"

"So, what else is new?" One-10 grumbles defiantly.

Just then a rising crescendo of warning sirens wail...as a tremor shakes the Underground City and rattles people's nerves. Even Bonzo, like a scaredy-cat, jumps back into the arms of One-10, who looks over with a questioning look to his always worried colleague. "I did nothing, I swear," One-10 protests again. But they both realize it's always the little tremors that come first that unsettle people the most, because they foreshadow a possibly bigger main event.

CHAPTER TEN

Trix and the Commander

Later, in another part of the Underground City at Mainlandia's General Council (GC) meeting, the "topside" issue is being hotly discussed. More pale faces mutter and nod.

A message crawl on the wall in the background reads, "No injuries reported due to recent seismic activity. Our Underground City will always endure..."

After all the eyes turn back from the crawl, the meeting continues. "Bottom line, we're fast running out of our old energy resources down here. So we must continue expanding our surface mining topside," states One-6 as she looks down, studying some notes on her handheld. She's Secretary to the GC.

Although she's barely 20, everything about One-6 is about perfection and business. She is a statuesque scientist with piercing dark brown eyes that are covered by spiffy mirrored shades—more for effect than anything else. Her head is shaved. Her white coat is as crisply starched as her manner. But she has developed many new technologies including that "wi-fi" antenna in a spray can that allows hot spots to be painted all over the Underground City.

"Even if it means more deforestation, species annihilation and pushing further into Thalandia?" asks One-10.

She ignores the comment but replaces her shades with reading glasses. "Our Scientist Council agrees with Cluster-X's slogan—Turning our desert into a power source," she says matter-of-factly as she scrolls through images on her handheld.

"You mean, expanding our man-made wasteland."

She reacts without looking up. "It's about our very survival, One-10. So thank you, we've all been refreshed and challenged by your unique point of view."

"Is sarcasm the only service we can get around here?"

She counters back. "Did you eat an extra bowl of slow this morning, One-10? Snap, snap, get with the program!"

One-10, ever the part-time dissident, murmurs under his breath, "Sure thing, Trix!"

"I'm sorry, One-10, you were saying?" She raises only an eyebrow.

One-9 gently elbows his compatriot to shut up. Calling someone by a name other than their official designation is slanderous.

"Sure thing...Six. I mean, One-6!" He almost can't help himself. He almost says Trix again, because she so looks like, and often acts like, a dominatrix. A brainy, almost nerdy dominatrix, but one nevertheless. He keeps his eyes down, trying to bite his tongue, not wanting to antagonize her more. But he twitches with unspoken mischief and fire.

He and his compatriot are in an outer circle around an inner roundtable where sit representatives for the five geographic Councils—the northern, eastern, southern, western and central areas of the Basin. Together, the geographic reps in their drab dress form the General Council.

Perhaps on purpose, One-6's chair is edged slightly higher than everyone else's.

"But, Madam Secretary, we can hardly keep pushing them back without expecting some sort of response," offers One-9 politely.

"That's right but rest assured, we've got a Plan-A and are working on plan-B and C."

Out of nowhere, One-10 presents the bloody spear that had pierced the engineer's back almost killing him. Broken in half, he hurls it surprisingly well from his position in the outer circle to the center of the inner roundtable. Hitting its mark, the dry-blooded spear trembles.

"So, that big plan, how's that all working out for you, One-6?"

While the other GC reps lean back aghast, One-6-Trix doesn't flinch, still not lifting her head. She doesn't respond for awhile. Finally, she peers up over her reading glasses, which she also wears totally for effect as she has perfect vision, and

she sniffs. "If you want theatrics, One-10, this is not the time
or the place. But I hear the Artist Cluster is holding auditions
for its new performance piece, Devo." One-6 signs off on a document and passes it along to the other Council reps to read
and do likewise.

"At the risk of sounding a little slow on the uptake, what are
you guys signing off on?"

One-10 watches as Trix slowly rises, all 6-3 and commanding. She motions to the center of the table with a laser stick,
and a holographic vignette appears—an army of soldiers are
led marching by hooded Cluster-X'ers toward the Thalandian
spear on the table. As the vignette plays out, One-6 reads
from her wristband computer. "Yes, we are getting reports
of increasing unprovoked Thalandian attacks on unarmed
workers on the eastern front." She pauses for more effect and
looks at another handheld. "There are also rumors that these
savages are even cannibals."

She waits for it. Whether it's true or not, her statement
has the desired effect, eliciting hisses and boos in the
Council chamber. And the GC reps each quickly sign off on
the document.

Flashing her dazzling whites, One-6 goes on. "So to launch
our new strategy, we're shifting more of our drone workers to
become Enforcement people. In turn, to deal with this increasing Thalandian threat, all enforcement will now come under
Cluster-X's authority, under the leadership of X-3."

"We're giving Cluster-X more enforcement power?"

"That's what they're there for, right, Commander?"

"Sorry, did you say 'Commander' because I don't think we
all got the memo?" asks One-10. So much for biting his tongue.

"Yes, the new order logically gives X-3 the title of
Enforcement Commander."

That spooky figure, with X-3 on his shoulder patch and
wearing that black cloak and hood that completely hides his
face, stands in the background and nods affirmatively. He is
the holy man who was listening in earlier with One-6 on the
two scientists' elevator conversation. He now seems to hold
that string of speckled worry beads in his left hand. His head
is slightly bowed, as if he's praying, as he gently caresses the

beads. The monk-like man signs the document with relish, and only says, "There are a lot of fake rumors around. So I say, carpe diem, seize the day, my friends, seize the day! And let's make our future extraordinary!"

One-10 grumbles, "I think I'm going to puke!"

The document returns to One-6 via X-3's equally shady and hooded confederate, X-33—the one who had made a threatening "eyes on you" gesture to One-10 at the Darwin auditorium.

Someone in the outer circle murmurs, "Let's just hope the first casualty of war isn't the truth."

X-33 glances over to identify the speaker but "Trix" doesn't acknowledge the comment, giving a "hold on" hand gesture to X-33. She then says with a satisfied grin, "Mission accomplished, we have agreement and conformity. Meeting adjourned." She turns off the holographic parade of soldiers around the spear.

As the other GC reps and the outer circle begin to leave, One-6 calls after One-9 and One-10. "Gentlemen, a moment alone, please?"

One-9 senses something is going to blow, as he shakes his head at his colleague.

When the others leave, she sashays over to her two fellow scientists. Under her white coat, they can see she wears seamed stockings that run down to her stiletto shoes. She sits on the roundtable near to them, slowly crosses then uncrosses her long, long legs until she's comfortable. She removes her glasses and puts a wafer thin communications headset on her shaved head. Her eyes seem to smile, but patronizingly so.

Under his breath, One-10 moans, "What, you don't scare me!" And, One-9 wants to smack his buddy upside his head for being so impertinent.

"Gentlemen, I and the Scientists' Council may allow you your verbal misbehaviors but beware, others may not be so understanding and forgiving. And, I wasn't being a smartass when I suggested you get with the program. It's for your own safety." She motions with her head toward the departing X-3, the new Commander, and his confederate. The Commander shifts the speckled beads in his hand to around his neck, as he leaves.

"Hello, did that thing in his hand just move?" asks a slightly stunned One-9.

"I thought they were worry beads."

"Those weren't beads, Dar, and it did so move!"

"Like I said, be careful. Anyway, what are we getting back from the chimpanzee and drone tests?"

One-9 coughs uneasily, hoping against hope that his buddy isn't going to get them into more do-do. But One-10 can't help himself. "Well, to be frank, the chimp kept peeing on the drone test subject."

"That's way too much information, One-10!"

"Sorry?"

"Uh, she's right, Dar!"

"Okay, right! I get it. Anyway, bottom line—the chimp keeps doing it, because he's outscored our Mainlandians, every single time! How's that for too much information, One-6!"

Topside, two mighty Thalandian warriors with painted blue faces poke the walls of another domed entity with their spears. They thrust with all their might but can't make a dent in it. Then out of nowhere, a portal on the dome once again seems to break down into individual molecules. And as the warriors thrust their spears at this section, their bodies fall through. With astonished looks on their faces, they are swallowed up by the portal, which for them feels like being sucked up into a big black hole.

A new slogan synchronously flashes on the dome's wall: "The influence of advanced technology far surpasses redundant magick, anyplace, anytime!—Your always concerned and caring Commander."

CHAPTER ELEVEN

A Little Enhanced Interrogation

Sometime later, in another area deep in the Underground City.

"Tell the others about the tests? Are you serious? How about never!!" whispers One-6 under her breath.

"But we're not making this up!" One-9 glances to his colleague and points to his e-device, as they huddle in a corner.

"Swipe that away," commands an irritated One-6 who then leans into both of them. "For now, let's zip it on the chimp/drone tests, okay?" They both comply by doing a combined zip-it gesture to her. She then sashays over to the other side of the room to her small audience. She has brought the two scientists and a few others to an observation room much like the room the scientists are using to observe their chimp memory test experiments.

"Gentleman, our new Commander has confirmed to me that officially we do not torture. And any rumors about it is just fake news," states a now stoic One-6.

"Then what in our moon's name are you doing setting up with the bench, water pails and towels?" asks One-10, who's just too honest for his own good. When he feels his colleague's stare, he says to him, "Hey, they invited us here to observe. I'm just observing. Unofficially!"

They peer through the glass window as a dark figure in a hoodie, X-33, oversees something sinister being set up. By the tone of his voice, X-33 is still a teen, but someone who has also risen up swiftly through his Cluster's ranks.

The two savage looking Thalandian specimens from topside are dragged in blindfolded. One of them is short, dark, hairy but powerful. The other is tall and lean, 6-6 of hard muscle with a full beard and flowing long hair.

"Uh, they don't speak our language, what can we possibly hope to get from them?" asks One-9, commiserating with his more outspoken buddy.

"The Commander tried the honeyed approach first. He fed them and gave them drink. After that, he had his people show reconnaissance maps to the prisoners of war, and politely asked them to point out their home base. They refused to respond."

"Home base? Prisoners of war?" One-9 asks innocently.

"The Commander says they attacked more workers today, so what else should we call it but..."

"How about fake?!" murmurs One-10.

"A first act of war," hisses the Commander, X-3, who also sounds youthful yet menacing. He steps up behind the scientists and now in a calming voice suggests, "Chill! A little enhanced interrogation never hurt anyone, right, Dar?"

"I'm not your, Dar," One-10 whirls to notice the speckled band back on the hooded one's wrist. The scientist peers up to the Commander towering over him with his face still shrouded in shadow by his hood. Another hooded confederate stands threateningly off his shoulder. "I mean, sir!" apologetically whispers One-10.

The word "Dar" is used in two ways, first as a term of endearment but only between close friends. It is also used sarcastically, at one's own peril.

"Sweet Occulo!" says One-9 when he sees the speckled band writhing on the Commander's wrist.

"You don't have to stick around to observe, Dar. Your choice."

But no one moves, including One-9 and One-10, who keep eyeing the speckled band that disappears up the Commander's sleeve. The opening inspirational strains of *Ode to Joy* rise up from surround sound speakers. And as they sit there wondering what next to do, the tall savage is led struggling to the board to be laid on his back in the test room. But "Trix" has something else on her mind. And, One-10 catches a glimpse of her almost catching her breath—did she really?—as she watches the heroic-looking tall savage being shackled for his enhanced interrogation. Then, One-6 whispers something quietly to the Commander.

The Commander immediately instructs X-33. "No, use the short one, my young friend. Let's see how much he really cares about his fellow savage's welfare." As teenager X-33 preps in the interrogation room, the Commander glances back to the two scientists. "And, if he really does care, he'll willingly point out their base, right?"

Still blindfolded so he doesn't have a clue as to what is going to happen, the short dark savage is placed on the board and shackled, unable to move. A towel is placed over his face.

At the same time, the tall savage is secured by chains attached to the ground like some real Prometheus. When his blindfold is removed from his face, this magnificent creature struggles even more at his chains as he sees his fellow Thal laid out on the board. In his seemingly limited savage mind, he growls, sensing this cannot be good.

Then X-33 rolls up his sleeves to reveal ripped young muscles. He picks up a container of water, and places it above the Thalandian's face. He looks to the observation room where his Commander orders via the telecom, "Show them how persuasive we can be, X-33!"

Ode to Joy pours gloriously into both rooms as the interrogator begins pouring water onto the cloth on the dark savage's face. The tall savage bares his teeth, roars and yanks at his chains as his fellow savage coughs and sputters. Trix finds herself being stirred by his ferocity—he tugs so hard on his chains that they cause him to trickle blood. She crosses her legs to stop the sensation she can't stop from feeling. Meanwhile, the serene Commander doesn't budge, with his hands clasped as in prayer. The boss of all bullies.

One-10 and One-9 watch shocked by the ritual. One-10 leans toward his buddy. "So what do you think about our evolution, now...Dar?!!!" He pivots his chair on a dime to leave as the interrogation rolls on.

And, to show how pissed he is, he lets one final firework explode from his chair, causing everyone in the observation room to almost have a heart attack. "Whoops, sorry, just an accident!" He's steaming and he may have to suffer the consequences, as he zooms out of the room by himself, but he doesn't care.

One-9 feels he has no option but to stick it out and watch as Beethoven's rousing music counter-points the persuasive "enhanced interrogation" being meted out. One-9's eyes well up but he quickly dries them—he can't help it, for there is no crying in science. Or at least, that's what he's been taught.

One-9 stays behind to watch the "not-torture" of the Thalandian savage. He stays as long as he can, until he throws up and is excused, returning to their offices. One-9 wheels in to find two new students, that frizzy-haired Artist Cluster girl and a young male teen, who are cleaning their office. His compatriot is staring through the observation window at the test chimp who continues to astound with his test results. Bonzo keeps setting off all sorts of chimes and bells, and even puts a consoling arm around another test subject...while he cackles.

One-10 hears the power chair enter but doesn't turn around immediately. "Come on, One-9. Many of us can't do simple math in our head. A young monkey left orphaned by the murder of his mother in the jungle can remember strings of numbers better than us. We synthesize our food and drink. We can hardly smell—then again our food has no taste or smell, so what does it matter. Our eyesight is getting poorer. We're losing all of our senses."

"Did you hear that?" There is silence. "Because that's the sound of no one above us caring, One-10!"

But he barges on. "For all our wonderful scientific progress, we've lost touch with who we were, and our connection to Nature. Technology was supposed to give us more freedom. Great, now we have the freedom to torture other beings. Where in Occulo, are we heading, One-9?"

"I'm sorry, you think I'm psychic or some sort of quack fortune teller now or what? Because our new understanding preaches that there is no such thing as extrasensory ability. It's a myth, a tale told when we're too lazy to find the rationale behind some event. What did our always caring new Commander write: The influence of advanced technology far surpasses redundant magick."

"Right, anyplace, anytime." He pauses to think. "Then again, didn't someone else once write, 'There are more things in heaven and earth, Horatio, Than are dreamt of in your philosophy.'"

One-9 wheels over to him. "You've been listening to transcriptions of some new radio signals?"

"From the Blue Planet in the 'Sol'ar' system, yes. Some priceless poetry."

"From that writer dude Shakespeare?"

"From his work, *Hamlet*, yes. But centuries after, the Hotspur Society, the group that sent the signal stream, suggests the famous William Shakespeare had literary collaborators, like Marlowe, for over half of his plays."

"Now that's teamwork!"

"You see what we're missing!"

The two working students keep quiet and try not to look up. But both their eyes light up for different reasons at the scientists' conversation. When the young male has a moment to himself, as his eyes dart shiftily around, he quickly sends a conspiratorial message on his own handheld: "Sir, I think, they're talking heresy!"

CHAPTER TWELVE

Garbage In, Culture Out

Their planet is called Occulo, because it lies hidden in orbit around its Star. And hidden is how Mainlandia's General Council of the Ten Clusters has always wanted it, as they are isolationists by nature. Outer space travel was never on the agenda. They've never even ventured to the unmanned satellites that have been left behind by some previous unknown visitors and that still circle above in low orbit.

But Occulo has a unique way of interacting, well more like "not interacting" with the world outside. Their planet is also affectionately called in old patois, Pu-bel, from the word Poubelle which means trash can. Through a combination of powerful magnetic forces and space eddies, Occulo has become a repository for invaluable space junk from everywhere.

Explorer vessels, planetary probes, discarded equipment, and satellites all find their way into Occulo's orbit and thus into the sphere of the Collector, the planet's giant space "garbage" collecting station. It had also most probably been left behind by the same unknown race. As a result, the Collector acts like a sort of space spider web, and so the planet continually scoops up a bounty of advanced equipment and materials.

Apart from that bounty, the Collector's associated satellites are continuously picking up digital signal streams that are full of untold treasures from all corners of the universe, including: the complete music catalogs of The Beatles and the Sex Pistols; the Hotspur Society's staged performances of Shakespeare's complete works, along with Darwin's *Origin of the Species*, and Confucius' edited works; Altair's tome on renewable resources; some performance art by rapper Red-manz and popstar Jùjué, both from Class M planets; an interstellar cookbook by a race called the Kanamits and titled *To Serve Man*; a stream of ominous alien DNA code from planet LV-426; an audiobook called *The Martian* which included upbeat dance songs like "Waterloo" and "Hot Stuff" and a rousing ode to a certain "Starman" and "Ziggy Stardust"; a punk rock opera called "American Idiot" which featured the story of Jesus of Suburbia; and, so much more—just a treasure trove which formed the basis of Mainlandia's culture and history.

One-10 now leans close to his science buddy. "So what did happen? No, hold on, let me guess. Torture-smorture, those bullies got nothing from those proud savages, right?"

"The short dark one almost died, and you're right, the Commander got zippo. I don't even believe they've attacked bases as One-6 and her puppet-master suggest."

"No kidding, Shakespeare. Apart from the fact that I find it reprehensible for our so-called advanced society to resort to it, torture just doesn't work. The zip-zap prod never worked on our primate test subjects, right?"

"Once again, I'm with you. Honey is always better than vinegar."

One-10 sighs as he gets lost in some reverie.

"What are you dreaming about?"

He recalls. "Remember real honey, from the bees who lived in our Basin before we wiped out their habitat? Remember its thick consistency, its awesome flavor with a hint of tang. Nothing like the synthesized gloop we now have."

"I so miss that, but what can we do about it?"

One-10 wheels over to the opposite side where the two students are cleaning and re-stocking the shelves. When they aren't looking, he inconspicuously presses his hand against a panel and a tiny compartment in the wall opens. He reaches in and gently retrieves a book wrapped in soft cloth. He quickly closes the panel.

"What, weren't we supposed to have burned all those old books?"

"As if?!" One-10 puts a finger to his associate's lips. He gently removes the cloth and opens the book, one that hasn't been opened in years. He breathes in the smell of its pages.

Then traces his fingers down the paragraphs. "Many myths from around our universe often say that when you ask the right question, that only then will the answer come." He finds the line he was looking for. "When our planet went dark, when night descended on our ancestors, it took the Shaman to ask, 'Do we have the courage to lift the veil of darkness?'"

One student, the young artist with frizzy hair, who has overheard them can't help but interject. "Then soon after the Zephyrian Crystals came to us from the skies and helped give us fire, light and new life..." She quickly averts her eyes and shuts up, going back to her work.

One-10 is impressed. "Somebody's been doing her home-work." The girl keeps her eyes down but smiles.

One-10 then turns to his buddy. "So what question should we be asking now, Dar? Because Occulo help us, we really are in some deep do-do!"

"No shit, Sherlock," One-9 actually jokes.

CHAPTER THIRTEEN

The Return of the Fire Horse

When the next shockwave hits, the Underground City vibrates a little on Mainlandia. But very few people initially react. They're all still too busy looking down at their handhelds or going about their daily drab of drudgery. The extensive use of wood in the City's foundations also helps absorb the shock.

Just before it hits, One-10 is in another spot of trouble. One of the two students, who'd been dusting his office, has turned him in for having a forbidden book—not the clever student, 451, with frizzy hair. So his office was tossed by enforcement drones led by X-33 but only one book was found.

One-10 is now fidgeting alone in One-6's cold, metal and glass office like a student waiting to be punished by his school principal. On his handheld, he says, "So, sue me, One-9. What's done is done!" He hears heels strutting in and his heart skips a beat.

As One-6 sashays in, looking down at the cover of the forbidden text in her hand, the big vibration hits, the one that had been felt on the beach by Aiya and Abana.

"Hello, if you felt that, this is hardly the time to jibber-jabber about my taste in bedtime reading."

She lies. "I didn't feel anything. But this is the exact time to nip a lot of things in the bud, One-10."

She walks by him all high heels and stylized lab coat, and opens the book. She adjusts her glasses and reads the title. "*A Book of Myths.*" She turns to a bookmarked page, and opens that and reads again. "*The Return of the Fire Horse* —What is this?"

"Okay, first off, One-6, this is all on me. Let's face it, I'm a bit of a pain!"

"That's putting it mildly," she mockingly chuckles as she reads on: "A dream about a horse is linked with freedom, strength, power and growth...it represents where you are in life. And riding a wild horse reflects strong sexual passion... Fire Horses are smart and self-confident and often end up leading others...What is this nonsense?" She's lying again as she's secretly intrigued, maybe even turned on by talk of passion. She squirms a little as she reads it. But she's a scientist first with big ambitions to pursue and, with the support of the Commander, a brave new world to create.

"Once again, One-9 knew nothing about this. It's just little old oddball me!"

She ignores his comment. "Let's face it, we here are brilliant scientists, Dar. But any student of science knows free will is an illusion. Or, just a fake belief as our Commander says. Most of us are just biological systems that obey physical and chemical laws."

The follow-up shock wave hits, this time a lot stronger. She still doesn't blink, and therefore, doesn't betray anything to One-10.

"You've got to be kidding me!" he says both to her comment and also to the shock wave.

"We've had ground quakes before, why always with all the drama, One-10?"

"Ex-squeeze me, if free will is an illusion, then why bother with anything?"

Just then she gets a message on one of her handhelds. She moves aside to view her caller then speaks aloud. "What's up, Commander?"

"We should take advantage of this and call an extraordinary meeting of the General Council!" he says on the speakerphone.

One-6 turns to One-10 and takes a deep breath. He's right. This isn't the time to argue about small heresies or philosophical discussions. "You're with me, One-10. And get your sensible partner to join us." She returns her attention to her caller.

As One-10 rolls out, he whispers on his headset to his partner, "Oh, brother what a nightmare!"

While she quietly replies to her caller. "All right, Commander, bring it on!"

The General Council is convening for an emergency meeting. The room is jammed as people wait for the other shoe to drop. The murmurs and whispers about things topside, including the shock waves, underscore the worry the audience is feeling.

The old electrical power lighting system flickers dim for a few seconds. And the audience all looks downwards as they ask in a babel of voices.

"What caused that shockwave?"

"Should we move into our bunker rooms?"

"Is the BIG one coming? Are we prepared?"

"What should we do?"

A now familiar hooded figure glides into the room caressing his speckled band that once again looks just like worry beads. The Commander pauses then whispers only into his shrouded young accomplice's ear, "Unleash hell!"

X-33 bows and leaves the room on some mission while intently keying something into his handheld. The Commander glides through the audience, head bowed down, whispering, "Be afraid, be very, very afraid." He keeps repeating it as if he is sowing the seeds of worry through a mantra. He glides to his chair, which has been set up at the right hand of One-6. But he doesn't sit. He stands, head bowed, hands folded serenely in front of him, but now looking like some executioner before he does his deadly deed. The speckled band has returned to his left wrist, now seemingly alive.

Another shock wave rumbles through the room, causing gasps and unconscious screams. One-6 looks at the contents of her glass that are shaking. She finally thinks this may be for real. But still she minimizes it. "No need for panic, our early warning systems report that it's just some sort of underground seismic shift."

One-10 adds, "What are we, ostrich birds burying our heads in the sand, thinking danger will just go away if we ignore it? It's the very nature of Nature, that as much as we try to control her, she will have her way. But we can take logical steps to minimize her impact!"

"Be afraid, be very, very afraid!" hisses the Commander as he leans into the microphone at his position.

"Hello, that's not what I meant. And that's fear-mongering, sir!" One-10 shouts out. Then he whispers to his buddy, "And I'm accused of being a drama queen, Dar!"

The vibrations rock on.

"As I said, Be afraid, be very, very afraid!" he repeats.

"What do you want us to do, Commander?" asks One-6.

Keeping calm, he slowly raises his hands up like some preacher. "What if this is not natural? What if this is a weapon that the Thalandians have created. After the personal attacks on our engineers and workers, what if this is their first major salvo in a war against us?" He uses the laser-stick to again reveal a holographic topography of Mainlandia's topside on the table. He directs the laser-stick to the east and causes a set of holographic waves to push in from the jungle east of Mainlandia's dirty new mining field. The waves then blow west across the Basin.

"That's just total bunkum, Commander. Our own detection systems show the waves starting and coming from the west, maybe even coming from below the sea, and then sweeping east across the basin," asserts One-10. "By saying otherwise, you're creating a false sense of fear."

The Commander waves his laser-stick to show the waves coming from the east again then swirling clockwise around the Basin to appear as if they are coming from the west. "Couldn't it happen this way?"

"In your dreams, sir!"

"But could it happen this way, if they somehow had new weapons?"

"Gimme a break, you're kidding us, right?!"

"Kidding is for kids, Dar!"

"But they're thousands of years behind us science-wise! Their most advanced weapons are crude spears, arrows and rocks. Now they've got some weapon that creates seismic activity? Hello! I hardly think so!"

"Why not? Why could it not have happened by accident? Think about how we fortunately discovered our Collector station and its satellites. We still don't know how they came to be left in our orbit. We were fortunate, but where would we be without them?" For effect, he points his laser-stick and throws images of fire down on the table. "And think back even further about how us finding fire, through the use of the Zephyr crystals, transformed us from similar savages to civilized people." He lets the fires burn. "So, I ask again, couldn't the Thalandians have lucked into finding a WMD—a weapon of mass destruction? It's not beyond the realm of possibility, is it?"

"Answer the Commander, One-10!" Trix advises.

One-10 looks around at the frozen looks on the GC members' faces, and at the imposing hooded ones interspersed among them. He mutters to himself, running a hand through his hair, and wanting to pull it out. Then he looks up and nods glumly to One-6, adding, "Nothing's impossible, I guess."

The hooded warmonger finally shows aggression as he thumps both black-gloved fists on the table. "There you have it. I sincerely believe they somehow have such a weapon."

And then another vibration rocks through the room.

"Now that isn't fake," whispers One-10.

"I say, let's declare temporary Martial Law. Let's be proactive and take on this threat before it hurts us. What say you, citizens? Let's seize the day!"

Having retreated to the back, One-9 and One-10 glance to each other. They sense each other's thoughts, understanding that like all of history's demagogues from the far-flung corners of the universe, that this shrouded one could bully and prod people, and walk them right into violence and war, even against all logic and their better judgment.

Desperately clasping his head in his hands, One-10 exclaims. "Occulo, help us!"

And, way, way over on Geto, "Occulo, help us!" suddenly pings around in Alkima's head, as the storm rages.

PART ONE

Geto's Paradise of Perils

Mainlandia Rules

Occulo Help Us

CHAPTER FOURTEEN

Enough, Already!

In amongst the still flying debris, "Occulo, help us!" now echoes in the back of my head. But more importantly, our people seem to have weathered it well. But, I shout out to the Nature herself, "Hello! Enough, already! Hello!" Mystikat joins me by almost growling back at the still blowing wind.

And strangely, right then and there, the storm suddenly stops, as if someone finally decided to turn off a switch. Or as if someone else has gotten bored with treating Geto's residents as if we are like flies to wanton stomping kids.

The menacing black and blue clouds just as quickly sweep away. Ready for a new painter to do his work. And a heavy hush of calm silence descends after the chaos, as our relieved island people gather our collective breath and let out a huge and almost audible sigh of relief. "It passé! – It's done!"

Following Abana and my lead, other teens start to help the adults and children unlash themselves from the trees. Personally, Abana and I have suffered only minor injuries. One big frond had caught Abana on his head and blood drips from it. I dab the blood away and smooch his cheek better.

"Am I going to die?" he asks with a fake worried frown.

"Anyone who can survive a Bonko bashing can handle a few fronds, you dope!" I gently punch him. He cracks up and the flash of his pearly whites warms my heart.

Our people start hugging each other and laughing and yelling in honor of still having breath. To them, we are heroes for raising the alarm call and suggesting using the ropes. As people massage blood back into their limbs, they come alive, as if they're rising from the purgatory of near death. They pat us on our backs or hug us. But that doesn't last long because

we hear cries for help, and notice that a couple of people in the
distance lie under fallen trees. Abana and I jump right to it,
somehow gathering amazing strength—who knew?—to lift
the trees off. Then, our fellow teenagers join in with all of us
ganging together to lift heavy and dangerous debris off any
trapped people. Soon everyone is freed. What a team, as we let
out another cheer of relief!

Soon, Alkima and Ma-Tu begin setting up the salves and
medicines he'd brought down from his mountaintop. He
has been absolutely correct in his prediction, so far. But he
said something else was also coming. Who knows what it
could be?

He shouts, "Aiya and Abana, first clean any wounds then
apply the salves. Ma-Tu and I will check for anything more
serious. Let's go team!"

"Let's deal with the children, first, Abana!" I direct.

The two of us take Alkima's magical salves and gather in our
fellow teens to assist. "Let's bring all the children here in the
middle, okay, guys?" motions Abana.

A couple of kids are crying from being hit by flying branches
and other debris. One little boy is being as brave as he can but
his grimace shows the pain he's hiding.

"Oo ye yi!" I say as I see he needs consoling. I tilt up his
chin and keep it raised as I gently peck his rosy cheek where
a teardrop has run down. Some distraction's in order. "You
want to see something cool?" The lad nods. I gently roll up my
shirt and show a jagged scar on my tummy, a remnant of my
natural but dangerous premature birth on Geto.

"Ga lee!" says the lad with wide-open eyes. I let him touch
my scar.

"My Ma-Tu told me I'm a survivor. That all of us on Geto,
our tribe, is a clan of survivors. So, I have a poem I want to
tell you..."

Several other injured kids push in closer to me, as I recite
something I'd written:

> The savage scar on her stomach was jagged
> It spoke much of her bravery and love of life
> There it remained, a remnant of her battle to breathe
> When she'd left her Ma-Tu's womb early

A reminder of life's struggle to avoid being blown out
Like a withering candle in the face of a stronger cold draft
And that savage cut on the smooth silk of her skin
She wore like a badge of courage
Like a wounded warrior who had been to the edge
And peered over at the possible gaping nothingness that lay below
And pulled herself back, screaming, shaking,
screaming for more breath
More time, more memories, more magical moments
before that breath was taken away again...

Abana puts a comforting arm around the lad's shoulder and he adds his own verse to my poem:

I bow down to your bravery
And only wish that your courage
Allows you to forever look up and kiss the sky...

My heart almost bursts as I feel on fire by his understanding. And, all the kids smile and blow kisses at the sky. Then we group hug. They feel better but the wounds still needed tending, so some further distraction is needed. So I beckon Mr. Mysterious, Mystikat, who immediately slides on over—he only seems to have one mode of motion and that's to mosey—as if he knows he's needed.

"Kiddos, we're going to play a game." I point to a nearby tree with a lot of branches. "Who thinks Mystikat can jump up onto the first branch?"

"We do!" A bunch of excited hands go up. One kid however says, "Not me!" Laugh out loud, there's always one.

But the sleek black cat knows exactly what to do. He moseys over to the tree and plays it out. Circling the tree, looking up at the branch then yawning and stretching, and even lying down as if he's about to sleep—what a clown. As he does this, Abana and I start treating the injured but distracted kids.

By the time Mystikat has shown his super amazing leaping ability by jumping up to and jumping back down from several branches—to the applause of the kids and parental units—the injured kids are all treated and bandaged up.

When it's done, Mystikat takes in the applause as if he knows he really was on show. But when the kids run over to pet him he skedaddles, with the kids on his heels to great laughter.

As our "medical" team, including two resident natural healers, work on the adults, I see that Alkima seems temporarily pre-occupied.

I wait until he takes a break to drink some refreshment. "What's shaking, Alkima?" He turns to me. And for some reason, I immediately remember the distress signal that both I and apparently Alkima had picked up—"Occulo, help us!" So I ask, "Okay, so who else needs help?"

"Our cousins on Mainlandia. But first things first, Aiya, let's finish taking care of our own. Then we go visit our cousins!"

There've been a couple of storm-related deaths but over the next few days, Geto's relieved but determined residents team together to rebuild our homes. There are plenty of natural resources like wood as we have an ongoing reforestation program that ensures that the resource is readily available. There are extra food stocks buried underground and in caves, and an abundance of fresh and desalinated water.

The further that Geto's exiled residents transition away from our Mainlandian cousins—genetically, emotionally and spiritually—the more attuned we're becoming with ourselves, with the soul of the earth, sky and sea around us, and with our people's ancient arts. It's as if we're simply being switched on to long lost and forgotten skills, abilities, and most importantly, instincts—as if we misfits, weirdos and outcasts are becoming higher beings.

For the loved ones that have passed away during the storm, there is no mourning, it's more a celebration of lives well lived—Don't mourn my death, celebrate my life. So, it's what we call "fais dodo," party time. And a big part of that is rebuilding our community to honor them.

Like our Mainlandian "cousins," Geto's residents have all the various occupations covered. We may be banished Rejexes, and many of us are now the naturally born children of these Rejexes, but we are also engineers, workers, artists and technicians in our own way. With focus and desire, a team of twenty can put a new house together in one day. So a dozen teams raise 50 homes in four days. And we sing and celebrate life as we work, unlike the drones and others on Mainlandia, I'm told.

We sing because we believe we have free will, that despite what may rain down on us, we can control our responses to even chance events. My Ma-Tu often tells me the same message when I've been hurt or disappointed by some situation: "Don't judge events as either positive or negative. Experience them, m'petite, celebrate them and learn from them." Additionally, Alkima also tells me: "See these events and experiences as opportunities to grow, and advance to self-mastery." Then he'll quip, "Just make sure to bring me some shrooms, sha!"

And so we people see the storm as a chance to start afresh on the foundation of what has been created before. Rebuilding our very workable hunter/gatherer/farming society and living by our holistic principles. And, we honor our lost friends by building several funeral pyres like our ancestors must have. We dress up in our finest cobbled together, steampunk creations— bustles, corsets, petticoats, suits with waistcoats, duster coats, tailcoats, and military-inspired ensembles with Abana leading the way, looking outstandingly handsome in a jacket and epaulettes. And also a lot of super cool goggles along with fancy hats, bowlers, and more glorious headgear. And in this finery, we tell stories and sing praises to those moving on.

Alkima, who wears a stovepipe hat crowned with awesomely gaudy feathers, recites, "When you arrive, the party is already under way, much fais do-do around the council fires, with our Rejex kin present, along with our ancestors. People from Mainlandia and Geto finally joined as one, again. So go prepared, loved ones, because les bons temps rouler!" And he dances a twirling series of spins, so fast, he appears like a spinning top while yodeling something wonderful.

The rest of us also spin and cheer, "Let the good times roll!"

The people also take big homegrown gourds that look like pumpkins, and we magically carve cool figures into them. I choose to carve my "fire horse" into my gourd. And I put a homemade candle inside of the hollowed out gourd, so that my equine creature seems to explode into being, galloping into life from the glow inside, its tail and mane aflame. And, our people also dance because the birds, creatures and also dem dangerous critters are also returning to Geto to rebuild their own homes and lives.

After each new workday is done, we celebrate our simple accomplishments together around big bonfires, reusing the broken trees. Everything gets re-used, nothing is wasted.

At the same time, Abana teaches me many of the ancient skills he knows from basic survival techniques to movement training like Parkour. And I soak it up, like a sponge, becoming more than I am, and loving just being around him and being directed by his hardened but gentle hands.

But one day, I see Abana wander off a little to look at the sea beyond Geto. There's a fishing boat back on the waters, returning to the shore. The crew recognizes him and waves at Abana. He makes a half-hearted attempt at waving back. He takes in a slow big gulp of air and sighs deeply, possibly remembering Azi, the girl he'd loved. He looks down, and toes the earth with his foot.

"Thinking of a lost one who you wish could be here, Abana?" asks a curious Alkima. As I stand behind my mentor, I also feel the weight that Abana's personal loss still has on him.

"Yes, lost ones, Alkima." He thumps his chest. "But their spirits are still with us, here in our hearts. It's all good." He turns around and grins at us. "What are you cooking up today, my friend?" Abana washes his hands and face off after a day of building.

"Poo-yee, don't ask, you probably don't want to know what's in it," I playfully hold my nose.

"Just take a drink, Abana," adds Ma-Tu, "It'll pick you up, believe me."

So Abana takes a big cup of Alkima's concoction, and slugs it back with zest. I do the same as I hold my nose. Haha! He does seem to look refreshed as he gazes at me with an open, melt-your-heart grin.

Without being obvious, I peek for any subtle signs that Abana is thinking again of Azi. But he seems focused. Or does he hide things as well as I do?

"You, good?" I ask.

"So I'm told, why?"

What a kidder, he is! But I wonder if somehow getting him off of Geto, away from any lingering memories and shadows, would help. "You know where I'd like to go?"

"The beach?" he grins.

"The beach?" No, not the beach, I want to shout but I bite my tongue. "Yeah okay, but I was thinking more of..."

But he interrupts me before I tell him my bigger plan. "Want to learn how to throw an opponent and fall without hurting yourself?"

How can I say no? I look to Ma-Tu who nods since all my chores are done. Then I start scooting past Abana. "Hey, last one there is a poo-yee rotter!" We two local heroes run off.

A little while later, we're back on the beach where the stormy chaos had started. The beach has been cleared and is starting to look like its former pristine self.

On the sifting almost crystalline sand, he shows me basic but very effective martial arts moves. After throwing me a few times, I stop him, "Okidoke, my turn!" It takes a few tries but I throw him down and I laugh out loud. "Wow, who knew?"

"Remember, the best techniques are the simplest. You just have to learn them right and practice them again and again."

We go at it, again, only harder. During one sequence, he doesn't pull his punch fast enough and he catches the tip of my nose, but enough to draw blood. I bend over, seemingly in pain.

"Aiya, I'm so sorry."

I wipe the drops of blood with the back of my hand, still bent over. I play it out, looking hurt. But he can't tell as my hair covers my face. He puts his hand on my shoulder but I just explode, my knee catching him lightly in the groin—not enough to incapacitate but enough to send a message.

"Gotcha!" He groans and falls down. "Didn't you tell me never ever to let down your guard?"

He looks up and cracks up laughing. I collapse on the sand next to him and laugh with him. "Too right. Like never!"

He rolls toward me, grabs me in his arms, and kisses me.

"Wow!" Alrighty then! One of those first kisses. Not always the best. Not always perfectly timed. Not held for that long, but always with enough feeling to remember. Even if the second kiss is a long way away. We look at each other, forehead to forehead. I nuzzle his cheek and smile. We don't say anything, like when we first met. Just smelling each other's scents, getting our bodies and vibrations into sync.

"Let's swim!" I blurt out after awhile.

"Quoi?"

"Why? Why not?!" I look up to our planet's solitary but very bright moon as it casts its super cool moonbeams down to dance on the water. "Let's be spontaneous!"

I'm up in a flash and strip down to my skivvies. He does likewise and off we plunge into the silvery sea like two young dolphins in a world of our own—splashing, diving, spinning, spouting water. We vibrate together, two tuning forks in sync for a few stolen moments. Something stronger and deeper really is building.

Back in the village, Alkima sits next to Mystikat watching the celebrations. Mystikat meows and Alkima rubs his chin. "I know, I know. It's Aiya's time and she wants to leave." When Mystikat then hisses, he adds, "Yes, I know, monsters await us!"

CHAPTER FIFTEEN

A Trio of Adventurers

Back at his mountaintop laboratory, Alkima hurries out of his teepee with ingredients in hand to continue prepping more potions and elixirs—he uses all sorts of natural minerals, plant elements and extracts to create his cocktails of herbal medicine.

Wearing a special white robe similar to the "holy" man's dark robe, he sits. On his table, along with his ingredients, sit a number of reflective materials. Like a wizard, he throws powders into more boiling cups, conjuring up his alchemic potions. As they mix and bubble, he stretches out his hands, bringing down energy from the sky and air around, chanting as he conjures. Tapping into all the natural elements around, and using the reflective materials near him, he creates a rainbow of refracted light around him. Bowing his head, a glowing smile appears from under his hood.

A while later, he sniffs the air, smelling us first then hearing us approach from afar.

He's invited Abana and me to collect some more natural ingredients he needs. I now have two yellow quarter moons painted around my eye—at night, they glow like the dazzling neon shells on our beach. Abana likes my look. Haha, I'm in full "hook and reel him in" mode. Wearing punk-like scavenging gear, we're super enthusiastic in our efforts, finding everything on Alkima's detailed list. We joke, compete and sing as we shimmy up trees. I practice some of my new "Parkour" moves, traveling up trunks and across branches better than before. Parkour means the "path" and like a wild creature I become at home in the trees. And, it's like a new me emerging, post storm. Meanwhile, Mystikat quietly shadows us, watching and moseying along.

We dig deep into the ground to pull out exotic roots. We spy some more of those flowers that make the purple haze dust but they are high up on a sheer rock face. A surprised Abana watches as I challenge him with, "Anything you can do."

"Go ahead, show me!"

I carefully but pretty easily ascend the rock face followed by him. At one point, I temporarily lose my footing but I have a newfound ferocity, and manage to regain that footing, and continue on upwards.

"I wonder who really needs protecting?!" he jokes as we reach the top.

He pauses. And I think I see a flash in his eyes, of him thinking back, but it's gone quicker than a blink of those same big eyes.

"What were you thinking about?" I ask.

He deflects me. "We can protect each other!"

I playfully punch him. "Wow, now you can punch like a little boy!" He teases. So I punch him in the gut. He feels it and is pleasantly pleased with how strong I am getting. "Okay, like a very strong little boy!"

"A strong, big girl, more like it!" I chase after him. Soon, after finishing Alkima's list, and on our way up to the mountaintop, we stop to rest and take refreshment. I liked how he looks at me. "What, now, you weirdo?"

"I have something for you."

"A present?"

"Yeah, let's call it that!" He yanks out a yellow slingshot from his backpack and presents it to me. "I've had it since I was a kid but I just re-colored it for you."

My eyes open wide at the beautiful gift. "You sure?"

"Absolutely. But its ownership comes with a little test."

"Shoot!"

"Exactly." Abana leaves me with a couple of projectiles and trots away. He now puts a fruit on his own head. "Relax, focus...then close your eyes." In my heart, I ask, "really?" and he nods "absolutely."

I focus as I swing the sling to get it going. I locate my target. Then close my eyes. I so don't want to disappoint him. Then I let it fly and while it doesn't hit the fruit right in the middle, it does enough to knock it off his head. He catches it and takes a huge bite out of its juicy center.

"It's now yours...let the good times roll!"

I run up to him and hug him. We hold onto each other, comfortable in the embrace. Our foreheads touch again but before anything else happens, a call echoes down from the mountaintop.

"Chop, chop, kiddos!" Alkima's commanding voice comes rolling over to us.

A few minutes later, with our collection bags in hand, we arrive on the top where Alkima stirs his concoctions. I blurt it out. "So like we're going on that trip soon, right?"

"Yes, soon enough. And it's really all because of you, Aiya!"

Out of nowhere, a strange black bird appears from behind us and flies towards Alkima, landing gently on his shoulder. It has a sprig of some wild herb in its talons. Alkima removes the sprig and crushes it in his hands before dropping it into one bowl. The black bird immediately flies off and disappears over the edge.

"Who's that, and where's Mystikat, he was following us?"

"He'll be along, soon enough. Did you find everything?"

We're bemused by Alkima's comment, but let it slide. "We got it all plus some extra things we thought you...we may need," replies Abana.

"Hold on, what about Ma-Tu, how much does she know about this, you know how she gets."

"We've already spoken. She's concerned but understands."

"This is so awesome," enthuses Abana.

We nudge each other in excitement.

"So who all's going?"

"Just you two, me...and Mystikat." Sure enough the black cat now appears, coming from the other side of the edge of the cliff, sleek and cool. He stretches as if settling into his skin for the day.

"Don't you want to know where our adventure is going to take us?" he teases.

"Mainlandia, right?" I blurt out.

"Right, we've got some people to meet. And a kind of treasure to find..."

"New peeps and a treasure, what's not to like?"

"And, we really are heading off our island heaven?" asks wide-eyed Abana.

"Yes, yes, and yes." Alkima turns back to his potions and slyly grins to himself.

"Except," I look to Abana, "He's going to show us it's not really an island!"

Early next morning, Ma-Tu helps me pack a shoulder bag. She makes sure her child is wearing several layers of clothes. My outer layering is a sheer, gauze-like covering that sparkles with glitter.

Ma-Tu then begins painting a yellow "tilaka" decoration on my forehead. At the center, she places a tiny, sparkling jewel. She explains that the area between the eyebrows is long known to be the seat of hidden wisdom. "The tilaka helps retain energy and strengthens the wearer's focus. It'll also help protect you, Yellow!"

"I'll also protect her, Ma-Tu!" Abana strides into view looking ruggedly handsome with a stylishly military look, with a vest and steampunkish, long duster coat.

"I'll take whatever help I can get," I smile as my heart leaps at the sight of my cute protector.

"You look gorgeous, Aiya!" he says and I can't help but blush.

Just then, we hear someone whistling and Alkima appears with Mystikat following.

"What an adventure! I feel like peeing my pants," I guffaw, as we all crack up.

"Ready?" asks Alkima who looks powerful and potent, in a flowing cape, and a staff in one hand. I always have a sneaky feeling he commands and controls way more than he lets on. We nod excitedly. Then I look to my Ma-Tu for any final words.

"Okay, listen to Alkima, enjoy the journey, learn from it and remember to always hold your head high and kiss the sky." I gently kiss her on the lips. Ma-Tu holds me close, breathing in the scents of her naturally born child, her super child. Her blood is my blood, it flows through my veins—shared flesh, blood, bone…and fire.

She also slips a sparkling crystal trinket wrapped in a saffron sash into my hand. Then she releases me into my future.

Alkima approaches Ma-Tu and moves his face close to hers. Their foreheads touch. And it finally becomes clear to me—doh?!—although I've always sort of sensed it, that the two of them are connected in a deeper way than I've ever imagined.

Mystikat snarls a sort of "chop-chop" as he prowls off, leading the way. Alkima and Ma-Tu separate. Then we, a trio of adventurers, follow the black kitty and merge into the morning mist like mystical specters.

PART TWO

Mainlandia Calls

CHAPTER SIXTEEN

An Adept's Daughter

"Okay, so like I, well, we have questions!"

"What a surprise!" Alkima winks.

We adventurers head up into a forested mountain range on the far eastern side of Geto, led by our black feline. "First, has Mystikat been this way before because he seems to know where he's going?" Abana asks as he hacks down prickly, poisonous vines in our way.

"He says he has..."

"Really, he talks to you, now?" I ask in disbelief.

"In his own way. And, he's got this natural interior compass...among other things."

I wonder what he means as I just sense Alkima knows way more than he's letting on.

Abana looks up, breathing in the air. "I can feel it getting thinner up here."

Alkima also looks up to the sun then to the lengthening shadows. "We'll break for camp when we start our descent."

But I'm adamant. "Hello, questions!"

"So you want to know what I meant when I said Geto wasn't an island."

"Well, there's that. And while I'm really up for an adventure, I'd like to know exactly where we're going."

"To an Underground City."

"Okidoke, and why?"

Mystikat looks over his shoulder and seems to raise an eyebrow as if to say "good luck" to Alkima.

He laughs. "We've been led to believe that Geto is an island, something removed from Mainlandia, a place to dump us oddballs...and keep us Rejexes separate from them."

"I don't get it, there's water all around us, and I'm figuring there's water on the other side of these mountains, right?" I ask.

"Appearances are often deceiving. And as someone once said, 'There are more things in heaven and earth, Horatio, than are dreamt of in your philosophy.'" Alkima stops himself for a second, realizing that he's picked up another thought from someone else.

"Which means exactly what?"

"Mystikat's scouted up here. And his sense is that, in reality, we're still connected to Mainlandia."

"So how does he actually speak to you?" Abana asks.

"We have a sort of mind link, just like you teens."

I jump in. "So he's 'saying' this mountain range is like a wall that keeps us here."

"Right. And we're heading to the other side."

"To meet who?"

"Someone who needs help...my brothers!"

We two look to each other with eyes wide open in astonishment.

"I thought they were distant cousins?"

"We're a little more closely related than I let on."

"Too cool!" exclaims Abana, but I was right—Alkima knows way more than he's telling.

Awhile later after we start our descent, we set up camp. Abana makes me spark up a flame from scratch, as he's taught me. And soon fire is ours...a roaring bonfire just inside a little cave Mystikat has found. Abana leaves then returns with a huge armful of kindling and puts it down. He looks back outside.

"It's going to get real chilly tonight. But you can snuggle up to me, Aiya!"

I like that but Alkima smiles as he points to the walls inside the cave. "Touch it, but carefully."

We two teens touch the walls and feel heat. "Wow!"

"This rock formation absorbs and retains the fire's heat. We'll be nice and cozy in here." He points to another part of the cave wall, and we see strange drawings on the surface. They're rough and crude, but they look like two beings in sort of bulky protective suits holding strange tools. Before we say anything, Alkima explains, "It's said they are depictions of travelers who came from the sky, people who brought gifts to our Ancients."

Abana notes, "Look, Aiya, this looks like the horse in your dreams, all aflame."

"What is this, Alkima, who drew it?"

"Shhh, this is all for another time. Now, we need to eat then rest up for what awaits us."

I can hardly control myself. "So before you were saying about your brothers?"

Not so far off we hear a wild creature howl a mournful death cry!

I tuck in closer to the fire and wiggle my happy toes— they're not so ugly after all—as I wait to hear Alkima's story. He passes us some of the food he's brought.

"Smell it first." We take in the scents of the food, which looks like a big dark cookie. We break it and share it. Then we munch, savoring the deliciousness. It seems at this altitude, things taste and smell different, and better.

"Yum!"

"Double yum!"

Alkima settles in. "It's not a long story. And it shouldn't surprise you. I've told you about the ten Cluster groups on Mainlandia, right?"

"Just the basics. People are bioengineered in labs into ten basic groups, from scientists to workers, right?"

Abana pipes in. "Since scientists are considered the top Cluster, they're all designated One-something, right? My Pa-Tu was a member of the soldier Cluster. What was your designation, Alkima?"

"I was bioengineered as a scientist. I was called One-11, and I have two so-called brothers—One-9 and One-10. But I was labeled a Rejex and banished to Geto before my fourteenth birthday. I don't believe my two brothers know it, but I've been getting those PIMs from them, that they're in trouble."

"And what was your Ma-Tu's designation, Aiya?"

Alkima cocks his eyebrow, waiting for what is surely coming.

"She was always very mysterious about it, not in a bad way because she said I'd find out in a very natural way."

"So what Cluster?"

"Cluster-X."

"What does that really mean?"

"It was originally Cluster-10 but then because its members were always involved in mysterious projects, they were nicknamed Cluster-X, as they became an increasingly secret brother and sisterhood." Alkima continues. "Aiya's Ma-Tu, her mother is an Adept. They're expert at many skills and adept at the manipulation of different things."

A streaming flash of images slam into my mind. How Ma-Tu healed her young daughter's early illnesses, sometimes just by laying on the heat of her hands. How she acted as mediator for disputes that arose on Geto. And, how she twirled sharp knives and never cut herself. "If Ma-Tu was created to be a member of this secret organization, what does that make me as a natural born child of...an Adept."

There's a long pause with no one speaking, then Alkima breaks it. "As I said before, it makes you a miracle, Aiya!" He breaks the breaded food. "You are that and so are you, Abana. And all of Geto's natural born children are miracles. All those improved tastes, senses, skills and instincts you're develop-ing, this is only the beginning...with you, our race is becoming more alive by going back to the future."

It all sounds so exciting to us two teens even if we don't quite understand what Alkima is on about. So I then ask, "Is there more food, please?"

Just then Mystikat appears from behind us and hisses towards the cave's entrance. Our trio looks that way. We don't hear anything. We lean in and listen harder. Slowly, we hear the beating of a pounding savage heart in the shadows outside. That's soon accompanied by the sound of steady, deep breath-ing and the misty exhale of warm air into the night's cold. Mystikat hisses louder at the shadowy threat outside. That is met by a deep, low growl that vibrates the ground.

Abana carefully pulls out his slingshot and begins to arm it. But Alkima puts his hand on his arm. "Not yet."

With his fur bristling and the reflection of the fire in his eyes, Mystikat prowls boldly out of the cave and into the cool night. His feline figure melts into the dark. We hear a full-throated canine growl that is met by an equally loud feline snarl. A fight kicks off and the growls and snarls are terrifying as teeth grind against other teeth and claws slash. The steamy hot breath from the two bodies clouds the air. And, we three in the cave think we can see sparks illuminate the mist.

Abana tries to get up but Alkima restrains him again.

The fight continues then more sparks fly. Then it all stops. The once fierce growls are suddenly reduced to a canine whimper that fade further and further into the darkness.

We wait and wait. And wait some more. Then we hear a meow and Mystikat appears heading back towards us. "Our little kitty kat scared off the big bad monster?" I ask.

Mystikat enters the cave and lies down in front of us by the fire. He has suffered some nasty cuts. As he licks them, Alkima is onto it already, pulling out a salve that he applies liberally to the wounds. The brave cat moans but laps up some water that Abana has cupped in his hands.

"He is so brave."

"And magical!"

"And, that's not even the half of it," Alkima replies to us, adding, "But stay frosty, kiddos, there'll be both friends and fiends ahead."

Later as we sleep, the children of the night sing the wild harmonics outside like they have for thousands of years. When I awake for a few moments, I realize I've never felt more alive than I do in this moment. My eyes twinkle with joy before I close them again and I begin dreaming again of my fire horse—his hooves cracking the ground nearer and nearer.

And, once again I see that creepy holy man way in the background. Then I see him throw a savage slash of rope, whipping it through the air. Soon, a third and fourth rope land again, pinning my horse down from all four sides, pulling tighter, almost strangling him. He snorts out in pain. And suddenly, it all shifts. Now it's me as the "fire horse" being pulled down by ropes from four sides, struggling and screaming to free myself.

That wakes up the two men who both lay their hands on me, trying to settle me down. I tremble and shake a little, as tears stream down my face—talk about a living nightmare! But soon their strong, soothing touch helps me go back to sleep.

Alkima looks intently to Abana and he doesn't quite know what his older friend is going to say. "Whatever happens, Abana, you must defend and watch over her, above all else. She is the spark to this new fire we're going to set. Whatever happens!"

Alkima unsheathes a knife and cuts his palm. Abana does likewise. Above the flames, they press their bloody hands together, sealing their oath, as blood drips into the fire.

"Blood oath, agreed!"

CHAPTER SEVENTEEN

An Invitation

The next morning, we adventurers start our descent down the other side of the mountain under an energizing sun and cloudless, clear sky. We feel refreshed as we joke and talk. I apparently don't look any worse for wear from my bad dreams. And, Mystikat's cuts are already healing. What a strange wondrous creature!

Abana takes the playful bait I offer. "Okay, Aiya, what are some reasons girls are cooler than boys?"

I giggle. "We can peek at boys without it being noticeable. If it's hot, we can wear a dress, although I think you'd look great in a kilt. But we can still wear a guy's clothes, if we want. If we wanna pee, we can hold it. And, we know how to dance." With that, I twirl around the two guys with grace and style, laughing my head off.

They have to laugh with me. "She does make some good points, right, Abana?"

"Too many!"

As we leave the forest behind, my jaw almost falls. "Wow, we really aren't living on an island!"

"No kidding!" chimes in Abana.

We now see Geto's boundaries. The land below us continues on and on into the beyond. We stop to admire the view. For all those times I have looked up to the stars and planets above, I've always imagined getting beyond our island. And now my wish is coming true. My feet and fingers tingle. "I can't believe I'm, I mean, that we're finally leaving our 'island.' Hello big world!"

"And Mainlandia is up ahead?" asks Abana.

"Past the Wall."

"The Wall?"

"To keep us out or maybe to keep them in?"

"I suspect a bit of both, Aiya. But we're going to have to find a way through it."

"Why can't we jump over it, Alkima? We've been practicing!"

"No, if we go over, we'll possibly set off alarms. And I'm pretty sure there'll be guards. Armed guards." Abana reaches for his slingshot but Alkima restrains him again, saying, "It'd be better if we don't announce our arrival to everybody."

"Good, because Abana knows about all that stuff, too."

"Yeah, I do serious stealth!"

"I was counting on that," says Alkima in a knowing way.

Abana looks around him and up ahead sees some wet mud. He runs over to it, glops some up and smacks some on his face. He glops some more up and runs back to us. He slaps glops of mud on our faces.

He sizes up our muddy faces and laughs. "What? It's a concept!"

Alkima and I, all muddied, look to each other and also laugh. "Yeah, this should guarantee me first prize at the Queen of Fais du-du party back home."

Abana then unrolls three lightweight capes. "Here put these on. They're good for camo as well as raincoats." We do as he tells us. "Now, let's get off this path until I can see where the Wall and its guards are located."

"And then?" I ask.

"Then we make our move, sha!"

Count me in. But I'm also thrilled because I seem to have found a way to get Abana off Geto. And hopefully leave his sad imprisoned past behind.

In the late afternoon, we see the outline of the top of the Wall not a hundred yards away. Abana puts his fingers to his lips to keep us quiet as he goes on ahead, crouching low in the undergrowth. He moves as smoothly as a slithering critter in the grass.

He returns a few minutes later with a devious look. "Okay, there are two guards every few hundred yards or so. I can find a way to distract them. But the Wall is very high, with what looks like barbs, maybe poisoned, on top. I couldn't see any gates or doors. But there must be one they use somewhere."

"Did you see any part of the Wall that was different, Abana?"

"A little way away from the guard post, this section was shimmering. Why, Alkima?"

"If we can distract the guards, I think that spot could lead to a hidden entrance."

Abana asks, "Alkima, I bet you've got some fire powder in your bag, something that can create a..."

Before he can finish, Alkima says "diversion" and pulls out a little bag of black powder. He hands it over. "It just needs to be ignited and the dried leaves and twigs around here should make for a good tinderbox, and a very natural looking fire."

Abana looks towards the guards and squints, thinking. "Okay, got it!" He takes off again with superfast speed and scatters the black powder on a big rock near some dried tinder. He returns to us unnoticed and points in the other direction. "That shimmering section is down that way." While he gets out his slingshot, he searches on the ground for some nearby pellets.

"No, let Aiya do it, Abana. We need you down there to show the way."

Abana grins approvingly. As I pull out my own new slingshot, he points to the rock, and I sense what he wants. I load my slingshot. "Relax, don't force it. Aim small, easy and true," Abana reminds me.

Abana takes off again, moving like a shadow, crouching through the trees and bushes. From a distance, he waves to me and I aim at the rock. It's a long shot, but my eyes crinkle with silent glee as I swing the sling and let the projectile fly. It strikes the rock and sends a spark flying. It takes a few seconds, then the other powder ignites and it spreads to the tinder. Flames come to life. As the two nearest guards see the flames and automatically run toward it to investigate, Abana waves for us to come to his concealed spot. Then we three plus Mystikat, who seems to understand exactly what we're planning, crawl low toward the shimmering part of the Wall.

Abana looks and strains to see a way in. "The surface is covered with these nasty barbs. They may also be poisoned. That's what I'd do." He carefully puts his hands on the Wall, but feels nothing. "I don't see a handle."

Alkima reaches into his bag for another sack of powder. "Do you feel any release lever?"

"Na-ah, and no rush. Because we've got maybe a minute or two...at most," he quips.

"Oh, great!" But the conjurer holds out some new black powder.

"What, so do we swallow it?" Abana asks.

"No, it's for Aiya. Rub your hands and breathe it in, sha." I do exactly that, breathing it in and opening up to its sense-enhancing powers. "Now put your hands on the surface, Aiya, and see if you can feel any tiny edge sticking out," urges Alkima.

I carefully place my hands on the surface, and feel with my touch. At first nothing. Time is ticking down. Alkima sees frustration in the tension in my hands. I shake my head quietly in frustration. Mystikat meows something and Alkima picks up his message. "Let it all go, Aiya, close your eyes and let it go, all the distractions...all of them." I'm guessing he means, forget about thinking about Abana and his lost love. So I try.

"Still no rush, but like we've got maybe thirty seconds!"

I put my hands back on the surface and my long fingers slide across the shimmering section like a creepy crawler. I pause. Run my fingers along a tiny edge that really can't be seen. Then open my eyes and glance back to Alkima that I may have it.

"Gently, push."

So I carefully push and a portal does open. We dash through it and the Wall quietly closes behind us. "Okay, we're in!"

On the other side of the Wall, on the westernmost fringe, we find we're in another forested area. But as we peek through the trees and beyond, we see the Basin below us, stripped of all trees and laid bare, with fires in the distance.

I'm thinking, What a nightmare!

"Great work, my friends."

"So, what now?" I impatiently ask, as I tap my toes.

"We wait."

"For what?"

"An invitation."

"Okay, so like, do these Mainlandians usually take long to get back?" I mischievously ask.

"Why, you have somewhere more exciting to go?"

Mystikat seems to smile as they both know they have me. So, I shut my trap!

CHAPTER EIGHTEEN

From My Cold, Dead Hands

Beyond our sight and east of Mainlandia's Basin, engineers and technicians, guarded by soldiers led by X-33, study and test the open-pit mining construction. Worker drones slash down more trees, making way by making savage incursions into Thalandia. They chop and mow them down, young and old, without any thought to replacing them. Those giant trees continue to bleed crimson sap that runs more red rivers from the jungle, coloring the dead land. The aggressive deforestation sort of contradicts the slogan: "Turning our desert into a wonderful, new power source!"

A couple of young engineers, with that three-gear symbol on their chests and who are mapping the area, need to move ahead into the forest. They're led by X-33 into the area. The Commander's young henchman gets a pop-up message on his handheld: "Do it, now!"

When they're led far enough away from the grid, these new oblivious engineers, who're hunched over looking at their handhelds, are suddenly attacked and struck by spears. As usual, and as obsessed as they are about checking out their schematics, they don't even see the attack coming. Zip, zing, zang, again!

From behind a thick undergrowth, the weapons hungrily eat into their unarmed flesh and bone. The engineers are struck down dead. Out of the undergrowth appears, not 'cannibalistic' Thals, but a couple of other Cluster-X'ers holding Thalandian spears. They wait for more orders from X-33 who motions with a chopping action. So, they then viciously hack off the limbs of their fallen fellow citizens. From under their hoods, they chant in unison. "Be very, very afraid." Then bloodied, they sneakily disappear back into the undergrowth.

X-33 sends a message back on his handheld: "Done, Commander!"

"We are so in the Right," the head bully replies.

The Commander deletes the message thread on his own device and then continues to calmly talk to his totally unaware audience. "I also propose that we lift the ban on guns for our law enforcement personnel, to protect us from our new enemy."

That does it. The people in the outer circle in the meeting room, including some of the General Council members, anonymously speak up. But keep their heads down as they ask.

"Is that wise?"

"Right here in our Underground City?"

"Is that even safe?"

"We haven't had a standing army..."

"Or needed weapons for a hundred years, why now?!"

The Commander earnestly whispers one of his catchy slogans: "Enforcement leads to peace and happiness. We can't have one without the other." Then he's handed a rifle musket from his weapons master, X-44, who has kept it under the folds of a cloak.

"Now that is devo-lution!" shouts one unmistakable voice from the crowd.

"Hear me out, citizens. It's written in our ancient 'Bill of Rights' based on the documents that the citizens of the Blue Planet wrote. We have the right to bear arms to protect ourselves." He brandishes the weapon, holding it aloft and gripping it tightly in one hand.

"Oh boy," exclaims One-10, as he recalls an image he has once seen from some radio signals from the Blue Planet. An image of a man dramatically standing in front of two signs—"Freedom" and "National Rifle Association"—and holding aloft a rifle, with the caption: "I have only five words for you: 'From my cold, dead hands.'"

"If war does break out with Thalandia, and they do try to invade our City, wouldn't you want to protect yourselves, and especially our young ones?" shouts back the Commander.

"But where fear is, happiness is not," retorts that unmistakable voice.

"That's alright, conversation is good. Speak up if you wish. But action is even better," says the Commander as he cocks the clunky weapon.

An audible gasp rises then falls back down into silence.

With every facet of life in the Underground City so controlled from cradle to grave, there has been no "reported" crime for decades. The rule is that any citizens who show deviance from the norm—green or blue eyes, left-handedness, above average IQ for one's designation, too much creativity, being gay or even too chubby, along with other oddball behavior and anyone tending to non-conformity and rebelliousness—are to be exiled to Geto. Conform or be cast out!

But sometimes, these "flaws" don't reveal themselves till the kids become young teenagers. So, Mainlandia is essentially creating a tribe of banished young teens, a small but growing tribe of outcasts, some who've now grown into adulthood.

Outcasts with an axe to grind.

Any other miscreants in the Underground City just mysteriously disappear with no questions openly asked or any answers given. So for all intents and purposes, as locked down as its society is, there is no crime or even acknowledged punishment. And never ever any torture.

But Thalandians, the savages, they're a different thing.

One-10 stands twitching uncomfortably, but he just can't help himself. He defiantly whispers out of the crowd: "The creation of false fear and bogus bogeyman always give Big Bully Brothers, or even Bully Sisters, the power to control others."

"Okay, that's one opinion. But the world would be a fine, boring place if we all agreed, no?" the Commander says. But he's on a roll, ignoring the criticism. "But make no mistake about it. The Thalandians mean war and we must defend ourselves." He presses the weapon's trigger and fires. People cringe. But it was all for effect as it isn't loaded with any ball. "And we must arm ourselves! Yes, seize the day!"

X-3 glances to her, and One-6 in all her glorious starchiness, shouts, "Seize the day! And we should not only vote on lifting the weapons ban but also on building a reserve of peace-keeping guns, right, Commander?"

The Commander then pretends to hear something on his earpiece. Then dramatically raises his hand for a pause. "Wait, shush!" The room goes deathly silent. With his face always shrouded, his head gravely nods up and down, playing it up. He raises his hand again for attention then relays the news as he gets it. "Brothers and sisters, more engineers have been attacked topside...The Thalandians have struck again unprovoked...murdered in cold blood...their body parts hacked off and taken..."

Those words "in cold blood" and "parts hacked off" strike home like a razor-sharp blade. They've all heard of rumors, maybe made-up stories, of the savages supposedly sacrificing others in cold blood to appease their Spirits, and then cannibalizing their bodies. And the Commander knows well how to milk that infecting fear, no matter how untrue.

He puts his hand to his hidden forehead, as if gasping in horror. "I also hear they eat the hearts of their victims...alive and beating!"

"Such savages!" screams someone.

The adept Commander raises the rifle again and adds with a glorious flourish, "From my cold, dead hands!" He, too, knows that image that One-10 recalled.

One-10's head shakes in dismay. He sees that a few of the Council members also shake their heads in disbelief at the Commander's theatrical display. But they bow their heads and keep quiet. It rarely ever pays to stand out.

The Commander barks, "So, hands up for the ayes!" The Commander's plants in the audience bully and jab people to shout "aye." And on that crest of a wave of fear, all hands, some more slowly than others, go up on the Council. He trumpets, "It's unanimous. The ban of guns has been lifted and we'll soon be able to defend ourselves and push back against the invaders. We are in the Right."

Jabbed further by his plants, the crowd with their heads bowed bay, "In the Right. In the Right!"

X-3 quickly types some words into his handheld, then presses a button on a remote controller. The percussive beats of marching boots rise up through the chants. The beats are strangely seductive. And, almost immediately, a crawl of red neon words flash and circle the council table: "To the happy beat of a safe new order." He's so marvelously adept in the ways of manipulation.

Clasping his hands, he solemnly prays, "Now, let us bow our heads. Make me an instrument of your peace. Where there is hatred, let me sow love; where there is injury, pardon; where there is doubt, faith; where there is despair, hope; where there is darkness, light..." He pauses, raises up both arms like some holy roller, adding with gusto, "All praise to the Darkness because..."

And bleating like sheep, they chant back, "Because out of darkness, comes new light!"

CHAPTER NINETEEN

The Prettiest Star

As manufacturing workers begin churning out six-shooter guns with revolving cylinders on a production line, the Commander's Cluster-X sergeants begin training the new enforcement members in the art of bludgeoning war. Deep down in the City's lower chambers, the sound of marching boots on metal rumbles through the upper chambers. Orders are barked out, the new recruits bark back some ancient military cadence. "I don't know but I've been told…Ene-mies lie better cold."

In the upper chambers, One-10 and One-9 feel the vibrations rumbling through their power chairs in another observation room, a secret one. One-9 glances into the test room that is now seemingly in darkness and quiet.

"Why are we here?" But One-10 doesn't respond. "You're up to something, I know the signs."

"What, you sense something?"

"Yes, I do. Kind of, I guess."

"Hold on, hold on. With all our science, formulas and math, you admit you actually 'sense' something, One-9?"

He seems a little confused as he screws up his face to consider the suggestion. "Well, I don't know if 'sense' is the right word."

"Then what is? Intuition, ESP? Isn't that heresy, Dar?"

"You've always been one with words. But alright, I do sense something, call it what you will."

"Admit it, you have a hunch I've been doing, what, some other tests?"

"Well, have you?"

One-10 makes his power chair turn around in a tight spin.

"Because, you're dangling your hand in one hot pot, Dar!"

"You're right, I am playing a dangerous game. And it's a risk but it's a move we've got to make, to go back to the future."

"Again with the riddles, what do you mean?"

One-10 has to check himself. He wonders where that thought has come from—"go back to the future?"—and he starts spinning again. Then stops and blurts it out. "Okay, I've been doing some really, really secret tests."

"On yourself? You mentioned that already, the chimp and the string of numbers test, right?"

"Well, not just on myself," he winks.

"Oh, brother, I have a 'hunch' I'm not going to like this. What in Occulo have you done?"

One-10 points to the darkness in the test room. His compatriot looks into it as light starts to infuse the room. Slowly, it fills up and what looks like a normal twelve-year-old girl now sits there across from the same cool chimp, Bonzo. Except, as the test starts up again, this new subject begins beating the chimp easily, racing through the test as chimes keep going off on her side of the test machine. Bonzo is being driven to distraction, losing out to a small girl.

The girl has the symbol of a "worker" hand clutching a hammer on the right breast of her jumpsuit, as she smiles at the chimp's antics. But she defuses the primate's irritation by giggling and sharing with him some of her tasty rewards.

"What are you showing me? Before, you were making the point that the chimp was reacting better than the worker, now you've got another worker there, an even younger one, but she's beating the chimp. I don't get it!"

"It's not rocket science, try harder!" Off One-9's shake of his head and a shrug. "Okay, here's a hint, check out the girl's feet."

One-9 leans closer and sees something very different. The barefoot girl, who is happily tapping her feet under the table in glee, has unusual webbing between her toes. "She's a Syndactyly?" It takes him a few seconds. "Holy, Charlie Darwin! She's a Rejex! So, what's she still doing here, why hasn't she been outed and banished?"

"We've got a few friends in certain places who are sympathetic to my ideas, well they're hardly my ideas. It's more like we share the same crazy, heretical ideas."

"That evolution on Mainlandia is actually devolution? You're back onto that!"

One-10 nods. "And they've helped me keep some of our Rejex kids hidden."

"Some? More than one? Here, where?"

"It doesn't matter where? The real question is why?"

"You're going to say something about 'lifting the veil of darkness?'"

"And if we say 'yes' then that little girl, when she is more grown up, I believe that she and people like her point us towards the solution."

"Are you serious? First, if they ever find out about her, or any others, they're history, gone. Second, you think the Commander and his puppet Trix want to hear anything about devolution? They've got a whole new show they're taking on the road topside." Then, he points to the rumbling below their feet. "And those boots we're hearing down below, which could soon be on your throat, One-10, they're just the beginning of Mainlandia's new order."

The boot stomps and chants seem to get louder as One-10 stares at the cute little girl in the room and puts his hand on the two-way glass, reaching out to her with a protective gesture. "Ain't 777 just the prettiest star? And right here with us!"

His partner's head spins and he goes pale. "Excuse me, while I throw up, will you, One-10!"

CHAPTER TWENTY

The Rejex and the Mainlandian

With his nose on the two-way mirror, One-10 checks out the young 'Rejex.' She has such potential but is so young, too young. Her time is not even close. He thinks of that question he and his partner have considered: 'Do we have the courage to lift the veil of darkness?'

Suddenly, he closes his eyes as he feels a sharp jolt in his head and gets an impression in his thoughts. As if someone or something is trying to break in. The impression is like a message that says: "Yes, you do...with a little help from some new friends."

He looks at the young girl, who is busy feeding the chimp and laughing with the primate as they play. One-10 whirls his chair around to One-9, but he's busy reading, peering down at something he seems to be hiding. One-10 looks around the room, even up to the ceiling. No one else is there. But the words come back again to him: "With a little help from some new friends."

One-9 looks up with a smile. "What's up?"

"Nothing! What are you reading, what's that book?"

"You're not the only one with tricks, Dar!" He reads: "You will never keep me down forever or break me, never—an excerpt from the Fire Horse story in *A Book of Myths*."

"But how did you get it back from One-6?"

"She just tossed it in the trash. With all the other distractions going on, I pulled it back out when no one was looking."

"Dar, I am impressed."

"You know, since we're talking about non-scientific things like hunch, intuition and maybe a sixth sense—the Fire Horse

story talks about this fiery creature coming in the time of great
need, accompanied by a mysterious rider." He smirks. "With all
that military jackbooting going on down below, today would
be a good day to turn up, huh?"

Then One-9 also feels a sharp jolt in his own head. "Jeez,
what was that?"

"Are you thinking, 'With a little help from some new
friends'?" One-9 tentatively nods yes. "So, you sensed and felt
it, too?!" asks One-10.

"What are we missing, here? Is being around the Rejex child
bringing this on? And what new friends?"

Then, simultaneously, they both get a surprise, a very strong
impression of another more urgent message in their heads. A
personal instant message that they can't explain but which
simply urges, "Good day! We're inside the Wall, can you send
someone to bring us in?" And then a follow-up from another
source, "Hello, and like, quickly?!"

Stunned, One-9 whirls to look at his colleague. "That last
one sounded just like you and your smartass mouth!"

"Yeah, no kidding!" He shakes and clears his head. "So, like,
we better get on this!'

Sometime later, a little used service dome entity rises from the
arid land on the westernmost fringe as afternoon and longer
shadows descend on the Basin. "451" the frizzy haired art
student, who impressed One-10 in his office, exits the dome,
eyes down intently looking at a GPS app on her handheld. She
carries a big bag over her shoulder and walks, almost eyes
wide shut, toward a location that the GPS is pointing to in
the forest. She approaches the tree line, still not looking up.
Suddenly, she hears, "Heads up!" But doesn't see a low-lying
branch as it whacks her on the top of her frizzy head and
knocks her down.

"You okay?" asks Abana who has quietly rushed out to try
and warn her.

"Ouch! That happens all the time." She rubs her head as she
finally looks up and shyly grins, a little sheepishly. "Hi, I'm
451. One-10 sent me to meet you. I'm one of his new students."

"I'm Abana. Sure you're okay?"

"I think, I'm so embarrassed. I'm a total klutz." She admires his military look.

Abana laughs. "Yeah, don't you just hate that?!"

"I should understand the science of looking up more often. I belong to the artist cluster. But I just happen to dig science, too. And like we all have to take Science 101..." she rambles, feeling a little nervous. She says quietly, "Okay, 451, shut up, already!"

They stand there, studying each other—the Rejex and the Mainlandian—amazed at meeting someone completely new.

He puts his hands out to take hers in a welcoming gesture. But she doesn't know what to do, and just continues to stand there, her eyes going back down to the ground. And sure enough, she doesn't see it coming.

I come flying down from behind the trees, run up to 451 and spontaneously embrace her. "Hi cuz, I'm Aiya! How are you? I've never met a Mainlandian. Are they all as pretty as you? I love your hair, who does it for you? But you're so pale!"

451 just freezes. Close human touch is just so rare for Mainlandians.

"Aiya, give 451 some breathing room, or you'll suffocate her, sha!" directs Alkima.

"Oh, okay, sorry." I back off. Now I and 451 study each other. I sniff the air in between us. My heightened sense of smell senses strange, antiseptic scents on the other girl. But I really like her cool jacket and point. "Ga lee, tres cool couleurs!"

"Hi, 451, I'm Alkima! And these are my two young friends Abana and Aiya. Mystikat meows to get their attention. "And this is our leader," he lowers his voice. "At least he thinks he is...May I present Mystikat!"

Mystikat goes up to 451 and brushes up against her, but she doesn't know what to do until I offer, "Just scratch him under his chin."

So 451 tentatively crouches down and does just that. She smiles when Mystikat purrs and when she feels the vibration of his touch. "We don't have felines in the Underground City." She looks up, smiling. "And, I've never met anyone from Geto!"

We continue to size each other up. While 451's skin really is so pale, her deep brown eyes are clear. And for her, my skin must seem so tanned and savage looking. "Uh, what's that jeweled yellow thingee on your forehead, Aiya?"

"It's a tilaka!"

Then I slowly put my fist out. Alkima coughs then motions with his head to 451. So she also holds out her fist and us two girls awkwardly fist-bump. And, no one gets hurt.

"So, okay, One-10 and One-9 sent me. But we'll have to wait until night to go in to meet them," says 451 as she points over her shoulder to the domed entity. But she's distracted by a beep of her handheld and looks down to it. It's just an intrusive pop-up message that keeps beeping, and which she has trouble getting rid of.

"Can you close that thing?" I ask.

"Do you mean, can I turn it off?"

"Yes, can you?"

"Well, we never really do that. We keep our handhelds on 24/7. It's the first and last thing I check on every day. We're kind of attached." But she considers our unhappy looks. "But sure, why not close it?!"

As she turns it off and stashes it, she has a look of relief on her face. She takes it in, takes a few seconds. "Wow, I don't feel like a handheld-zombie anymore...I feel kind of, free!"

Alkima smiles as he leads us back to the cover of the forest. "Have you tasted home-cooked food, 451?"

"You have natural food?" asks the girl as she licks her lips. "Wow, you really are so different! And I think I'm going to really, really like you!"

Even though 451's tummy grumbles, I'm still staring at her when Abana nudges me. "Uh, Aiya, the food, I think she's starving! Hello!"

CHAPTER TWENTY-ONE

Down the Rabbit Hole

We sit in the forest, in the shade of great overhanging trees. One casts down blossoms, not quite like Geto's trilling glitter blossoms, but bright yellow star-shaped flowers that lay down their own dazzling blanket.

"I've never seen anything like this," exclaims 451 as she gazes up and lets the flowers fall onto her face. "We're always so busy looking down at our devices, we rarely ever look up. Although, downunder there's no real reason to look up. There isn't any beauty like this!" She lets more flowers gently fall on her face.

I share some of Alkima's food with 451 who tentatively tastes the cookie-like munchies then immediately says. "Yum, I've never tasted anything like this either! Can I have another piece, if it's okay?"

Abana has found a dried out gourd and is testing its sounds when he taps on it.

"Hey, I've got some disguises for you from One-10, he figured you'd need them." She pulls them out of her bag. "Artist's rainbow jackets for Aiya and Abana."

"What about Abana's mohawk haircut?" I ask. "Will he stand out?"

"Us artists are allowed to be kind of weird, so he'll blend right in!" She pulls out another coat. "And, a scientist's lab coat for Alkima. But what about cute Mystikat?"

"As Confucius said, 'The hardest thing of all is to find a black cat in a dark room, especially if there is no cat,'" muses Alkima, but it confuses 451.

I jump in, "Uh, don't sweat it, Alkima's just showing off. And he's always quoting from this. I show and hand her my dog-eared copy of Confucius' sayings. "As for Mystikat, he'll be fine, he's great at skulking around, right, kitty?" Mystikat rubs up against my leg, as 451 graciously accepts the gift of my book.

Then we three try on our coats and continue chatting. Jazzed, 451 looks on happy as she fixes the collar of my jacket to make it look just right. Then she hears Abana hitting the gourd to create a sort of percussive back beat. I start humming.

"We don't really hum downunder..."

I then sing quietly along to Abana's beat. 451 finds it strangely hypnotic. She leans back and then lays down, craning her head up to the sky, maybe for the first time in her life. She listens as yellow-starred flowers float down onto her, covering her like safe blanket.

When we stop, she whispers, enthralled, "That's beautiful. Your voice, I've never heard anyone singing, well not in person."

"You're not allowed to sing?" Abana questions. Off 451's sad shrug. "Then we'll have to teach you, right, Aiya?"

I've been considering 451 and Abana's eyes twinkle as he watches my mind working. "Okay, watch out, here it comes!" he laughs.

I catch him studying me and it stirs my heart. "First I have a new name, a nickname, for you. 451 is like so uncool." I move my hand slowly so as to not frighten the girl. Then stroke her shock of frizzy hair. "How about Frizz?"

"Frizz?" 451 rolls it around on her tongue and chuckles. "Frizz...I like it, Aiya." She then stares at my tilaka. "Uh, can I get one of those, too?"

"Can you?! You bet!" I yank out some yellow powder and mix it with some water in a little bowl that Alkima gives me. When the mixture is ready, I place my hands close to Frizz's face but hold them there until she nods okay. I apply the paint and then put an extra sparkling jewel I also have in my pocket on her forehead. As the mixture hardens, the jewel stays in place. When it's done, I hold a reflective crystalline stone in front of Frizz's face. Her eyes glint as she sees her reflection.

"Cool, eh?!"

"But what does it mean?"

"It represents the mind's eye—my Ma-Tu says it's the gate to seeing things as they really are."

"Because the way in is through the door," adds a pleased Alkima who delightfully applauds his young friends.

"Wow! Performing music. Real food. Looking up. Seeing things. Confucius. There's so much I don't know about." Frizz lamely tries to throw out her arms.

Then, I throw out my arms with my usual goofy enthusiasm. "Mainlandia. An Underground City. My cousins. There's so much that we don't know about either. And so much I want to see." Spontaneously, I kiss Frizz on the cheek. Not an intimate kiss, but a friendly kiss nevertheless.

Frizz freezes. Words are stuck in her throat. I sit in front of her smiling, totally at ease with my move.

Abana breaks the silence. "Don't worry about her, Frizz, she's just friendly and will smooch anyone who she likes."

"Yeah, 'cool,' I think." Those are the words that come out but Frizz trembles inside. As Mainlandians hardly touch, a hug, a kiss, or any similar show of affection is unheard of. Frizz's mind races. 'What is this thing called a kiss? Why did Aiya kiss me? And, why is it still sending tremors through my body? I can still smell her exotic scents, wow!'

Frizz still doesn't move, so I then quickly peck Abana to show that he's right. "That's just me, Frizz!" Abana likes my spontaneous show of affection towards him and he kisses me back. I smile, happy about my forward move and his response.

But Frizz feels awkward and averts her eyes as she's unable to shake the after-effects of these open gestures.

Alkima checks out the lengthening shadows and breaks the kissing reverie with a cough. "We should pack up, kiddos."

Once we're ready to move, Frizz's forehead crinkles with worry.

"What is it?" I ask.

"I've heard One-10 and One-9 say we've got troubles downunder."

"Then some cool change your way comes, Frizz! Right, Mystikat?!" I say.

The feline meows and seems to smile. And, all together, Frizz inconspicuously leads us towards the dome. But I hear a whinny coming from the creeping shadows. "What's that?"

"That? Equines!"

"There are horses here, I've never seen one, not for real, anyways!"

"Yeah, they test-tube breed them, then train them up here."

"And then what do they do with them?"

"Well, they break them first before taking the poor creatures downside to work in the mines." Off our looks. "It's the rules. The equines can also sense when there may be a shaft collapse. Like most of us, the workers down there don't have much of a sense of smell."

"Can we see the horses, please? Quickly?"

Frizz takes a moment. "Okay, but real quickly." She crouches down on all fours and leads us past the line of trees to overlook several fenced-in corrals. In the first one, a group of equine beauties stand still under the darkening evening. When one of them, a big dark red stallion, smells the air with flaring nostrils, he stomps the dry earth. His eyes open white and steely. Unafraid, the creature rears up protectively in front of his small herd.

Light from a waxing moon bathes his glistening body. As he rears, his mane and tail seem to glow like embers. And, I'm mesmerized. I can't move. My heart beats faster. Blood pumps at my temples. A fine sheen appears on my forehead. There in front of me rears a magnificent "fire horse" like the creature in my dreams—my lifelong symbol of freedom.

Amidst his stomping and snorts, I first softly whistle to get his attention. Then murmur to him, "You're so awesome!"

And that stops him. He settles down. Pauses, then prances forward to smell the air in between us. Once he catches my scent, he stomps a percussive beat with one hoof—*tap, tap, terap!*

My friends let me have a moment with the creature. And, as separated as we are, I feel a powerful connection. Not like the heart one to Abana, but still powerful. We stare at each other, not moving, for the length and breadth of a few extended moments.

"I think he gets you, Aiya," Abana finally says.

"We really have to go!" says Frizz, who gets a beep on the handheld she's turned back on.

I feel it way down inside of me. Confidence in knowing. So I whisper to him, "See you soon, Big Red!"

Our group quietly backs off, then heads to the Dome. Frizz gets a buzzing pop-up that reads: "Praise the Darkness—fourteen days and counting!"

I see my new friend's concern. "You're scared of something, Frizz?!"

"It's just this thing coming up in fourteen days. Scares the bejeezus out of us." Checking her handheld. "I'll tell you, later!"

Alkima pulls us back for one more moment. "Aiya, do you have anything to offer, on this, the edge of our most splendid adventure?"

"Ma-Tu gave me something before I left." I take out a note, look it over and read it. "May the Ancients smile favor upon us on our journey. May Nature, our mother, protect us even when we are far from her embrace. May our Magick help defeat intolerance and ignorance. And, may our hearts aflame always guide us."

I say something in Frizz's ear. On the count of three, the two of us then chant together. "Laissez les bons temps rouler!"

As we step forward, our Conjurer removes something from his bag of goodies and rubs his hands together. He shakes his closed fists, then dramatically throws two fireballs along the ground toward the Dome. We stride forward between the guiding lights of fire. Frizz then is about to give a voice command to the Dome. But she pauses, sensing the significance. "This will change us forever, right?"

"Here goes nothing, and everything," says Abana.

And Frizz commands, "Designation 451, open" and the portal opens to invite us down the rabbit hole into our future—unknown, definitely dangerous, but oh so mysteriously exciting.

No matter what monsters await us, I whisper, "Bring it on!"

The Commander sits alone in the dark, spinning and twirling a wicked-looking sharp weapon with his right hand. As an Adept, he has amazing dexterity, and the gleaming tool spins between his fingers as smoothly as the knife did in Ma-Tu's hand. Wrapped on his left wrist is that ever-present speckled band. After a few more twirls, he doesn't even watch what his right hand is doing. He doesn't have to anymore. He's become one with the tool and weapon. So he focuses on the band on his other wrist as it slithers up his arm.

Out of nowhere, his shrouded head jerks back. What? Two balls of fire streak across his inner vision. He shakes his head. Is he daydreaming? The speckled band feels the tension in his body, too, wrapping itself tighter on his forearm, while hissing a warning. The two fireballs keep streaking across the Commander's mind's eye. But, just as suddenly, his body eases, the tension drains out as his left arm and his fist relaxes.

He repeats three words. "Bring it on!" As he expertly throws the knife into the dark, hitting something squishy soft, the Commander then adds with a chuckle that escapes out from under his hood, "Because, time has come today!"

CHAPTER TWENTY-TWO

Without a Spark

As our quartet, with Mystikat in tow, whoosh down in a service elevator, Frizz receives an e-message from One-10. She sends a reply back. Looking up, she tells the plan. "One-10 is going to meet us at a performance art gathering. He thinks it'll be the least obvious place."

"What sort of performance?" I ask, kind of thrilled.

"Well, we've been working on it for weeks. But, if you feel like humming or playing some music..."

"What do you usually do?"

"The last one was like a rap, a rhythmic reading about the wonders of algorithms. Hardly singing."

"Sums and stuff, really?"

"Yeah, sounds kind of boring. The algorithms, that is," teases Abana.

"That's the rules. Our painters can only make still life art. Our storytelling evenings are about the people who make scientific or mathematical discoveries." Off our pained looks. "I know, I know, but it's all we've got to play with. That's our canvas! Unless we do it on the Q.T., if you get what I mean?"

"I'm sure we can whip up something cooler, right, Abana?"

"You bet. So what tools will we have?" asks Abana, getting stoked.

"You can use laser sticks that can make holograms based on whatever has been programmed into them."

"Laser sticks? Holograms?"

"Think of them as really 'cool' painting tools."

"Wow, that is neat, using science and art, not just one without the other," I enthuse.

Alkima asks, "And where will you say we're from?"

"One-10 said to say that you're friends visiting from the northern sector."

I nudge Frizz, point to her hair and then gently let it back down like my own. With our long hair flowing, we look prettily alike. "See, we could be cousins."

"Yeah, like kissing cousins!" adds Frizz, who awkwardly pecks me and then feels her heart pound and mouth go dry.

As we exit, Frizz reminds us. "Best to keep your heads down until we get to the space."

We all do that and we pass anonymously by two enforcement officers who are too busy looking down at messages on their own handhelds. One moans, "What's up with all these new pop-up orders and slogans?"

"Yeah, we already get the picture."

"Shhh, be careful what you say, citizen!" he whispers.

Led by Frizz, our group notes the wisp of disenchantment. She tells us, "I know, right?! Something small is already going on."

"Then all we need is a jumpstart," encourages Alkima.

"Something to spark our move?" I add.

"Can't start a fire without a spark," agrees Abana.

Soon, as Frizz takes us down some steps to a cave-like room, she explains how Occulo's orbiting Collector has been retrieving space junk and digital signals for decades. "The Orbiter has been the major supplier and source of our history and technology. We get stuff from all around the universe. Our group just got illegal access to these video-streams from the Blue Planet. From a time period called the 1960s. First, there were these black and white streams of a sport called football. From mob games like The Royal Shrovetide match to organized games with this famous team called Tottenham Hotspur. The Spurs played the 'glory' game in these all-white uniforms. And, one of their players had a cool saying, 'It is better to fail aiming high than to succeed aiming low. And we of Spurs have set our sights very high, so high in fact that even failure will have in it an echo of glory.'"

"Oooh, I so like that. Here's to setting our sights really high!" I see Abana and Frizz's eyes light up with that. Then, thinking of the joyous mob aspect to the Shrovetide games, I blurt out, "Those mob games sound like our game Bonko. That's where I met Abana." I wink at him then look back to her. "I hope you also get to see that one day, Frizz."

"Me, too." She smiles hopefully. "Okay, then there were these Beatnik parties." She quickly downloads one and shows it to us on her handheld. It's also in black and white and has swirly shapes and paisley designs.

The people wear Beatnik clothes and there's a band playing, but the sound has been corrupted. I watch the stream, intrigued and planning. I note the audience do finger snapping after the band stops playing. I snap my own fingers like them. It takes a few turns but I get it. "So, okay, let's do like a neo-Beatnik night! Can you send out a message to your friends that they have to find-make-whatever, and wear something suitable?"

"Sure thing, but what sort of clothes are you talking about?"

"Things like they're wearing in the video. Boots, short skirts, cool hats. And lots of colors. I can help you make some other things."

"Cool. And, this is a laser stick." She hands it to a fascinated Abana who excitedly looks at the menu on its handle. He makes ocean waves appear on the floor. Then, he looks up to the ceiling.

"Got something going, Abana?" Alkima chuckles at his crew. "But, Frizz, can we get the audience to leave their own handhelds shut off and out here while they watch the show, with no distractions?"

"Yeah, I guess!"

"I can stay out here and explain to them what to do," suggests Alkima as he lets his young practitioners take control.

I repeat a bunch of words I can lip-read off the Beatniks' mouths: "Yeah, big daddio. Don't ever change, kitty kat. Just keep swinging. Dig it?!"

"You can read their lips and words?"

I nod, as Abana views the video, saying, "And I think I sense the beats they're using."

"This is going to be way fun," Frizz enthuses.

"You ain't seen nothing yet!" I gently punch her.

Excited and trembling, Frizz starts personally messaging her friends on her wristband watch.

"What do you want me to do, One-10?"

"Stay out of trouble!"

"Look who's talking. But seriously, what?" asks his colleague.

"Try to look after her, entertain her, keep her busy, until her family unit comes to pick her up."

"Sorry?" One-9 throws up his hands and turns his power chair in a tight spin. "She's been living right here?"

His compatriot shrugs. "Best place to hide, Dar!"

"And where exactly are you going?"

"You don't want to know. The less you know, the better."

"Okay, okay, you're usually right, even if I hate that. But am I going to hate what you're up to even more?"

One-10 lifts a mischievous eyebrow, wraps a long silk scarf around his neck, puts on a beret and turns his power chair around. "You know it! So, how do I look?"

As One-9 gives a tentative thumbs-up, the ominous sounds of marching boots thump louder and closer in the depths of the Underground City.

Awhile later, Alkima stands outside the "Cave" venue, asking the Beatnik-inspired artist cluster members to leave their handheld devices with him. They all wear rainbow jackets, but they come in different styles—some wear three quarter versions, some bomber jackets, some have rainbow stripes, others have rainbow swirls. They're all quietly excited as they murmur in hushed tones, in expectation of something different, maybe even special.

"What's going on, big daddy?" says one to Alkima.

He's caught off guard but blurts out, "Just dig it, brothers and sisters!"

"Yeah, too groovy, big daddy!"

He hands out Beatnik hats and accessories from a table, as he also puts a beret on his own head, and tips it stylishly on its side. Catches a glimpse of what he looks like in a reflective surface and then tips his hat back the other way. 'Okay, I'm smoking,' he grins!

Inside, the dimly lit Cave has many comfy mats laid out on the floor. Frizz signals for them to sit down and get comfortable. On a small stage, Abana and I prepare, checking several items that lie on a table. In the middle of which lies a monkey's polished, gleaming skull. Frizz joins us onstage. Our trio looks very snappy in our Beatnik wear as both of us girls wear stretchy "go-go boots" and "mini-skirts," while Abana wears skinny pants and pointed shoes.

Abana picks up the skull and begins tapping a smooth percussive beat on it as I hum a sweet melody, something the trilling trees do on Geto.

I nudge Frizz who begins to recite some words from a piece of paper in a sort of rapping voice. "The weight of your fear makes me bow low/The hammer of your mantra makes my heart slow/ As your words reach out to always say no-no/And so the art inside me dies/Until I lie back and look up to the skies and rise..."

Frizz gestures for the audience to lie on their backs and look up to the ceiling where Abana adeptly uses laser sticks to "paint" a galaxy of shooting stars and suns going nova. White light seems to shoot into crystalline shapes and fractures into rainbow slivers.

The audience murmurs with "ooohs and aaahs" as Abana's light show enthralls them. He's a natural, an alchemist with this new technology in his hands.

In the background, Frizz and I improvise another verse of words, overlapping each other in two-part harmony.

"Star bright/In the far night!"

"Shooting star/From afar!"

"Open our eyes/And silence our cries!"

I pick up the monkey skull and beat on it as the audience begins repeating the verses. "Star bright/In the far night!"

The whole room erupts into life with sounds, percussive beats and words, and eye-opening visuals.

In the back of the room, but not yet officially introduced, One-10 rolls in and positions himself just behind Alkima. He watches transfixed, with his own beret now slightly cocked forward. Alkima is still trying to get his just right.

As the impromptu performance segues to an end, Frizz starts snapping her fingers in appreciation. Abana and I join in. And soon the whole room is finger snapping. Or, at least trying to finger snap.

With a look of elation on her face, Frizz spontaneously hugs me. Then, she also hugs Abana. Spreading the love, and perhaps so much more.

Soon the words "eyes wide open" filter out of the audience and everyone is rhythmically chanting it, "Eyes wide open!"

Even One-10 and his long-lost brother Alkima chant it. And the words hold so much more hope and light than the Commander's own mantra of fear and non-light, "Praise the Darkness."

CHAPTER TWENTY-THREE

Happiness Is a Warm Gun

The Rite of Spring Sacrificial Dance by a man named Igor Stravinsky breaks the next morning's misty silence, as it plays on a geodesic-shaped speaker system set up on the Basin's expanding cleared ground. Controlled fires continue to burn in the background.

The rousing sounds accompany a hooded Cluster-X as he oversees the maneuvers of the rearmed enforcement drones in their new dirt brown uniforms. Doing the goose-step in shiny new boots, they march in tight formations, chanting, "In the right! In the right! In the right!" And the great music blasts its clarion call to arms. As they march and chant, they morph into soldiers, into an army of One, an army of Darkness.

"I don't know but I've been told/You'll get my gun when I'm dead cold!"

A distance away, barging bulldozers come out of a nearby domed entity and thunder towards the forest's edge, ready to raze more trees and vegetation.

The Cluster-X'er barks more sinister orders from under his hood to the drones who adjust their rifle muskets on their shoulders.

"Fix bayonets. Ready, aim, fire!" A volley of musket fire clouds the air. "Charge!"

The soldiers charge with gleaming bayonets leading. And they viciously attack dummies that look like long-haired, savage Thalandians.

"Hoo-ah!" they growl after they tear the dummies to shreds.

Meanwhile, on the move down below, the Commander enjoys footage of the maneuvers on his handheld, cackling with delight. "Hooah! That is so excellent! Nice touch, X-33!"

He puts away his handheld and glides through the weapons production factory with X-33. He lovingly picks up a new rifle, checking its sightlines. Removes a glove and touches the weapon's cold metal with a bare finger. He likes the cool sensation, reciting, "From my cold, dead hands." He purrs with approval as he sees X-33's questioning look. "That quote—you like it, sir?"

"Very nice one, Dar!"

The Commander puts his glove back on, then smoothly glides down some stairs to a heavy iron door. His confederate places his face close to a panel for a retinal scan. The door swooshes open. Inside, another hooded creature, X-44, ushers him in to a table covered by a sheet. Like some slick magician, the hooded weapons master dramatically whisks away the sheet to reveal various revolvers.

"Commander, these are based on the designs that we got from the Blue Planet, replications of weapons used in their early 1800s." He eagerly points to one gleaming six-shooter and invites the Commander to try it out. "The Colt revolver gave one the ability to fight off multiple attackers. Not only did this special weapon help in the protection of pioneers in the American west, it became a vital tool for their military and law enforcement."

"And what are we without our tools?" the Commander agrees. He picks up and holds this smaller weapon awkwardly.

X-44 picks up a gun belt and holster from the table and straps it on. He holds his hand out to his Commander. Then, he gently takes the Colt back, signals for his leader to step back. He starts spinning and slinging it around like a gunslinger would. Smooth and efficient. Showing off even.

He walks his boss to a nearby indoor target range. He loads the six-shooter. "Sir, this will alter the way we conduct our campaigns."

He slides the gun into the holster, then uses a laser stick to create a holographic Thalandian savage with a bow and arrow, thirty yards away. "Sir, you could put those shooting earmuffs on if you want."

The Commander shakes his head and folds his arms. "No, I'd like the full effect."

The holographic Thalandian and X-44 face off, weapons at the ready. Then, they both discharge their weapons—a revolver against a bow and arrow. And X-44 has obviously been practicing as he shows dexterity, firing off all six shots, hitting a target dummy behind the holograph. And like a performer, he blows the smoke off the hot gun barrel. He deftly spins the revolver around and holsters it again.

"Welcome to our revolution, citizens!"

"Happiness is a warm gun, right, Commander?!" smiles X-33.

"You will go far, my son! And, you too, X-44!"

They then walk their boss over to the dummy behind the holograph that has six holes in its chest. "Sir, as you suggested, now that we've lifted the ban on muskets..." X-44 continues his pitch. "We can move onto these new weapons, which we can call The Peacekeeper series!"

When X-3 claps his hands in glee, his confederate X-33 whispers, "Be afraid, be very, very afraid...right, sir?!"

X-3 distractedly nods as he also hears some glorious orchestrations in his head.

As the weapons master safely wraps up the Colt and holster, he glances up suddenly. Hello, he thinks he hears his Commander humming. X-33 hears it, too, but he shakes his head at the weapons master, giving a subtle zip-it gesture that suggests to not even go there. Like totally forget about it, because he was not humming! Period.

Alkima, Abana, Frizz, One-10 and I have stayed up all night, buzzing from the performance, and just hanging out in the Cave. The new curfew means that only authorized personnel are allowed to travel the corridors of the Underground City at night.

All of us, except One-10 in his chair, lounge on the mats as we sip refreshing drinks that Alkima has served up—a little water, some special powder and presto!

"So you really are kind of brothers, right?" I ask Alkima and the scientist.

"Although we had different birthers, our embryos were created from the same source pool. So yes, we are like brothers!" admits One-10.

"Does that explain the telepathic messages?"

"Is that what I've been getting, telepathic messages? All I know is that I've been getting this pounding in my head and then these messages come to me, they're like thoughts, someone else's thoughts. It's like something has been switched on," marvels One-10.

He wonders if he's rambling, but a smiling Alkima motions for him to go on. "Thanks, because I've been so wanting to let it all out. I've got this theory that really does border on heresy, that our bioengineered evolution is really devolution. I've been doing strings of numbers tests with chimps and they score higher than the average Mainlandian. In fact, they score higher than me. Well, almost. All those things we did naturally, things that we no longer have to do, senses we no longer have to use, these are all things we've lost to our science and our unbridled progress. And why?" He throws up his hands. "Because we have conquered all the outside impetuses that required fast evolutionary growth—predators, unpredictable natural disasters, famine, and all those kinds of stimuli have gone. Well, mostly."

On a roll, he slugs back Alkima's concoction and breathes in to calm himself. "And, at the same time, our decision-makers in their selective wisdom, they decided that certain traits were to be dominant and others were to be considered abnormal..."

"You're talking about traits like non-brown eyes, left-handedness, above average IQ for your designation," adds in Alkima, who knows all about this, having been banished himself.

"Yes, all of those. They also started to eliminate any genes that could result in disease, even childhood ailments like measles and chicken pox..."

"Great in theory, but if you expose the immune system to less, then you could start seeing autoimmune conditions."

"Exactly. Now, in the almost twenty years since you were exiled to Geto, Alkima, it's gone way further. All sorts of so-called 'recessive traits' have been included. So this master bioengineering plan continues to evolve, or should I say, devolve."

"But, disagreeable traits and undesirable behaviors still keep cropping up?"

"Well, one person's odd behavior is another person's natural way, right?" One-10 shrugs. "And, no matter how much artificial selection we do, Nature will have its way!"

"Now they want to banish anyone who displays too much humor, who sings, who's considered too touchy-feely, who is too gay..."

As I see Frizz twitch at the words "too gay," I add, shocked, "So, they don't like happy kids?" I remember what Alkima said about him laughing too much.

"No, they don't do happy down here," deadpans One-10.

"They would've exiled you, Aiya, for singing," says Frizz. "Or the lot of us for what we did last night, if we did it in public."

"What about the ones who aren't exiled to Geto, what happens to them?" asks Abana.

"Who knows? And more and more people just seem to be disappearing," notes One-10.

"But why? Who makes these decisions about dominant or recessive traits, and for what reasons? Shouldn't happiness be kept around to balance out sadness? Shouldn't weakness in one person help strengthen another? Couldn't esthetics and function work hand in hand?" I plead.

"Too true!" One-10 glances over to Alkima, impressed with my enthusiasm and logic. "Aiya is sensing exactly what I've been thinking. That is the problem here—science, the very essence of what I'm about—and over-reliance on it is failing us. It's put that veil of darkness over our eyes, put us in a straitjacket, and burdened us. In our rush to create uniform order and stability, we've lost touch with who we are, with our imperfections, with what makes us different..."

"Right, aren't those the things that make us whole beings, the yin and the yang, and isn't life really about that struggle. Don't imperfections make us strive harder?" I ask.

One-10 raises a bushy eyebrow, totally impressed with my take. "The truth is, I've come to realize we are overly edited beings here."

"So, there's no room for anyone or anything unique or unusual," Abana notes.

"No room for mystery or magic, how boring," I add.

"Yeah, we really don't do happy or different!" shrugs Frizz.

"And what's with this 'Praise the Darkness' thingee?"

"They say it's about honoring the solar eclipse coming up. That we can overcome the darkness that's coming, with our science. So they turn off all the power down here to correspond with the darkness above. It's really quite scary with all the lights and everything off. You never know for sure if they'll switch it back on. But I think that's their goal."

"To show they have ultimate control!" offers Abana as Frizz and One-10 both agree.

To which, I counter, "Then we'll have to give them something different and light up that darkness!"

Just then, some drone workers who've finished their shift cautiously enter looking around them. "We hear something special is going on here? There is going to be another show, they haven't shut you down, have they?"

Frizz confidently steps up. "No, the show must always go on!" Welcoming them in, she says, "And, if there ain't no audience, there ain't no show!" And, then she directs them to us, her new friends. "Too right, eh guys?" She sure has that, right! Go, girl!

CHAPTER TWENTY-FOUR

May Peace Reign

As the young artists and drones huddle in small working groups, trying their hand at performance art with help from Abana, me, and Frizz who's a natural, Alkima and One-10 consult together.

"I think your buddy One-9 is right to express his concerns, because we are playing with dynamite here," Alkima points to the young Mainlandians. "With them but also with this whole idea of lifting the veil."

"Be careful what you wish for, right?"

"Because a pebble in a stream really can cause far-reaching ripples," Alkima cautions.

The big overhead screen on the back wall suddenly whirrs to life.

"Speak of the devil," hushes One-10 to everyone in the room.

The vidcast begins. X-3, the Commander, appears and he must be wearing special neon contact lenses because there's a spectral glow from under his hood.

Abana and I watch, amazed at our first sight of a big-screen vidcast. I almost freak out to see that the 'holy man' from my dreams is now some living, breathing and spooky reality. And, his sudden appearance shakes my very core for some other reason I can't really explain. There's just something about him....

The Commander, wearing a white cloak and hood, glides gently and quietly through a birthing ward, complete with different colored test tubes being gently shaken, not stirred. A fine, cool mist keeps them cool as warm breath escapes from under the Commander's hood. He traces his fingers along the tubes' casing.

Frizz notes that the rattling, speckled band has disappeared from his forearm.

"Good day, my fellow Mainlandian citizens." He clasps his hands together, then releases them. "May peace reign over us." He beckons with one hand for the camera to follow him. "Shhhh, let's see what we have here." He now slides over to rows and rows of baby incubators. He stands over one as a nurse reaches in and carefully hands him a cooing little baby, fresh from its surrogate. He very ably and gently puts the swaddled babe into the crook of his left arm, looking very much at ease, and oh so adept.

"Hi there little chubby one, coochy coo!" He then turns back to the main camera, ready for his close-up. "So, how are we today, my friends? Very well, I hope! Because the tremors we experienced caused no serious damage. Our structures, built with our own sweat and scientific ingenuity, stood strong. And they will continue to shelter and keep us all safe, including this precious little one." The cute baby seems abnormally quiet.

Alkima, a master of observation, whispers, "The child looks sedated."

"This is a quick reminder that our friendly new curfew is in effect, every day, even on weekends. Remember, we are, In the Right—repeat it after me, In the Right," the Commander pauses for the viewers to repeat the line, as he gently rocks the unmoving child. "This curfew is for the benefit of all of us, to protect us, to maintain Mainlandia's peace and way of life. A way of life we've strived so hard to create, a life without disease, a life of comfort and ease, without the harshness topside. So, if you see anyone trying to disrupt our order, please report them. Think of the future of this young baby. Plus, fun rewards will be given out—like special versions of the GOH videogame. I will be chatting again later about also safeguarding ourselves against a wicked new virus. In the meantime, don't forget to take your 'calm' pills, which are now freely available throughout our City in lovely, new dispensers."

Using some sleight of hand, the Commander produces a pale pink pill in his other gloved hand. He holds it up for effect, then appears to pop it into his hidden mouth but in truth he's being deceptive.

"He dropped it on the floor. That's pretty sneaky," I sneer.

"Remember, all you need is...peace and pills for a good night's rest and general happiness." The Commander strokes the still unmoving child on the cheek and hands it back to the nurse. He straightens his robe and looks right at the camera. "And also remember, at the end of night, comes light. So, praise the Darkness!"

That spooky spectral glow lights up and then fades away, with the screen going to black. For a split second, no one says anything out loud.

I say to Abana. "He uses strong gris gris." When Frizz wonders what I mean, I explain, "Strong magic."

"Possede, a man possessed," offers Alkima.

"I feel like I know him, do I?!" I look to Alkima but he has an enigmatic blank stare. So I look back to Frizz. "So, when again is this Darkness thingee happening?"

Instead of answering, a feisty Frizz now shouts back at the screen, "Soul assassin!" She grabs the pill dispenser in the room and throws the 'calm' pills all over the floor, stomping them to dust.

And then a few more of the young Mainlandians chime in, "Soul assassin! Soul assassin!" They help Frizz stomp the pills to smithereens.

One-10's eyebrow rises up and he surprisingly reaches his hands out to Alkima, "So it starts, Dar!"

"Welcome to the change, brother!"

Way, way down in the Underground City, statuesque One-6 stands alone in the dark in an observation room, watching the Viking of a Thalandian prisoner. At first, he doesn't realize she's there. In this room, there is no plate glass, just a buzzing electric force field separating them. She watches him mix mud from his prison's floor with water and some ground up clay. His hand paints a figure on the wall, a man-like creature whose left hand is raised in a sort of closed fist gesture—in defiance.

He paints a sort of halo around the figure's head. Then uses clumps of blue pigment from his own knotted hair to create blue eyes for the figure. He reverently steps back from his painted figure and falls to his own knees in supplication.

Quietly sighing, One-6 is enthralled, she can't explain it, she doesn't know what it means. And yet she squirms uncontrollably.

The savage slowly turns his head around, having heard her sigh, but he can't locate her. So, he sniffs the air, and smells her. He can also hear her heart thumping. Then in an instant, he attacks the force field and is bounced back. He attacks again with the same result. He lets out an unholy cry and Trix shivers in the dark. Even with her reduced sense of smell, to her he feels of the jungle, and she can sense his savagery and... his nobility. She sighs again. And leans against the damp wall for support.

Defeated in his attempts to break free, the savage returns to look at his wall painting and kneels again, then slumps in defeat to the ground. The two of them stay there unmoving for moments on end. Separated by space and philosophy, and everything else in between.

Then, Trix gasps when a hand gently touches her on the shoulder, and beckons her back towards the entrance.

"Shhhhh, it's me, the Commander." She sees the neon glow under the hood. "Do you know what he painted?"

"A family member?"

"What he drew is the reason why we must maintain our vigilance. Look closely, One-6, the figure has blue eyes, a sure sign of a Rejex. And his left hand is raised in a sinister fist of rebellion."

"Why would the Thalandians know about our Rejex?"

"In the early days, we used to try and change them—surgically and otherwise—to make them fit in...for their benefit of course. And when that didn't work, we first exiled them to Thalandia. Now, of course, we send them directly to their own place of isolation. Better to keep them all in one place. After all, they're not really our enemy. They can't help it that they're different. They just don't belong here, infecting us. In a way, I feel sorry..."

"Are there Rejex still living in the jungles of Thalandia?" she interrupts him.

"If there are, we should be afraid. Very, very afraid!" warns the Commander as he turns to leave the room.

"Hold on!" Her words do make him halt. "Why should we fear Rejex among the Thalandians? They're not suited for uptop living, just like us. They don't know how to hunt or to fend for themselves. They'd probably die of starvation or thirst or be killed by the savages."

He turns back, shaking his head as he stabs a finger toward the wall painting. "Or be revered and followed for being different."

"What are you not telling me, Commander?"

"All in good time." He then poses his own question. "But what were you imagining, One-6, when I came in? Your own illusion?"

"I was thinking of the Thals looking up to the sun."

"Beware, there is a tale from the cosmos of a god who flew too close to the sun."

"I was thinking of their life without technology, of living with ancient magick."

"Science is our magick! The most powerful kind."

She goes on. "Of sitting around fires and looking up to the stars and telling tales like the one you just told."

"Come on, you know stories are just illusions to keep little children and people...happy, as you put it."

Her handheld beeps and it breaks her reverie. She glances at it and sends a message back. She turns on her high heels, back to being all business. "Please!" she says as she brushes by the Commander. "Allow me my illusions. Like it's rumored that you have yours, Commander."

He glares at her from under his hood, and he petulantly stomps the ground with one foot.

CHAPTER TWENTY-FIVE

The Disc

Curfew bells bing-bang-bong through the corridors.

"Prison's out for now," quips Frizz.

"I need to show you all something," says One-10 to us. "Actually, two things. One of which is a most revered Talisman." He points to the golden Disc on his coat. "And, second, something potentially even more valuable than that." He checks his timepiece. "We have the time. Are you up for it?" There was genuine excitement in his twinkling eyes, as if he was awakening himself.

We all nod in agreement. "Okay, let's bounce!" smiles Frizz who can't contain her own excitement, smooching everyone in her new group.

Leaving Mystikat behind to watch over the working groups, we exit the Cave wearing more muted grey clothing, and keep our eyes looking down at handhelds that One-10 had brought us. Better to blend in and not seem different. Led by One-10, we walk through the corridors to a set of elevators and ascend back up to a higher level.

Our group arrives at a high security level and before the doors open, One-10 advises, "Just follow my lead, you're my guests for a tour." He's about to open the doors when he looks to Abana. "Did you say you were going to use some of that purple haze thing in your performance tonight?"

"It's something that Alkima and Aiya showed me. It can be used for all sorts of things including a way to cloud the mind of an opponent. I've got some with me. Why, what are you thinking?"

"I have an idea but the less you know now, the better. But when I tap the Disc on my coat, you'll know what to do, Abana."

Okay? Check! One-10 touches a keypad panel, the doors open and he leads us to a retinal scan panel on a glass wall. The device scans his eye and an electronic voice speaks: "Welcome, One-10. How many guests do you have?"

"Four, including a fellow geek from our northern frontier."

"Welcome all to Occulo's Museum of Science."

The glass wall opens and we follow One-10 in.

Wow! Inside, we're amazed by the dazzling array of "space junk" that Occulo's Collector station has apparently retrieved over many decades. The items are openly displayed on glass shelving units that are being inspected by other small groups as they also tour through the displays.

One-10 proudly points out some of the artifacts. "That's the brain of an Altairian probe from which we were able to download a lot of their history—as you can see, its silicon configuration looks like a real animal brain. That engine over there is part of an unmanned satellite we believe came from the system of Wolf-359. And, those solar reflectors must've torn loose from another passing craft—we're using its design as a basis for our secret solar grids. For me, it's a way cleaner, better option than mining our tar sands."

I look at the very basic, grey rectangular panel. My face screws up, unimpressed. Frizz admits, "Yeah, it is kind of boring, isn't it?"

"We're working on our own solar power system but it's way more fun."

Frizz looks around to make sure no one is listening. "How, tell us, please!"

I look over to Alkima, who motions to go ahead. "We've got these Mlap trees with their great big fronds, you know, their leaves. And we, Alkima and me, sort of just suggested to our Rejex engineers, what if we could make solar panels that look like the leaves of a Mlap. The trunk could conduct the collected power to a storage unit. And that way, instead of having plain old, boring solar panels sticking out like a sore thumb, why can't we blend in the real Mlaps with the solar powered ones?"

"You've built them already?"

"It's just theory as we don't have all the materials to build them right now!"

"But you could potentially create like an energy forest!" she enthuses.

"Absolutely. It's like art and science combined. And, you could build them here."

"Wow! That's what's so cool with you guys coming here. You're bringing your art, punk attitude and passion to our, you know, boring functionality."

One-10 winks, impressed, and keys in some notes into his handheld. He then wheels through the displays, explaining other neat, cool stuff. Some are ancient. "The Zephyrian Crystals were dropped like gifts from the skies, giving our once-primitive Occulan ancestors the ability to change their lives and ultimately ours."

I am sort of stupefied, as the other part of our life begins filling in—about our history, our ancestors and their inspirations.

"How did we find the Crystals?" I ask, glancing at my mentor Alkima who notes how I used the personal possessive "we."

Frizz is itching to jump in but restrains herself. One-10 graciously allows her. "Go ahead 451, I mean Frizz, tell them a story."

"The fables have it that during our early Thalandian period, when winter's dark coldness had descended, a shivering child cried out for warmth to her mother. The child's mother and father looked up to the skies and asked the moon goddess for help. The story goes that the moon wept for the child's pain and shook her haloed brow. Then the night was suddenly filled with exploding showers—like shooting stars—and glittering gifts fell from the skies. Thousands of sparkling crystals were found blanketing the ground. Crystals that were used to create the gift of fire and warmth and life," says the excited frizzy-haired teen.

"Awesome!"

"And what's that?" asks Abana who points to another display that holds in its hand-like mount a golden disc that shimmers with light. Abana unconsciously reaches out to touch it but a nearby security bully boy grunts to warn, Hey, back off. Abana withdraws his hand but he and I both stare at the disc, our bodies touching in a comfortable, casual way.

For a brief second I wonder if he truly has left his past behind. Hoping, with all my heart, that this possibly dangerous but oh so exciting adventure has made him leave his sad past behind.

I peek at him for any sign, but instead Abana blurts out, "It's just like the disc on your coat, One-10!"

The scientist motions around him with both arms wide open. "Nearly all of these objects came to us from our skies. Some just appeared on the ground. Others were scooped up by the Collector station that the Ancients left behind and were transported to us in the unmanned delivery shuttle that comes down here monthly." He wheels up to the Golden Disc's display. "The Blue Planet has also sent out many satellites and probes and radio signals over the years—they seem like they were a very eager people, eager to reach out, to communicate."

"They were but now?"

He shrugs. "We haven't received anything new from them for decades. Perhaps they experienced some cataclysm, natural or otherwise. But this Golden Disc was salvaged from one of their Voyager crafts, and we've used it, along with other separate radio signals, as the basis for our modern science."

"Wow, here's to the Blue Planet then," I whisper.

One-10 signals again to Frizz and she rambles on. "This amazing disc has over a hundred embedded images, starting with ones of scientific interest. They illustrate mathematical and physical quantities, the Blue Planet's solar system and its sister planets, along with human DNA. Those initial designs along with the subsequent radio messages, that included Darwin's *Origin of the Species* communicated in digital language, have helped catalyze Occulo's technological progress."

I wonder, "So it was like the people of the Blue Planet seared the message of their very soul into this disc...and then sent that message in a bottle and tossed it into the cosmic ocean, hoping that one day it would be found, right?!"

"Message received loud and clear."

"What else is on the disc?" asks Abana as he circles around to view the back of the disc's display.

Frizz can't stop. "Ta-da, recorded music!"

Just then, there's a whirr and a giant screen emerges from the wall and crackles into life. Abana and I almost jump back, as a pop-up promo appears: "Success is ours—if we all pull together as a team." There's a pause in the message.

"He'll be back," spits out Frizz. "He always is."

"So you do have music here?"

"Well, we can't play it in public unless approved. We can't even play it in private unless approved. I don't know if even The Commander or One-6 can play it for personal enjoyment. But the Army has been using some music for its topside maneuvers," explains One-10.

Abana and I peer at the disc from the backside.

Alkima, who's just been observing, gestures knowingly. "Yes, there's actually two discs there, back to back, which I remember seeing as a child visiting here. It's an optical illusion that it's only one, but two were retrieved from Voyager."

One-10 motions for us to look closer.

So Abana and I look even closer. There are two discs back to back. Abana said, "Cool, hidden in plain sight. Often the best place to conceal something."

I ask, "So what type of music did the Blue Planet send?"

Frizz jumps in. "Pieces from artists like Beethoven to a man called Chuck Berry whose tune 'Johnny B. Goode' was played by One-10 at our recent commencement. It was as if our ears had been closed like forever. And then this rock and roll music just blew out of the speakers in the Dar Hall." She looks around her then says softly, "It really did just rock our socks! Thanks One-10, sir!"

"You're welcome, Frizz."

The security drone is distracted by some other visitors, so Frizz takes her opportunity to quietly sing while subtly wiggling her hips. "Deep down Louisiana close to New Orleans/ Way back up in the woods among the evergreens/There stood a log cabin made of earth and wood/Where lived a country boy named Johnny B. Goode..."

"Your singing voice is pretty good already, you're a natural!"

"Until I met you guys, I never realized that if you don't sing or hum or express yourself, you don't vibrate, you're not alive. In fact, you're kind of dead! Look at me now, an art student who loves science and now music. What a combo, eh?" She surprisingly giggles and wiggles her hips again.

Everyone is momentarily silenced by her spot-on observation and pleased with her spontaneity.

Alkima adds, "If I also remember, this second disc is rumored to contain additional music selections, as well as images of paintings from master artists and sculptors, and poems by great writers. Plus all sorts of other delights."

"Treasured stuff that very few of us have been exposed to," sighs One-10. "I'd love to get my hands on it!" He mischievously looks to Alkima and gently signals toward the discs with a motion of his head, and a wink.

Alkima then glances at me and I read his mind: "U know what 2 do, right kiddo?"

I do. So, I look over to Abana who takes a few seconds. But he soon gets it, too. And we get ready for our silent sneaky play.

The big screen crackles into life again with another pop-up promo: "One voice, one thought—simplicity rules, okay!"

Frizz curses something under her breath.

Then onscreen, the Commander's glowing eyes appear once again, shrouded by his still white hood as he begins his vidcast. His tone has softened even more, as he glides through a classroom of young students who're all seriously typing into their handhelds, heads bowed down at mini-workstations in several rows.

"Dear citizens of Mainlandia, I wanted to follow up with you, my friends. You know we care about you, so I'd like to talk more about a terrible 'virus' and how it is adversely upsetting our harmony and balance, affecting our hard earned scientific progress. Here in our comfortable Underground City where everyone has food on the table and a roof over our head, we all know our jobs and our place in life. We have no undue expectations on us. Nothing is left to chance. If you really, really think about it, we have a happy lot and a safe long life. We are blessed and give thanks to our great god of science and technology for giving us decades of no lack, no starvation, no disease, no pressure to be anything more than what we are created to be."

He lightly and gently brushes his gloved hand across the heads of the students as he slides between the rows of workstations.

"But all that is being threatened by this virus. In short, we're starting to be infected, my friends, and we should be concerned. First, we're being infected by foreign bodies—the Thalandians and whomever else they have recruited to work with them. Already, foreign thoughts, alien ideas and dangerous behavior—murder, rape, cannibalism—are trying to creep into our peaceful way of life."

The Commander stops and seems to look at one student's work. He puts a gloved hand on her shoulder. "A gold star for you, little Dar!" He tips up her head and she smiles on cue. "Isn't she so perfectly pretty?" He pulls out a handkerchief and it looks like he wipes a tear away from his hidden eyes. "Excuse me, while I take a moment." He regains his composure then continues on walking as the camera expertly follows him. "Do we want instability? No. Do we want the rupture of change? Again, no! But I can hear you already out there. Yes, you are afraid. But we have the right to be afraid. Of fake news and false stories. But you can trust me, we will not let this happen. We will fight and we will resist any changes to our harmonious order. So stay the course, my friends. Trust in your leaders. And, once again, think of our precious children, who are our very future."

He gives an open arm gesture over the students' heads. Then he slams one hand into another, and as one, all the students stand up from their workstations. "We will keep Mainlandia moving forward, always forward—for a better Mainlandia, for an endless enduring dream and a thousand points of light." He pauses for effect then adds, "May our god of science continue to bless the children!"

In unison, they all chant in that singsong kids' way, "A thousand points of light!"

To which he further adds, "And more!" Like a grand holy man, he seems to bless the children reverently with his right hand. "Let us have a momentary silent prayer about that, shall we, everyone." Everything is totally quiet for a few seconds. Then he abruptly brings his head up. His eyes glow even more, almost seductively. "Now, everyone smile for the camera, kids!"

Like human automatons, all the kids chant, "Cheese!"

Some weird wave of sounds rises up around him, and buzzes through the air in a crescendo. Then the cheesy smiles fade out as the screen shifts to black. The weird waves of sound keep buzzing for awhile then also fades to silence.

That silence is broken by several observations.

"What's he on about? The Thalandians barely have language skills. And as for conscripting others, who else is there?" One-10 asks.

Alkima offers. "Those weird sounds, I think he's trying to use some form of subliminal stimuli."

"I really, really don't like that guy!" says a perceptive Abana.

"I don't know if I should say this, Aiya, but your Ma-Tu and I knew him when we were younger. He wasn't always like this."

"But why would she have known him, Alkima?"

"Because like your Ma-Tu, he's an Adept, m'petite."

"What does that mean, again?"

"That he is very, very good at the art of...manipulating absolutely everything."

And then we jump when we hear the sound of another PMV frantically nearing us.

"One-10, we so have a problem!" One-9 zooms up. He's about to break out with some breathless news when he sees Alkima. His excitement turns to a quasi nod of acknowledgment. "Uh, greetings, sir!"

"They're visitors from the northern frontier, Dar," says One-10, glancing at the guard and covering.

"Oh, right, welcome!" One-9 looks around but the guard is still busy elsewhere. So he motions for us to approach him and he speaks under his breath, "It must've been an accident. They found one of the children, 777! They broke in and abducted her from her parental units. Gone!"

"That's not good, that's not good at all."

"What child is this?" I ask, naturally concerned.

"She was the other gift I wanted to show you. But first, we need get out of here and assess the danger of this new event."

Abana looks to me. I read his PIM and nod, yes. He sticks his hand into his pocket and quietly removes some of Alkima's purple haze dust.

One-10 speaks up. "Uh, we should get back to work at our offices, people!"

Secretly, Abana throws some dust in the direction of the security drone. I edge toward the golden disc display.

A few moments later, our group has left the Museum, blending in with others leaving and coming. But I pause for a second, and suddenly hold my own temples. I'm feeling something very strong coming in. My knees knock a bit.

"What's up, Aiya?"

"I don't know, maybe just a little overwhelmed and tired."

"You sure, it's nothing else," asks Abana worried.

"No, just too much excitement. I'm good. I think!"

My companions grab my arms to steady me, and we all walk on with our heads bowed.

Meanwhile, somewhere deep in the Underground City in the room where the Commander concocts his own strategic formulas, he now sits alone in the dark. Leaning back in a cushy chair, he switches off a replay of his recent pre-recorded vidcast. He calmly relaxes into his surroundings. Very slowly, surround sound speakers spark to life. And Bach's *Brandenburg Concerto No. 2 in F* starts filling up the room. As he gets into the piece, the dark Commander conducts along with the beautiful music. And, yes, he hums along!

In the background, obscured by the dim light is a neon tank that stands upright like a giant test tube. It's fed by pumping tubes of oxygen and nutrients and other liquids. And if one looks really, really close through the opaqueness, one can see an unmoving but large human-like creature inside the tank, monstrously hooked up to all the tubes and floating in some sort of cryogenic suspension.

CHAPTER TWENTY-SIX

Zen and Zine

Back in the two scientists' private office, our group collects our thoughts. Alkima prepares some more energy drinks while Frizz keeps watch on the security camera.

"Do you think the Commander now knows about the girl?"

"Do one legged ducks swim in a circle?"

It takes his buddy a second. "Of course, funny image. But so what should we do? And what about the other ones? I'm beside myself, the poor thing."

"Let's not panic, One-9!"

"Panic? Panic? You haven't seen real panic, yet, One-10!"

Alkima interrupts the two of them. "Okay, Dar, what exactly are we talking about?"

"Yeah, who is she?" asks Abana.

While sipping Alkima's special drink, I'm still recovering from my throbbing temples. I eye the scientists' gestures. The two seem genuinely concerned about this child. One-10 glances over to me. And then I get it. "Wait, what exactly have you been holding out on us?"

"Who is this girl?" asks One-6 on a video conference call. "And, what are you saying, Commander, that there may be unidentified Rejexes here in the Underground City?"

"Let's not panic, One-6..."

"Okay, I'll try but explain, please!"

"Well, I told you we used to send the Rejexes to Thalandia. But not all of them, as we decided to study some of them here in, shall we say, secret labs. So for awhile there were young Rejexes under our control. We didn't try to alter these ones. We just studied their behavior patterns."

"Are you still doing it now?"

"You're not seeing the bigger picture. Something harmful this way comes, and we should be very, very afraid."

"I thought you said don't panic!" she blurts out as the Commander shrugs.

Our group huddles around a wall screen airing a recording of the earlier encounter between the young girl and the chimp. We hear the interaction between the scientists and how they notice her playful feet that show two digits fused together, almost webbed.

"She's a Syndactyly?" Alkima's head whirls around to his scientist colleagues. "Holy, Charlie Darwin, is she a Rejex?! And what in darkness is she still doing here?"

Insatiably curious, I use Frizz's handheld to check the word "syndactyly" and sort of figure out why she'd be considered a Rejex, as she doesn't fit the norm. Then I look up something else, the word "zen" which talks about seeing things clearly. Hmm, I sneakily think to myself.

Then the little cutie seems to smile right at the camera as she plays with the chimp. Even for one bred to be a drone worker, she's radiantly pretty and bright. And we watch her transfixed. The gap between her teeth makes her even more endearing.

"So, like, what's her designation...Zen?" I can't help it, as I've created a cute name for him.

One-10 smiles. "I like Zen, good nickname, thank you."

"Well, it rhymes with One-10 but it says that Zen is a way of being, that it emphasizes the value of intuition. I believe you, Zen, are highly intuitive, no?"

"Thank you, Aiya," Zen responds and takes a moment to glance at his "brother" Alkima who is proudly impressed. Then Zen continues, "As for the little girl, she's a drone worker although she was incorrectly designated and her talents kept hidden. Her official designation is 777."

"777?" I close my eyes then quickly open them. "Okay, I'm going to call her Heaven. I feel like she's my little sister."

"How many others are here, Zen?" asks Alkima.

"Almost a dozen, all with characteristics that we've been able to hide. If they showed left-handedness, we taught them ambidexterity. One had blues eyes, so we used contact lenses.

If they were too smart, we'd teach them to dumb it down."

"But why keep them here?" I study One-9 and work it out—Zine rhymes with 9 and has a nice balance to Zen—so I add, "Why keep them here in danger, Zine?"

Zine catches himself laughing, at his new designation but then shrugs and motions to Zen. "It was your call...One-Zen." They both chuckle out loud. Something I bet they haven't done together in a long, long time.

Zen zooms his PMV in a few tight spins then stops. "It's hard to explain but even though I'm a scientist and my life is ruled by absolutes and equations, my logical mind tells me that our Rejexes should be with us. I don't know, it's an emotional statement, a feeling, I guess."

"You're combining logic with emotion, Zen!" says Alkima.

"Why not, I got a sense it's what's meant to be."

"It's like I was thinking before, Geto's art and magick should be mixed up with Mainlandia's science and technology. That us Rejexes should be growing up alongside our brothers and sisters," I suggest.

As my friends agree, I pick up a laser drawing stick and create a generic Occulan being, then focus on its heart and split it apart into two separate jagged halves. The being starts to weaken and double over in pain. I bring the two heart halves back together, and the being grows back in strength, reaches up with its arms and cries out loud, its whole body shimmering with life and energy.

"Wow, that is so beautiful!" cries Frizz.

"Aiya is right. I've felt it for awhile. When I started receiving your telepathic cries for help—'Do we have the courage to lift the veil of darkness?'—I just knew we had to come together. Together we can lift the veil!" trumpets Alkima.

"Then we'd better make some moves before the Commander's Darkness descends."

I point the laser stick at the televised image of Heaven. I then reproduce a holographic copy of the sweet smiling girl right in front of them. "We've got to get Heaven back!"

"And move her and our other Rejexes to where?" asks Zine.

"To a much safer location," Zen says firmly

"Maybe close to uptop?" suggests Frizz.

"Zen, it would seem we have a small window of opportunity to act. That the Commander and our leaders wouldn't want to panic the citizens any more, so they'd be looking for any other Rejexes very quietly."

"Perhaps, but they won't be above using torture—for sure—to get the information they need," declares Zen.

"But, even if we can safely collect the other Rejexes, what do we do about Heaven? There's no way we can get her back by force."

"What we need is a…"

"A bargaining chip?" suggests Abana with a wink.

"Sure but a really powerful bargaining chip," says Zine.

I spin Zen's vehicle around. "Something like this?" Abana reaches into the satchel attached to the back and carefully retrieves the stolen second golden disc. He holds the shiny disc aloft with a beaming smile.

"You didn't?" asks Zine.

"Sure, we did!"

"This good enough to trade with the Council?" I ask.

Alkima looks on proudly at us, his young warriors, as he takes the disc gently into his hands and inspects it. "But before we give it back—and since it was hidden in plain sight, I don't think they'll be missing it just yet—don't you think we should copy its contents. You know, might come in handy some time. Just in case."

"Sneaky, Alkima, I like the way you think and the way your protégés act." Zen reaches out and gently touches us all on our cheeks. We're surprised by his overall show of affection. When he settles back into his PMV, he glances over to his scientist partner who gives a worried "what now" look. Zen looks to the small group, gathers himself and says it. "You know we're not just talking chump change here, but a real revolution, right?"

"Better late than never, Dar!" quips Alkima.

"Okay, as one of the Blue Planet's musicians says, 'Let's rock and roll!'" enthuses Frizz.

Then, we huddle to draw up our plan of action. First is to round up the other Rejex children. Next is to hold a meeting at the Cave to map out a plan with our other neophyte revolutionaries. Then to contact the Council with our trade offer.

Then a buzz comes over the intercom. We look up to the security cameras. Armed officers are at the outer door. *Pound, pound, pound!*

"Holy crap," I whisper. But be careful what you wish for, eh?!

CHAPTER TWENTY-SEVEN

Some Strange Genie

Inside the private suite, Zine commands, "Zen, you go. Take them down through the disposal shafts. I'll deal with them here."

"No need to be a hero, Dar!"

"Frizz, hand me that medical bag." Zine points and she grabs it, not having a clue what he has in mind. He takes it and withdraws a syringe and vial. "Don't worry, Zen, it's a solution I've been working on. It temporarily allows the user to avoid being exposed by any Mainlandian lie detector test." He quickly gives himself a shot as Zen looks on stunned. "As you know, I helped develop the detector test, so this goes hand in hand with it—a counter-acting agent. Now you guys go. But don't forget about me, right?!"

"I'll stay with you Zine, I'll just play dumb. I'm only a first semester student. What could I know?" offers brave Frizz.

Zine reaches out to give her a shot.

"Just in case?" she asks and he nods as the thumps on the door increase.

"Okay, play stupid, don't be brave. We'll be back!" says Zen.

"Welcome to the down and dirty of the revolution, right?!" adds Frizz who can't help herself and hugs Abana and then me last. I sense Frizz's heart thumping and that she wants to kiss me full on. But she keeps composed. Then she raises her closed fist to Abana and me. We do likewise in a communal gesture of defiance.

With that, Zen's hands find a secret seal in the office wall, it opens and our group disappears through the wall, and we leave Zine and Frizz behind to deal with what waited outside. But as we descend, my temples begin to throb again. Who's trying to contact me? From where and why? Because the message is garbled and doesn't make sense. Oh, well, it'll have to wait.

On Geto, miles and miles away, that thing that doesn't make sense is afoot.

It was thought that the first sign had happened during the recent lacrosse-like game of "Bonko" when the sons of two soldier Rejexes had squared off, ready to fight. Abana had defused that possible ticking bomb at the time. But the danger hadn't gone away.

And that hadn't been the first occurrence. It had actually happened several times before the game and each of the events was very similar. Other Rejex soldiers had exchanged harsh words, differences of opinion, and possible displays of elevated testosterone levels.

Now another more dramatic event is flaring up on our island paradise.

While working on strengthening the "island" homes in case of another storm/tsunami, a group of Rejex workers decided to form two teams and compete to see who could finish the job first. When one team was erroneously accused of cheating, all hell broke loose. There was a fistfight. At first, just healthy physical fighting, like how ancient cultures would blow off steam. But it escalated to one Rejex falling and accidentally smashing his head against a rock, killing him. And, now, some strange genie has indeed escaped its bottle.

Back in the Underground City, as our group descends in order to rise back up in the service elevators, we arrive at the mining level.

The air is so choked full of soot and carbon, I feel my nose clogging up, and my lungs bursting for fresh air.

"Here, tie these scarves around your mouth and noses," says Zen, as he hands them out. "These are some of the awful mineral mines where only our poor drones and our other beasts of burden work," he explains against the din of pounding and drilling.

"This looks more like what other races used to call a penal colony," observes Alkima.

Zen turns to study these workers more closely. Then he sees someone. "That was one of my students from last semester. He just went missing after some rumors that he had gotten into some sort of trouble. Now he's down here…"

"Doing his time?" asks Abana.

"So this is where some of the out-of-control young Mainlandians are being sent!" suggests Alkima.

"Hey, what's that?" I hear something else. I strain to listen. "What is that sound?"

Zen's face screws up and twitches. In between the dull, rhythmic pounding of loud metal drills, there are poignant non-verbal sounds.

"It sounds like something crying."

Zen figures out what it is. "You'll see soon enough, Aiya, but be prepared."

As we walk, Zen shows his pass to security drones. Zen's PMV leads us round a corner to an underground quarry where more sounds of "crying" blast my eardrums. It isn't crying but the neighing of several horses that are being used to pull loads of dirt and rock.

Their powerful bodies strain and sweat. They snort at the suffocating air. But their resolute equine spirit keeps them working—they will haul and work and serve till they drop and die.

Abana and I are immobilized by the sight. I tell him that a poem had come to me during the night. "What we're seeing is almost exactly what I saw in my dreams, and what I wrote down." Abana bends in close to me, and as we watch the magnificent beasts of burden before us, I recite my poem:

My nostrils flare as I twist and turn
Screaming, as they pull me down
With chains and whips, they try
To conquer me, bend me to their will
By putting out the fire in my soul
With teeth bared and hooves flashing, I try
To break free of my oppressors
But they've cut me off from the Source...
Now forced to breathe their tainted air;
And force-fed their synthetic food...
I work for them, one of many
Horse to horse, taken below the ground,
When once we were free to roam,
And now we work to bring back lumps
of long dead flesh...

"Wow, that is beautiful, Aiya."

"So are these creatures. But why are these men and horses really here, Zen?"

"They say they're just mining special minerals needed for use in our daily lives. But I get a feeling something else is going on here but I don't know what it is."

"Materials for weapons?" asks Abana.

"Maybe but I can't even get close enough to inspect what they're digging."

One mighty horse, covered in soot, appears, pulling a covered wagon.

His appearance makes me gasp. "Oh, no, that's the one, Big Red, who I saw uptop. He is magnificent. I wish I could touch him. He seems so upset."

"Don't even think about it, Aiya, the guards here take no prisoners when it comes to breaking the rules."

"But why use horses? Surely, mechanized vehicles would do a better job?" asks Alkima.

"These equines are special. They can sense noxious gases."

"So they're used like canaries in the old mines of the Blue Planet, right?" says Abana.

"Yes, just like that."

"That's awful. For the canaries back then and for the men and equines here!" I sigh.

Big Red's ears perk up when he catches my whisper. Even though he is straining to pull his load, he feels me. He manages to turn his head and gazes at me. There is fire in his eyes, but not fear.

I catch his glance. "He's so proud and furious."

"He's feeling exactly what you're feeling, Aiya. Have patience, little lady," says Alkima.

"Alkima's right. The revolution won't happen with us feeling sorry for ourselves. Let's move on," offers Abana.

"True, Abana, let's head up."

Big Red sees us move and stomps one hoof on the ground to get my attention. And, as equines do have tear ducts, there is a tear slowly dribbling from his eye.

It almost tears my heart out when I see that.

CHAPTER TWENTY-EIGHT

Go Johnny Go, Go, Go

"Aiya, allons, let's go!" hisses Abana.

First I linger. Then I defiantly step forward to reach out to touch Big Red as he crosses near us. A security bully strikes me on the arm with the whip he's been using on the horse. The leather draws blood from me.

But I suck it up, fierceness of purpose in my heart, and I keep moving forward. The drone clumsily pulls out his new revolver and points it at me. "Back off, citizen, or I will shoot!"

Abana, after checking quickly to make sure no one else is looking, has circled him from behind. In the din of pulverizing drills, the workers and guards are more focused on their own tasks. Abana reaches out with his strong, deadly arms and puts a sleep hold onto the guard. He falls into the shadows unnoticed.

Bleeding from my arm, but not caring, I reach out and touch Big Red, stroking his forehead. He licks and cleans the blood off my arm. Our eyes and spirits connect, something different than what I feel for Abana. I feel his power even under the weight he is pulling. I wait till the drills start pounding the ground again and I shout below the loud noise, "We'll be back, Big Red, I promise! For you and all your fellow workers!"

With that, our group backs off and leaves the noise and the suffocating air of the underground "penal" colony behind without any further incident.

At her very ordered, somewhat emotionless apartment, One-6 kicks back in a shimmer of smooth satin that caresses her skin. Even without makeup, she's stunningly natural. Artificial selection has worked wonders with her external looks.

As she moves to sit down and relax, she puts on a prototype headset that's being developed. It projects images directly onto her retinas. They're all images of her work, but she's distracted.

She removes the headset and tries to kick back. But she can't get the Thalandian savage out of her mind. "Grrrrr!" Her stomach churns. She needs to see him again, maybe even touch him. She's a scientist. She needs to know. She's always been naturally curious. But she knows it's not prudent to return to see him. But she's secretly kept a filmed copy of him doing his wall painting. She watches the clip again on her headset and it brings it all back to her again. She exhales at the sheer rawness of the scene and how he reverently gives it up to the wall mural he's created.

She glances at her profile in the reflective surface of her handheld. She notes how perfect her face is, symmetrical with cheekbones that can cut glass. She peers closer at her reflection, and sees something else in her eyes. They're moist and sad in their depth. "What is going on?" she confusedly asks herself. She tries to shake the feeling, but fails.

She tells herself, "I'm a scientist, a purveyor of formulaic logic and algorithms. These feelings of concern for the savage are, well, illogical and wasteful."

An e-message beeps her and breaks her out of her daydreaming. She dries her eyes. She's been invited, more like summoned, to another one of the Commander's many private rooms. This one isn't like the dark and dingy private room where the Thalandian savages had been interrogated. This observation room is clean and colorful.

Entering, but looking down at her handheld, she strides up to an observation window where the Commander stands with his back to her. He's gazing through the window to a comfy four-poster bed with drapes enveloping it. She looks up when his voice crackles into life.

"When you asked me about what we should fear about any Rejex among the Thalandians, I suggested that it was on a need-to-know basis. Well, it's time you need to know because we'll have to go before the Council again."

She points through the window to the room and bed. "You trying out some other interrogation techniques, now?"

He gently raps on the glass and inside the room, a very maternal-looking drone nurse parts the drapes to reveal someone asleep under the covers. There is a big, stuffed, furry canine toy on the bed.

"You've taken a child?"

"A very special child. One of our own, a living, breathing Mainlandian Rejex."

The drone nurse gently lifts back the covers to reveal the little girl that One-9 and One-10 had previously observed, 777.

"I don't get it. You told me that it's now law that all Rejexes, upon detection and examination, are instantly exiled to Geto?"

"That is the law, of course. But this one slipped through our fingers, kept hidden by her parental units who've strangely disappeared before we could find them. Anyway, 777 is a blue-eyed Syndactyly. From what we know so far, she's only appeared to be an average student in school. She hasn't displayed any special qualities, so it made it easier not to notice her." One-6 looks back down to check some more information on her handheld as she listens. He continues. "It was a sheer accident that she was noticed—she wears permanent brown contact lenses that hide her true eye color. But when she took her shoes off in class, a fellow student gave her up."

One-6 keeps looking down as she asks, "What's her designation?"

"That's the interesting thing about her. She shouldn't belong to any of the regular worker clusters."

One-6's head jerks up. "She's a young Adept, one of your Cluster-X'ers?"

"That's what her DNA shows. And so the plot thickens."

"You're not going to interrogate her, are you, like you did with those Thalandians?"

"No way, she's going to get our VIP treatment."

"That's unusual. But, on another note, if memory serves, there've been very few Cluster-X Rejexes, right?"

He raps again on the glass, and the nurse puts the covers back over the young Rejex. He now turns toward One-6. Even though she's seen him many times, the initial sight of his glowing eyes under his hood is always unsettling.

"Just one other in our recent past. But let me back up a bit."
He touches a remote control and a screen turns on, showing
old clips of young Rejexes when they were first "outed" in
Mainlandia. "I previously told you that our scientists tried to
change the Rejexes, but that didn't work. So, they were exiled
to Thalandia. But we also kept some here for testing."

"Why don't I know about these experiments?"

"The scientists were sworn to secrecy." He points. "But
watch this!" He strokes the remote again.

The clip shows some young Rejexes who're being tested for
extra-sensory perception. Like with the chimp tests, buzzers
go off and lights flash.

"They were showing heightened sensory perception?"

"Incredibly heightened. But, not all of them, of course. And
that's when my adept elders got interested. There were signs
that other possibly advantageous traits were being switched
on in these young oddballs. But the tests didn't last long
because it was too chaotic to have these Rejexes around."

"They upset our harmony?"

"Apparently, some of them were just wild children. Our
science teams couldn't handle all the disorder they rained
down on them. They'd shout, scream, sing, bang on walls,
stamp their feet then sing some more. Others would strip
naked, paint their bodies and vomit their food. My reports say
it was like amok time. Our adepts said enough was enough.
And so these Rejexes were sent to Geto."

"So, why bother even sending them to Geto, why not just
exterminate them when they're uncovered? And why are you
so interested in this young girl?"

"Too many questions. Suffice it to say, this young girl does
interest us because some of my fellow group members now
want to start testing her abilities, given the new outside threat
we're facing." She whirls from looking at the screen to him
but before she can say anything. "Let's not kid ourselves," he
snickers to himself. "If their abilities, especially the abilities
of a young adept, can be used by our new army to defeat our
enemies, yes, we will use them. Are you kidding me?!"

"If you're talking about possibly using their DNA and genes,
that's horrifying!"

"Cry me a river, build me a bridge and get over it, One-6."

"Thank you for being so unequivocal, Commander." She turns to switch off the screen manually, as the shouting and yelling is getting to her, but she hits the wrong button. Chuck Berry's music suddenly turns on, accidentally, and very loudly. She stops, and wonders. A smile parts her lips. "So, each to his own illusion, right, Commander?"

The Commander now fumbles to find the remote to turn it off. Having been found out, he hits the wrong button and the raucous music only gets louder. His face would show embarrassment if you could see it. After more fumbling, he finally manages to turn it off. "Uh, it's just some homework!"

"You're usually much more adept at obfuscation, sir. By the way, who was that other adept Rejex? Or, is that also on a need-to-know basis?"

"It is, but I can tell you they were exiled to Geto."

She cocks her eyebrow, thinking about the scientific permutations of a Rejex adept living and growing in an isolated but free environment like Geto. "Are we done here, sir? I have some of my own work to do."

"We may need your help, One-6, so keep yourself available. No scientific excursions uptop or anything, okay!"

She turns to leave but can't let it go, whispering the new words she's heard. "Go Johnny go, go, go, Johnny B. Goode." And she notes that the Commander's left foot uncontrollably taps.

CHAPTER TWENTY-NINE

Our New Dawn Rises

As Zen and our group exit an elevator, Abana tenderly but firmly ties a part of his sleeve around my arm wound. I love his care and attention. He kisses me but only on the forehead and quickly. In my heart, I want more. But now is not the time or place. But at least he doesn't seem to be thinking of his lost love.

As we move down a corridor, we see some drone workers quietly finger snapping at two student artists, who finger snap back. But even though they keep their heads down, a security guard-bully spies their gestures.

"Hey, you, what was that?" The two drone workers quicken their pace. "Hey, I'm talking to you!" Then he sees the two artists finger snapping again in support of the workers. He roughly grabs one of the artists, while he pulls out his communications device. The artist tries to pull away but the stronger, bigger guard just throws him on the ground and steps on him with his foot while he tries to use his communicator. The poor artist whimpers, and I kneel down to comfort him.

The guard-bully aims his baton at me but doesn't see what hits him. Abana's youthful power takes down the guard and knocks him out, using a martial arts strike to the temple. He then firmly tells the artists, "Go, go, go and use the finger snap only between ourselves when we can't be noticed, okay?" Relieved, they scoot off.

I smile, proud at the way that my ever so strong companion has taken care of two dangerous situations without blowing our cover. I can't help myself, and passionately kiss my protector on his lips. A short but very soulful kiss.

"Time for romance is later, kiddos. Let's get to the Cave!" Zen suggests as he gets a message on his handheld.

"Quickly!" adds Alkima.

"Oh, great, they're both against me," I groan as I move my butt.

We find Mystikat alone in the Cave with a low-lying light spookily sending his long shadow onto a wall.

"What've you been up to, my friend?"

He gets up from sitting next to a handheld left by one of the young performance artists. Mystikat presses his paw on the device and it whirrs to life. I pick it up and read its meaningful message: "Night fades, our new dawn rises!" At the same time, the device starts playing a crescendo of finger snaps in an orchestral way. It is a pretty impressive mini-production.

"Wow!" say Abana and I together.

"This is really how it does begin," predicts Alkima.

Looking at his own handheld, Zen happily informs us, "All the other Rejex children are safe together. They're being quietly taken with their paternal units to the northern frontier. Actually, we're going to hide them close to the undermanned military base up there."

"Brilliant strategy," says Abana, "Stashing them right next to a military base."

Zen agrees. "And there they'll await our instructions."

"But first, we eat, we must stay strong," says always-caring Alkima.

The artists have left food for me and my friends. We snack on the synthesized but supposedly beneficial bites. Alkima mixes up some powders to put on the food to make it more nutritious. We sit quietly, huddled together at a small table.

"I know for a fact that there are Council members and cluster leaders who share our view that things must change in Mainlandia and not change in the way that the Commander and his new Army want. But, we can't be taking on their Army, can we?" Zen asks.

Abana interjects. "My Pa-Tu taught me that armed insurrection was one of the few options that the oppressed have had throughout the galaxy. I remember him reading from some writer I think was called Shakespeare."

I add. "To be, or not to be: that is the question: Whether 'tis nobler in the mind to suffer/The slings and arrows of outrageous fortune/Or to take arms against a sea of troubles..."

"And by opposing end them...Yeah, that's the dude," Abana adds.

Impressed by us, Zen offers, "I've also extensively read how non-violent, civil disobedience has also helped start revolutions all over the universe. It was used on Altair in the winter food protest." Zen quickly checks his facts on his handheld. "Also Wolf-359's moon had a mining revolt as did the moon in Barnard's Star in the constellation of Ophiuchus." He looks up. "On the Blue Planet, one brave man named Gandhi used the weapon of nonviolence to help defeat what was, at the time, the greatest empire on the planet, the British Raj."

As Alkima rubs Mystikat's throat, he adds, "Active nonviolent protest may indeed be an option."

I use one of Frizz's handhelds to Boodoogle Gandhi, and read aloud, "Gandhi's strategy was called Satyagraha, which means truth-force. Wow, all this stuff about him. I think he's my new hero. And then these other guys, too. MLK Jr., John Lennon, Mandela, they all used peaceful ways to protest against injustice and inequality. The Dalai Lama says, 'If you want others to be happy, practice compassion. If you want to be happy, practice compassion.' Wow!"

Alkima adds, "Wow, indeed," as Mystikat seems to purr in agreement.

Zen's handheld beeps. He reads the message and wipes his forehead in relief. "My friend One-9, Zine, has been released. Frizz says they didn't get anything out of him, that the inhibitor solution worked. She's now with him, returning to his place. But she says there are rumors that the Commander has the little girl."

I feel my head pounding at my temples again.

"What is it, Aiya?"

"Nothing...But Heaven is in a terrible, terrible situation. They could bully her into doing things she doesn't want to do."

Abana carefully removes the golden disc from Zen's satchel. "Once we have our plan in place, we'll start the negotiations, don't worry, Aiya."

"Okay, if we're all agreed, when the artists and others return this evening, we'll talk to them about starting up rotating strikes. But, first we need to rest," says Alkima in his always-paternal way.

"To sleep, perchance to dream," recites Abana with a smile.

"I have to go see Zine." Zen gives us one of his communicators. "So contact me there." He starts to motor away and then stops. "At the risk of overlooking all the danger and obstacles ahead, this is so exciting. Thank you for responding to my silent pleas for help!"

He motors off. I snuggle up to Abana to snatch some needed rest. I mumble to him. "I'm sorry. You didn't have to come along. Bet you'd rather be back on that beach under our moonlight or sitting under the glitter trees."

"Sure that was special but that's in the past. Now I'm meant to be here beside you." Those words excite me but then, perhaps remembering his blood pact with Alkima, he adds, "To look after you, and make sure the change happens!"

I don't want to show any disappointment. "My Ma-Tu used to sing a song to me, and its words went: 'There's nowhere you can be that isn't where you're meant to be. It's easy. All you need is love...' I think that's true."

"I'm happy, are you?"

"I'm happy here with you," I say, but in my heart, I hope that first kiss was only the beginning. My lips want to reach for his. To kiss him again, softly and longingly.

"Then here's to a long and beautiful friendship," he says.

And in those words, my heart sinks. I feel that resistance in him again, as if he is definitely holding onto something he hasn't yet given up. Again, I don't push him even though part of me so desperately wants to. So, I curl up next to his warm body and we fall asleep together.

Alkima smiles, watching over us. He takes out some more powders to mix. Mystikat jumps up on the table and joins Alkima in his work. "So, what've you found out, my friend?" He meows to Alkima. "Yes, I knew X-3 when we were both young. He took over as Commander-in-waiting when the designated X-1 disappeared from Mainlandia."

Mystikat meows more urgently.

"So, they have new guns and other even more deadly weapons that they're developing."

Mystikat now hisses.

"You're right, we've got to be on our guard. And to be very, very afraid." Alkima drinks a potion that emboldens him and makes his eyes sparkle. Then, as he mightily cracks a solid small ball in one hand that crumbles into more powder, he chillingly warns, "But even an all-powerful leader has his moments of doubt and pain!"

CHAPTER THIRTY

Even on Geto

"Dar!" says Zen.

One-9 appears at the door and makes hand signals to a relieved Zen who gives an affirmative nod, explaining, "It's okay, I've turned the sound dampeners on." He says to Abana, "They stop any hidden eavesdropping bug from recording."

Abana is impressed. "I so dig how you guys are starting to use technology against technology!"

"Excellent, so we can talk freely," Zine says, then motors in with a cut on his cheek and a huge grin on his face. "The inhibitor worked. As far as they know, I know nothing."

Frizz, who follows behind him with a relieved look, adds, "It wasn't as easy as he's making it out to be. They tried to play with his head, and frighten him, but he held out. He's my hero."

"But, Dar, what's with the cut?"

"That's nothing, you should see the other guy!" Zine gently rubs his face.

"Zine, my brother, good one. Another joke, wow!"

"Change is afoot. Okay, what's the plan?"

"Civil disobedience."

"Civil what?"

"There's going to be another artist performance this evening and plan details will be interweaved into it."

Frizz suggests, "If we want representatives from the various clusters to be there tonight, we should get on it. I've already been compiling a list of possible people to reach out to. It'll be simple to send them a group invite E-mail tonight. Should I?"

"Go right head, Frizz!"

"We should also file plans for an official scientific visit to the southern frontier, you know, the furthest possible from where the Rejex kids and their paternal units are being hidden," says Zen.

"Smart misdirection, very smart, Dar!"

"But what about the little girl, 777? We didn't see any sign of her where we were," asks Frizz who is already busy messaging her contact list.

"So, we're going to trade for her, but how?!" asks Zine.

"You'll see. But first things first, let's file that scientific trip with the authorities. Then, we've got to be ready to be on the move in an instant." Zen leans over to his brother, who doesn't quite know what to do. Zen awkwardly, but genuinely, hugs him.

"This really is happening?" Zine says.

As his buddy nods, "You so got that right!"

Barriers on Mainlandia are beginning to crumble just like different barriers on Geto are also tumbling down. The usual bounds of the golden rule, well, rule on Geto. People have always paid respect to each other. But the workers' rumble, the one that had ended up with one worker being accidentally killed was bringing down that wall of civility that had previously reigned. Amda, the offending party in this incident, isn't imprisoned. He's fully aware of what he's done, blowing his cool. He's brought to an outdoor meeting that's being chaired by Ma-Tu who, as a counselor acts as a judge, wearing a flowing white robe—representing an assumption of innocence.

The meeting is informal but there's obvious seriousness in the air. Out of respect, many of the young lads wear stylish jackets with button-down panels and epaulettes.

"Tell us what happened, Amda. And, has anything like that happened to you before?"

Bowing his head, this muscled and tattooed son of a soldier Rejex barely speaks above a whisper. "First, I want to apologize to the family of my friend. If my life is forfeit, I am happy to die. Second, it was an accident. I had no plans to act that way, to lose my temper." He looks up to Ma-Tu. "Yes, this has happened before. But just not with me. Even Abana has showed some anger. And, not just us children of soldier Rejexes, but some of our other Geto sisters and brothers, too."

"Amda, can you think of anything that started this chain of events?" He shakes his head.

As a relative newcomer, herself, my gal-pal Ayuna gravitates to other incoming Rejex. She encourages a young lad named Armen who finally and shyly raises his hand. He's also a newcomer on the island, having been recently exiled from Mainlandia. He'd belonged to the engineer cluster. Ma-Tu opens her palms up to him. "What are you thinking...it is Armen, right?"

Geeky, bespectacled Armen, who'd been bullied mercilessly on Mainlandia, speaks haltingly but wisely. "Yes, Ma-Tu. So, like, I love watching Bonko. But I noticed that after those red-sky morning solar flares, a few weeks ago, that the game got testier. I made some personal observations," he takes out his handwritten notes. "You're welcome to them. But I believe it's a fact that while the psychological effects of CMEs—coronal mass ejections or solar flares—are usually temporary, they can include emotional mood swings, headaches, anxiety, depression and a general feeling of being unwell. There's also incidences of chaotic thoughts and confused thinking, as well as other erratic behaviors."

He glances up, adjusts his specialized glasses and smiles goofily.

"Okay, Armen, we will suspend this hearing until we've looked over your research." Armen puts his hand up again shyly. "Yes, Armen?"

"One more thing, please." He digs into his satchel, removes all sorts of odd things that he piles up on the table in front of him. He keeps digging deeper. Finally, he nervously laughs to himself. He removes his own glasses and finally pulls out a pair of dark glasses and holds them up. "This is only a prototype of course, but as you can see, they're very stylish. The frames can come in all sorts of colors, and in different shapes—round, rectangular, oval, square, letterbox...." He puts the prototype glasses on. "But most importantly, they have a very practical function." He stares up to Occulo's sun. "Not only do they protect against our sun's UV rays, but they also create a subtle force-field that counteracts the effects of outside electromagnetic waves." He removes the glasses and says with a huge grin,

"I've also started developing special glasses that can be worn by Bonko players... without breaking."

"Wow, talk about showing initiative, Armen, that is wonderful. It's unfortunate they treated you like they did and exiled you from Mainlandia. But, we're so happy you're now with us." And, led by my pal Ayuna, the small group quietly applauds Armen who blushes.

The Commander watches through the observation glass as 777 plays with some puzzles. His fearsome, teenaged confederate is working on his handheld and projecting some images onto the wall-screen for his boss to read.

"Sir, our informal poll today of random Cluster members show a majority would be happy to have an X-1, again." X-33 points to the analyses and data that the Commander glances over. "If my data is correct, sir, we haven't had an X-1 since the last one left under suspicious circumstances 15 or so years ago. Did you know the citizen, Commander?"

"I did. But what's your play, my young friend?"

"Why don't we have an election, sir? I'm sure you'd be unopposed and when you win, we can make the majority happy to have an X-1 again, someone to lead us into our new future."

The Commander looks back to the observation room as 777's nurse enters the room with some food on a tray.

"Sir?"

His interest is intrigued further when the little girl puts her hand out for a drink, but continues playing with the puzzle with her other hand, as she slurps the liquid from a twizzle straw. In fact, she completes the puzzle without even looking, as if she has memorized the individual parts and where they were lying on the table. The Commander rises, approaches the glass and speaks pleasantly into the intercom. "Hello, 777, you are looking very cute today in your new outfit."

The little girl, who wears a funny liquid mustache on her upper lip, puts her drink down and smiles a big thank you towards the glass.

"Wouldn't you like to play an even more fun game?"

The little girl's eyes open wider.

"Nurse, could you please come out here and get something, thank you."

He turns to X-33. "Give her the Zephyrian Cube, level nine."

"Absolutely, sir. But I don't think anybody under the age of 18 has ever solved that."

"This one's unique. In fact, let her look it over then do it blindfolded."

"Right away Commander." But, X-33 pauses to point to several bagged items with "Caution" labeled on them. "Also, those are some newly confiscated items which may be of interest."

As he turns to leave, the commander says, "Thank you for these. And, good idea on an election, X-33. Make it happen, but make sure there are some other candidates, you know, just for show—the usual suspects. This is long overdue. Good work, Dar, I like your initiative. You shall be richly rewarded. Perhaps some personal music—something to hum along to?"

As X-33 grins under his hood and leaves, the Commander inspects the bagged items. "What secrets do you hide, my pretties?" There are medallions, talismans, trinkets, odd toys and puzzles...all unauthorized. He puts them down to watch 777 easily solve the Cube blindfolded, just like he thought. He glances back to the bags, and a couple of them catch his attention. One, he opens and smells. "Cat scat?! Hmmm, that is different." He puts the contents under a highly specialized scanner and it begins its tracking.

Then, he sees a bigger plastic bag and reads "from the mines." It contains a whip with what looks like dried blood on it. He uses his gloved hands to carefully remove the whip and examine it. He brings it under his hood to his nose and his head yanks back, affected by the scent. He brings it close again with the same adverse reaction. "My oh my, what do we have here?" He then turns back to the window, his eyes glowing, his adept mind twisting and on fire, as he watches the young adept, 777.

CHAPTER THIRTY-ONE

Dear Occulo

One-6 goes for a walkabout alone down some upper corridors. She's dressed down with no make-up or seamed stockings. Wanting to be incognito, she wears something close to what a worker drone would wear. She keeps her head down, lost in thought, thinking about conflicting images, the sweet unabashed Rejex girl smashing up against the sinister control of the Commander. She exhales, feeling guilt, maybe pain, for being a party to his view for Mainlandia's future. His flashy slogans—"We are One, Indivisible"—crawl along the neon, moving signage on the corridor's wall. She also sees what looks like graffiti saying "We (heart) the Commander," but with a rebellious line slashed through the heart.

She shakes her head, feeling she, like One-10, is about to play one dangerous game.

Walking along this way, she's mistaken for a regular Mainlandian heading home after a hard day's work. An artist student glances around, sees no security person looking and finger snaps at One-6 who doesn't pick up on it at first. When the student finger snaps again and two other young citizens finger snap back, One-6's senses are perked up but she keeps walking. She glances back over her shoulder as the young people give subtle hand signals to each other after the finger snapping.

One-6 feels excited, her body trembles, sensing she's in on something. Although she doesn't have a clue what it is. She keeps her head down, but memorizes the signals they were making and quietly duplicates them. She continues to walk the corridors for hours on end. By the end of her walkabout, she even finger snaps to some kids and they finger snap back with a smile, playing along. But, her gut is in knots. "Dear Occulo, what am I doing?"

Later in the evening, Frizz's electronic invites have gone out. The secret finger snapping gestures have gone out, spreading like quiet wildfire. Like an undercurrent, the message ripples out—"The Cave, at 9 bells, be there or be freaking square, soul bro!"

Everyone tries not to make too big a deal of it. They keep their heads down as they approach the performance venue. But, heading inside, the excitement is palpable. You can touch the electricity crackling from the ground to the air. It zips through the corridors, frenetically jumping and bouncing off the walls as it shoots along looking for its connection.

Inside, *Johnny B. Goode*, *Dark Was the Night* and *Melancholy Blues* and other Voyager disc tunes play as a sort of opening salvo.

Outside the Cave, young security drones, who are in on it, stand guard in inconspicuous ways. Pretending to be painting and repairing the walls. But, they're prepared to take action if anyone else finds out what's about to go on.

At the door to the Cave, the crackling, electrical impulses drape themselves over the audience like a gossamer cape, as the young people enter, hearts beating.

Inside, Abana has set up a couple of kids on percussive instruments on a riser to the right of the stage. Abana, who's such a natural storyteller, has also set up laser sticks to project swirling images on the walls and ceiling, including images: of solitary stones being dropped into seemingly still waters and causing ripples to float on out; of various shackled beings, including the mythological Prometheus, stretching up and straining at their chains; of shadows of beasts of burden throwing off their yokes and harnesses.

The stage is covered in blazing white sheets.

Everything is put together. Ready to go. A great, heavy hush of anticipation descends onto the room. Total quiet. Then, percussion creates the sound of jack stepping boots approaching. Closer and closer. Sounding real, and almost scary in its immediacy.

A small group of performers in military wear and in tight formation appear, and menacingly march across the stage. Back and forth to the percussive beat. Their faces are covered in hoods. But you can catch a swash of green neon across the bridge of the eyes. In their hands, they hold very authentic-looking muskets.

Slowly, two figures emerge from two large egg-like objects on the stage, breaking free out of their white, protective shells that have blended in so well to the white backdrop. Rising up from the stage floor, these two figures roll over in front of the marching figures that halt abruptly in their stride.

There are spontaneous gasps from the audience. These are immediately stifled in throats when the soldiers point the rifles at the two figures in front of them. But, the two figures uncoil upwards and pull out very realistic yet synthetic flowers that they show first to the audience. Through the magic of performance art, their white faces appear to cry falling, painted tears. There's a collective exhale of "oh my!"

Then, the two figures, wearing skintight white, approach the pointed weapons. The percussive beat rises in urgency and dread. The soldiers cock their weapons. The audience's eyes open wide.

"Noooooooooooo..."

Frizz and I, the two figures, place the flowers into the barrels of the weapons and the closed buds somehow open, magically. Then, we gently caress the cheeks of the soldiers, their faces still hidden by the hoods. Slowly, the soldiers back off, uncocking their weapons, laying them down then embracing us, the two white civil disobedient protesters.

The audience finger snaps, and some even whoop it up.

The soldiers and resistors start to fade from the stage, locking arms in peace.

More images explode onto the walls—images of protests from other cultures, and scenes of more peaceful disobedience. The theme of protest swirls in vibrating colors, images and scenes. Innocence against realism, peace butting up against violence and the inherent danger of tanks and other weapons.

Out of nowhere, great swashes of bloody red spray across the white stage. The audience reels back in shock. Then, there are more moving images of resistance and reaction.

Abana appears with a resonant voice. "Common sense pleading with reactionary fervor. Art with attitude calling to science and technology to be more forgiving."

Frizz now reappears on stage. "But, in the face of fearful odds, in all these images taken from protests from across the universe, the peaceful way won out."

I walk out to join them. As we speak together, other figures around us appear and mime what we speak. "Flower power will bend the angry snarl of weapons."

Like a congregation responding to an inspired gospel speaker, the enthusiastic audience choruses, "Aye!"

"In time, it will soften the iron fist of inflexibility," I say.

"Aye, that it will!"

"It will bring the fiery passion of art back to the coldness of science and technology without humanity."

"Right on!"

"We will hold peaceful strikes across all our cluster groups. Fight the power with non-violent resistance. Power to the people."

And, everyone chants, "Right on!"

Alkima, Zen, and Zine, off to the side, join in with us young people.

So does a disguised, but dressed down woman with a scarf over her head and hiding in the shadows at the back. "Right on!" she says spontaneously, then catches herself and moves further back into the shadows, not wanting to be noticed.

"Power to the people!" echoes around the room.

Us three on stage then put our fingers to our lips to hush everyone. The lights dim. Now extremely adept with the laser stick, and like an artist wielding his with a flourish, Abana points one to the back wall.

A hologram of a jagged halo of fire appears over the audience, sizzling and twirling.

On the stage, the percussionists hit their skins. *Tap-tap-terap! Tap-tap-terap!*

The sound of hooves, beating the ground, grows and grows but no one can see anything. They look on in wonder around them and above. Where is it, what is it?

Tap-tap-terap! Tap-tap-terap!

Then it comes from behind. An image of a big, dark red horse crashing through the air and through the dancing circle of fire. Leaping into the Cave, and over the heads of the seated audience. The horse lands on the stage with embers of flame coating its body. It rears up on its hind legs, its mane and tail glowing, its eyes aflame.

"Ahhhhhhh!" The audience is mesmerized by the hologram's sheer strength, beauty and grace, as it paws the stage and inspires us all.

Abana, Frizz, and I scream, "Power to the people, right on!"

CHAPTER THIRTY-TWO

The Fire Horse Alive

As the crowd cheers and finger snaps, Zen whirls his head around to the place where the tall, discreet woman had been standing. He'd spied her in the back in his peripheral vision. But, when he looks directly there, she's gone. Having slipped out with those who had work details to do. Zen feels a shiver of discomfort.

"What is it, Dar?" asks Zine.

"Thought I saw someone who shouldn't have been here, ordinarily."

"But, you got to admit these are not normal circumstances."

"True enough," he turns back to his associate and they surprisingly high-five. "Wasn't that performance something else?"

"Dramatic performance using holographic technology. Art and science working hand in hand. Who knew?!"

"Somewhere, long ago, someone once said that science is just magic made real."

"That is brilliant, I like it!"

On stage, I proudly ask for quiet, saying, "Hush!"

The audience hushes to my call. Abana and I hold up tiny memory sticks. "On these memory sticks, we'll soon have tonight's performance uploaded. Thanks to our scientist sponsors Zen and Zine, formerly known as One-10 and One-9, for the use of their recording devices and other tech gear. Take a stick with you on the way out. Be careful who you give them to, but make sure other like-minded Mainlandians get to see this."

Abana speaks. "Shake them up, inspire them, bring them onboard, make them look up!"

"For a series of rotating strikes to have an impact, many of us will have to get onboard. But, understand, in the history of non-violent resistance, there have always been sacrifices to be made," Frizz adds. "But, if we truly want to stop these bullies. If we want to throw off this yoke of super technology without humanity, if we want to bring back our banished cousins and have our peoples reunited, then we have no option but to act."

I say, "But, be patient and don't make a move until you get word."

There are murmurs of questions—when, how, where?

"Patience, friends. All questions will be answered. But first, we're going to make a small strategic move that won't please the authorities. Once we've dealt with that, then a few days from now, the strikes will start," says Abana who stands strong and powerful on stage, making me proud to be on the same team. "When you see this sign, it'll be time!"

He points the laser stick to the back wall, and a much smaller fire horse appears and rears up again. Frizz then moves her hands together and amazingly creates a fire horse shadow on the wall.

"The fire horse alive, it's our sign, watch for it!" I shout.

Awhile later, Zen, Zine, Alkima and our powerful new trio of teens, followed by Mystikat enter a secret suite close to the southern tip of the Underground City. We trio of performers are exhausted as we slump onto a big soft couch in the sound-dampened room.

"What is this place, Zen?"

"Yeah, I've never been here, Zen!" questions Zine.

"Just call me Mr. Surprise, my friends." Zen motors around in the dark and lights some candles, then he brings a big, thick blanket over to the kids on the couch. "Sleep, children, we'll take care of things for now."

We finger snap and giggle—"Yeah, big daddio!"—as we huddle under the blanket to nap.

Abana is positioned in between us two girls. He kisses Frizz on her cheek, then turns toward me and spoons me into his body, as if he is some powerful magnet. With his big arms around me, I feel he could just crush me. And, not just physically.

I mischievously whisper to him. "Be careful, Abana, you have my heart, so don't hurt me." I glance over to Frizz and just for a second, I get the feeling she feels the same about me. But, she turns away into a fetal position on the other side of Abana.

He then tickles me. "I've toughened you up, little lady, so I'm betting you can handle a lot more than a squeeze from me."

I can't help but giggle but a little question slashes deep in the back recesses of my mind, asking, "Humor, distraction, whatever. Why does he pull me in then still keep me at a distance?" But, I'm too tired to chase that question around. I close my eyes, safe in his protection.

Zen, Zine and Alkima huddle themselves under a big candle's glow in another part of the suite, away from us kids.

"So, what is this room, Zen, you didn't say?"

"I had some engineering cluster students build it for me. Told them I needed a room with sound dampeners for some loud experiments. But, my real goal was that one day I could hopefully listen to music and other performances privately without anyone knowing." Before Zine can say anything, Zen puts his fingers to his lips, then motors over to flat wall and touches it. The graphic LED lights of sound equalizers and volume controls jump to life on a module. He removes another memory stick from a secret compartment, then plugs it into the module. Zen chuckles, pleased with himself and his hidden treasures.

Alkima grins. "It's said, secrets are things we give to others to keep for us."

"Then I give you one of mine." Sounds crackle to life. "I got it from some of the radio signals our Collector station in the sky captured. It's called Ravel's *Bolero*…" says Zen as Zine finds some refreshment and brings them over.

The three men, the three brothers, listen to *Bolero* and sip their drinks. The music is ecstatic, moving, pulsing, powerful.

"Wow!" says Zine. And Alkima, who has Mystikat on his lap, pushes back, his eyes smiling.

"I come here on my own to listen to something, anything that will temporarily remove the dirt I feel on my skin whenever I hear that Commander of false chaos speak. This place is an oasis, a peaceful place of retreat where I can't hear what's going on outside and they can't hear me. But, quite by accident, I also discovered the walls effectively block the tracking of any outgoing communications. Who knew? So…"

"We can contact the Commander, offer our trade, set up an exchange. And feel safe that no jackboots will be coming here to knock down these walls and arrest us?" Zine mischievously suggests.

"You read my mind, Zine."

"Well, not really," he jokes.

"We should get started. But, I should make the call as they won't recognize me or my voice," says Alkima.

"Which should turn them into having a right old mind freak!" says Zine, rubbing his hands with some glee.

Zen pulls out a handheld communicator and hands it to Alkima. "I've coded in the number. It's disposable and non-traceable."

"Who knew you were such a smooth criminal, Zen?"

"I've read that much crime is due to a repressed desire for some sort of esthetic expression."

"And in our case, when our crime succeeds, it'll be called virtue!"

"Just hit talk, Alkima."

Alkima does and leaves the communicator on speakerphone mode. It doesn't take long.

"This is X-33, how may we be of service to you, citizen?"

"I have a trade the Commander will want to negotiate. In fact, he can hardly say no."

"What? Who is this? Where are you calling from?"

"Call me Harlequin. Get him on the line as quick as you can, if he wants to retrieve one of Occulo's most prized gifts."

At his own office, the Commander is already listening in on the conversation while calling up a file to see if any of Occulo's prized icons have gone missing or been damaged. He gestures to X-33 to keep talking.

"Just one moment, he's coming. You did say Harlequin, right? The faithful valet, the amorous one, a quality that often led him into difficult circumstances. But situations he was able to get out of through his wit, cleverness and joie de vivre, no?"

Zen and Zine look to each other, surprised that X-33 has this knowledge.

But Alkima is on a mission. "Blah, blah, tell him time is ticking, please!"

The Commander sees a big, negative cross come up on his screen. No cultural artifacts are reported missing. He hisses a response to the speakerphone. "You're playing with the wrong man, Harlequin! You do know who you're dealing with!"

Alkima holds up the golden disc we kids have taken. "I do. And I hope you're not ultimately remembered for being the Cluster-X'er who lost Occulo's second golden disc!" There's silence on the line. Zen and Zine smile at Alkima's gambit. He goes on. "I'll exchange the disc intact for the young girl, 777, unhurt."

X-3 calls up live feeds of the museum and zooms in on the Voyager Disc displays. At first glance, the optical illusion makes it appear as if nothing has been moved. But, then X-3 sees that only one disc is there and the other one really is missing. He snarls under his hood and slams his desk with his fist with great force.

Alkima pushes him. "I hope that wasn't your right hand, X-3. Because if you've damaged or hurt it, you wouldn't want to rely on your left hand. Unless, of course, you are really left-handed. Are you? I mean, you haven't been hiding that, have you, X-3?"

The embarrassed Commander's right hand throbs. And he reaches to turn the speaker feature off with his left hand, when he hears Alkima's taunt. He stops and lets his throbbing, right hand reach to turn the speaker feature off. But, he stops when his personal handheld buzzes, with a priority, pop-up message. He signals for X-33 to read it.

X-33 picks up the handheld and whispers the message to him. "One-6 says it's urgent that she come see you, Commander!"

"Tell her I'm in negotiations, but I'll be finished soon." He considers Harlequin's request.

"Tick, tick, tock, X-3," baits Alkima.

"Where and when do you want to make the exchange, Harlequin?"

"That's better. At dawn, get your assistant to take the girl to the southern frontier, near the 'Forbidden Zone' sign at the coordinates I'm sending you now. Leave her there with the big dark red horse from the mines. Tell him to stay back at the dome portal. Once the horse and girl have entered the forest, you'll find the location of the disc on a memory stick attached to the sign. One girl can't mean much to you when it comes to getting your disc back, so let's not have any change in the plan. And, if there is any deviation, your golden disc will be destroyed before you find it. So stick to the program!"

"Absolutely." He pauses then goes for it. "But, have we met, Harlequin? You sound familiar."

"We are not familiar or similar, X-3. Don't disappoint me or you will go down in infamy." Alkima disconnects. He fist-bumps his brothers, Zen and Zine.

The gambit is played.

CHAPTER THIRTY-THREE

Harlequin

In One-6's private suite, she's plugged in one of the Cave's memory sticks and is watching a replay of the evening's performance art, wrapped in a thick, comfy coat. She still shivers from the emotional impact of the performance. She's transfixed by the scene when the two eggs crack open and the two flower-power girls emerge to try and stop the military advance. She puts her hand to her mouth in fear when they point their muskets at the protesters. Then, she tears up when they place their flowers in the guns.

She pauses the action. What's going on?

She gets up and paces the room, obviously conflicted.

She impatiently checks her flashy timepiece. Tick, tick, tock...

"Crisse colis de tabarnak! Sacre bleu et viarge!" hisses the Commander, summoning up some old patois. X-33 is taken back by the mix of curse words. His master shakes his left fist at his comm device, shouting, "Va te faire foutre, trouduc!"

Then he instantly changes. His eyes still glowing, he calmly says, "It's nothing, I just hate losing."

"Who is this Harlequin, sir, and why do they want a little girl with webbed feet?"

"I can't quite place his voice, but I will...remember who he is. As for the girl, we have much bigger tasks at hand. Make sure the exchange is made. We cannot let this Harlequin have the disk for a moment longer."

"Do you think he knows what's on it, sir?"

"Just make sure the exchange is made, X-33, and make sure her tracking chip is working properly before we let her go." He relaxes back into his great, swivel chair. "This will be a one-off move by this Harlequin nutjob, and he will pay!"

"And One-6's request?"

"I'll meet her alone."

X-33 bows and, like his Commander, he glides out of the office.

Not long after, the Commander, who has changed into a silk hoodie and pants, sees One-6 standing under the security cameras. He lets her in. She's now dressed in her usual domina-trix-scientist wear. Curve-hugging lab coat, seamed stockings, hair pulled back, and stylish nerd glasses. All business.

The Commander has poured two ample glasses of very rare, green liquor. She recognizes the "green fairy" liquid.

"Isn't the green fairy illegal?"

He smoothly slides over with the drinks and gives her one. He signals with his hand towards a wall panel that reads his gesture. "So is this." And, a lush cello piece by Yo-Yo Ma playing Bach begins. "A couple of the perks of making a lifelong commitment to serving one's fellow citizens," he boasts.

"Do as I say, not as I do, Commander?"

"If you prefer. But I am so glad you came over to talk. I've been wanting to do this for awhile. You know, to open up, away from it all."

"Away from the 'be very, very afraid' and other such things?"

"You're being provocative, One-6! But, I like it. And I know you have something to tell me or ask of me. But first, relax, take a sip."

They clink glasses and she asks, "What are we celebrating?"

He motions for her to sit in a comfy couch that's shaped in an L. She sits at right angles to him, while she sips the green fairy liquor. It's intoxicating, like drinking something cool that's aflame.

"What are we celebrating? This little beauty," he says as he opens an ebony box on the crystalline table in front of them. He removes a shining, six-shooter revolver. He is more comfortable with the weapon this time. He's obviously been practicing—being an adept, it hasn't taken him long to get it—and he twirls the gun around as smoothly as X-44, the weapons master, had.

His actions make her nervous. When he points the gun, she flinches.

"Impressive, isn't it? Not only as a piece of functional wizardry. But, also esthetically." He traces his fingers along the barrel in an intimate fashion. "Look at its long lines, its detail. A beautiful, efficient tool you can fit in one hand."

"Want to hold it?" he offers and she squirms more. He sees her reaction and laughs. "I did mean the gun."

"I'm a scientist, Commander, not a soldier."

He reverently brings the gun close to his face. She thinks he's going to kiss the freakin' weapon. "This is the product of our science, One-6." He does kiss its cold metal, then puts the weapon back into its ebony box. He leans back into the very comfy couch. She can't see his eyes, but she can feel him looking her up and down and it is unnerving. After awhile, he gently says, "May I say, you're looking exquisitely lovely tonight, One-6. But, I digress. You wanted to tell me about something, what is it?"

She has come to fess up and talk about what she'd seen earlier that night in the Cave. But his actions are dissuading her from speaking up. "You know, it can wait. I'm sorry, I didn't realize how tired I was." She fakes a yawn.

"But, for us who are passionate about a cause, the night is still young, no?"

"I think I should go before I bore you by falling asleep."

"Why are we beating about the bush, Trix?"

She knows that her fellow scientists, One-10 and One-9, call her that under their breaths and it kind of amuses her. But, hearing the hooded one before her saying it is starting to creep her out.

He continues. "Let's talk about the elephant in the room." She squirms some more. "Come on, you know."

"No, I really don't." Maybe she does, but she doesn't want to let on that she does. Better to play dumb in the face of the ultimate intimidator.

"We're ignoring an obvious truth."

"And that is?"

"Well, throughout the galaxy, the ruling classes have always enjoyed what they thought the masses unfit or unworthy to partake of. We have listened to glorious music and sipped fine liquor here yet we are totally in control. As much as we love and need them, can you imagine the chaos if we allowed the masses to also share these treasures?" He lifts his head and she catches his flashing neon eyes. She feels like a doe in the incoming headlights as he edges closer to her. "I'm talking about pleasure for pleasure's sake. You and me together. Cool skin to skin. What do you say, Trix?" He moves his head close to hers. She can smell some intoxicating body spray he's put on. Its effect is sucking her into his vortex.

She purposely grips her glass so tightly that it breaks and cuts her, allowing her to somehow break free from his stare. She looks at her cut hand. "I have to go." She gets up.

"But, you called me."

"I'm sorry, I'm feeling sick and I wouldn't want to throw up on your beautiful, brushed, velvet couch."

One-6 almost runs out of his office. In the corridor, she finds herself gasping for air and leans against a wall, feeling weak at the knees. For someone who always has it together, things sure are getting edgy. She looks at her hands as they tremble. She breathes deep to steady herself and relax. When that helps, she reaches into her pocket and pulls out the performance art memory stick. She looks at it and drops it to the ground. She is about to stomp it to bits but stops. Instead, she picks it back up, puts it away and scurries off into her night...

For the Commander, however, his night is just beginning. He messages someone and then waits, happily listening to unauthorized music and drinking unauthorized liquor. A little while later, someone else buzzes his suite's door. He looks up to the security camera and it appears like One-6 has returned. Her face is masked in shadow, but the figure has a similar white lab coat and seamed stockings. X-33 stands behind her.

On his intercom, X-3 welcomes his visitor. "The door is open. That'll be all, X-33!"

The female enters with a veil covering her face. Holding a shoulder bag of goodies, she stands trembling, not saying a word as the Commander circles around her, checking out her look.

"I'll be calling you One-6, if you don't mind."

"Your wish is my command, sir," she barely whispers.

"Did you bring the toys I requested?"

"Yes, sir!"

"The whip?" She nods. His neon eyes light up. "Dance for me, One-6."

"Sir?"

"Weren't you trained?"

"I'm new, sir."

"Even better." Then, again to her. "Dance for me, One-6."

She puts the shoulder bag on the velvet couch. He turns up the music. And, she begins to dance in her high heels and seamed stockings and lab coat.

She's awkward, all long legs and gangly arms. Her performance is kind of pathetic and sad, like a marionette with him as the puppet master pulling the strings. His neon eyes squint, as he drinks liquor. "You are very alluring, One-6!" He then whispers, "In vino veritas. The truth will out." Slightly buzzed, he loves the control he wields as he conducts her to dance the night away, while thinking, Power to the ruling class, right on!

CHAPTER THIRTY-FOUR

I Am Rejex!

Our group finalizes our plans well into the night. The rotating strikes will start in a few short days.

"Zine and I will stay here. We'll be your ears on the ground, your contact source. But, take these handhelds—they run on long-lasting cells," says Zen as he hands me, Abana and Alkima three devices.

"This is so exciting. I'm going to come back here after we make sure the exchange is made," says Frizz.

"I want to go there early, scout the area, see what's what, so we should get going!" a totally focused Abana says.

The two scientists accept hugs from our foursome as we disappear into a private elevator to the Basin uptop.

"Here goes nothing," says Zine.

"And, everything," adds Zen, not knowing their new friends had said that exact same thing.

At dawn, on the southern frontier, the portal of a large, domed entity opens and X-33 appears with a leash on Big Red. The little girl stands beside them. X-33 seems unaccompanied as he gives the leash to the girl and points toward the "Forbidden" sign near the forest's edge about a hundred yards away.

Heaven, dressed in bright yellow, takes the leash—"Come on, horsey!"—and leads the horse away from the dome.

Halfway there, Heaven and Big Red hear a distinctive whistle. It's from me. It stops Big Red who responds by pawing the dry earth. I whistle something else, and he somehow understands. He kneels on one knee and lets Heaven get onto his back. When she's secure, another whistle makes him rise and pick up his pace. As they near the forest, Frizz still wearing her white outfit, appears with a welcome on her face. Heaven happily recognizes Frizz from when she'd been with Zen.

Behind Frizz, shirtless Abana and I stand ready. Abana wears war paint on his face. He's on total alert.

As Heaven and Big Red reach Frizz, suddenly some dirt mounds strangely start to move. Abana senses what's going on way before anyone else. He slaps Big Red on the hind to get him to gallop into the safety of the forest with Heaven. Then, he yanks out his slingshot and projectiles. "It's a trap!"

Sure enough, three special ops soldiers emerge from the mounds of dirt where they've stayed hidden for hours. Two of them carry muskets and start firing at the escaping horse and girl. "Shoot the horse!"

Abana automatically and protectively pushes me to the ground. But Frizz, who's still in front of us, bravely stands in between Heaven and the horse and the soldiers. The musket fire catches her full in the chest. Red spatters all over her white outfit. Abana throws Purple Haze at the soldiers, then ducks and rolls on the ground as they lose sight of him. He fatally hits one of them under his helmet, right smack in his exposed throat with a slingshot projectile. He strikes another with an improvised, wooden spear he's grabbed up from the ground. Both soldiers gurgle in their death throes.

Alkima appears and helps me up.

The third soldier fumbles around trying to get his bearings. Abana's pissed. "Aiya and Alkima, get Frizz out of here. I'll be right behind you!"

Alkima and I pick up Frizz and carry her body away. Alkima can see the damage from the old-style, soft metal bullet that has hungrily buried itself into Frizz's body—bones are shattered, internal organs and tissue have been shredded. It's just awful.

Abana approaches the still blinded soldier. In the distance, he sees X-33 and some other soldiers running towards him. But, he doesn't panic as his body quivers with anger and vengeance. He then drives his fist hard and upwards into his nose to disable him. Then, as the soldier's head flies back, Abana uses a martial arts hand thrust to his throat, breaking his windpipe. Abana stands over the three vanquished enemy soldiers with their high-tech helmets and reflective shades. He yanks out his spear and turns to head towards the forest with X-33 and his other men fast approaching.

But, as our pursuers enter the forest, Abana's carefully rigged, explosive devices using powders made by Alkima, start blowing up—*boom, boom, boom*—halting their charge. Abana shouts, "I knew you'd lie and cheat." He'd suspected their duplicity and had also come prepared.

X-33 scurries away, fearing all the crap he's in. "Merde, shit, shit!"

Way into the forest, and safe for now, Alkima's trying to clean Frizz's wounds, but he grimly shakes his head. The rifle musket's shot has torn through some major arteries and he can't stem their flow. He's, at heart, a scientist who's also skilled at applying salves and creating special foods and drinks. But he's not a skilled surgeon. It shows in his eyes, how helpless he feels.

Poor Frizz's white outfit is now covered in great gouts of blood.

Alkima gives her an anesthetic liquid to drink. "It'll help with the pain, little one."

Mystikat snarls. This skirmish is over, but the battle is still to come. Closely attended by her rebel friends, Frizz coughs up thick, gooey red. "Is Heaven safe?" I gravely nod. But Frizz sputters, "It looks worse than it feels, really. Just let me sleep a bit, but make sure you wake me when the party gets started!"

I bend over and gently kiss Frizz on her lips. Frizz forces a happy smile. Then, she slips away into that forbidden sleep.

Abana holds his spear in both hands and savagely snaps it across his thigh. Next, he lights its splintered end and, like a flaming torch, holds it high. With Frizz's spilled blood on his body, and in honor of her, he shouts, "We will rock and roll!"

Alkima solemnly says, "Frizz, the first martyr of the Change."

Empowered by Frizz's sacrifice, I also smear her blood on my face and unleash an unholy, banshee cry—back across the stripped Mainlandian Basin to the towering and shimmering domed portal. Mad as hell, I roar, "I am Rejex!"

PART THREE

And Everything Under the Sun

CHAPTER THIRTY-FIVE

To the Place

Mystikat leads our little band deeper into the jungle and further into safety. Now freed, Big Red proudly carries Frizz's covered body on his back, as if he knows he's carrying a martyr who's spilled precious blood for his freedom. The little angel, Heaven, holds back tears as she grips my hand tightly.

Near a small pond, when Mystikat halts, Abana signals for everyone to pause as he walks a little ahead and checks out the surrounding area. I can't help it, but my heart thumps as I watch him smell the air, listen to the jungle and to the hidden creatures above and below. He takes in everything around him, like a totally alert warrior, my personal knight. He seems to sense we are safe for now but he feels my gaze on him. He glances back and smiles at me. "Okay, this is far enough. We can make camp here, little sis."

I think to myself, "little sis?"—that's what he calls me! Then I quickly realize I'm being selfish, and nod back to him.

And, as we begin to settle in, Heaven claims, "And we can build like a funeral pyre for our friend Frizz!" We all agree as I hug the precious little thing.

Alkima collects fresh water and prepares drinks. Abana scrounges for food. Heaven and I collect branches and twigs for the fires we will build. Big Red stands watch over Frizz's body, keeping eyes and nose trained on the way we had come.

Upon his return, we build a pyre on a raised platform of branches, while Alkima prepares the food and Heaven feeds and waters Big Red, her new equine bud. When we're all done, we begin wrapping Frizz's body in my shimmering shawl.

"Can I keep a lock of Frizz's hair?" asks Heaven, and I let her by snipping some off. The little girl gently puts the curls away in a tiny hiding place. We, her new friends, now place Frizz's body on the pyre along with fruit and other small food stuff for her journey.

Alkima looks up while proclaiming, "Go your way to the land of our Ancestors, sweet friend, where they wait for you with open arms, there on the edge between this world and the next. Look, there they stand! Ancestral spirits, welcome this one to the place where we all must go…"

We all hold torches Abana has made and dip them in fire to light the pyre together. It crackles and explodes into flames as Big Red stomps the ground and Abana plays on a handmade flute. There isn't much sadness. We are at peace with memories of our newly-passed friend who's graced our lives, even for a short time. And, as is the way of Geto residents, we eat and drink while the flames burn.

Mystikat, however, is distracted. He moseys over to the edge of the pond, on its far side.

"I haven't had real food like this, like ever," says a wide-eyed Heaven as she licks her lips.

"No more synthetic crap food for you, like ever," I assure.

"Isn't Mystikat hungry?" she asks.

"He's a real mystery, that one, always doing his own little thing," I reply.

Mystikat sits there motionless, his fur bristling in the breeze. After awhile, he stands up, arches his back and hisses at something in the jungle. We hear him and are immediately up on our feet. Abana yanks out two slingshots but I already have mine ready.

"Go stand near Big Red for protection, Heaven!" I tell her.

We load our slingshots. Alkima shouts a Thalandian greeting he digs hard to remember. "Kia ora!" Hesitatingly then again, "Kia ora rā kōrua!"

Tree branches rustle. The sound of heavy footfall approaches in the grass. Our breathing goes silent.

"Kia ora?"

Mystikat snarles. Big Red snorts.

The undergrowth parts and an older but sturdy man with striking green eyes appears. He's accompanied by a couple of tall, muscled and armed Thalandians. I thought of Abana's

story of Min fighting the giant Gang Jun, and I prepare myself
for battle.

But, the older man smiles and raises his hand, palm
forward in peace. "Namaste, I am Two-19! At least, I was a long
time ago."

"You're an engineer Rejex, right?" guesses Alkima.

"That I was. Now, I'm just a man with no name."

"Could you tell your friends to put down their arms and
we'll do the same, Two-19!" shouts Abana.

The man makes a slight signal with his head and the two
Thals lower their spears. He then approaches Mystikat whose
fur still bristles. He kneels down in front of the feline. He
slowly puts out his hand. Our brave feline tentatively sniffs it.
The man pulls something out with his other hand and presents
it to Mystikat.

"It's a sort of Thalandian catnip—guaranteed to work, trust
me," he explains as Mystikat does take a fancy to the treat.
The man now rubs the purring feline's fur. "He makes a great
watchdog, your feline!" grins the man with no name.

Sizing him up quickly, I say, "We'll call you Nonamé."

"I like it. Nonamé, it is. We didn't want to interrupt your
celebration. The people here practice a similar one when their
loved ones pass on."

"We're finished, it's done. Our brave friend is now safe with
our Ancestors," offers Alkima.

"We've watched you since before dawn when young Abana
set up his explosives. Can we approach?"

Alkima looks to us and when we hear Mystikat meow, we all
nod in agreement. Alkima beckons for Nonamé to approach.
His two guards follow but stay behind him several paces.
Proud, long-haired warriors, they stand on guard, keeping an
eye on the jungle.

Abana feels an immediate kinship with them, steps close,
and raises a closed fist to them. "Salve, brothers!" They recip-
rocate his gesture of fraternity

Nonamé warmly greets everyone's hand with his two hands.
"I've heard all your names." He gently rubs Heaven's cheek,
then strokes Big Red's forehead. "We used to have equines
but the Mainlandians took them from us. And, the ones they

didn't want, they slaughtered, so that we wouldn't have them. Such a proud, beautiful creature. It would be great if his kind could run free here in Thalandia again."

"We know where more of them are! Uptop!" I now say, warming to him.

Alkima offers him refreshment, which he takes and sits down in an ancient lotus position. "I'm the last of my kind, the last of the Thalandian Rejexes. All my fellow Rejexes who were sent here have died. It's been a little lonely at times. But, I'm so very happy to find myself surrounded by four of my kind. Welcome, cousins."

"You have an adopted clan, here, Nonamé?" asks Alkima.

"When we were exiled here, some of the Thals took us in. We were just children and young people. They were kind to us. But, some of their leaders were understandably scared and didn't want to have anything to do with us. So we, and the ones who took us in, relocated to the southern frontier. Our new friends gave us basic shelter and they hunted for our food. And, we taught them our technological skills and language."

"Your two friends speak our language?"

"A little, but I sent two of my people, one of whom understands our language well, into the Underground City to find out what was going on. They planned to play it dumb and hopefully not get mistreated. Unfortunately, we haven't heard from them." He sees Alkima glance at Abana. "Why, do you know something or heard anything?"

"We were told that one of two captured Thalandians might've died. The other one, a tall, long-haired man, is being kept for further interrogation," I exhale.

"Why did you send them into harm's way? Did you sense something or got some sort of thought impression?" asks Alkima.

"Yes, I did, it was very weird, but I couldn't get it out my head, that someone needed help. I can't explain it. These words just bumping around in my head—boing, boing," he smiles.

"We have a lot to share, Nonamé. But quickly, as we're about to start something downunder!"

Nonamé jumps up and summons us. "Okay, since we don't have much time, come see what I've built with my friends."

"You have a village?" I ask, totally excited.

"Sort of, but not really. And, we don't actually live on the ground. Come, come see!"

I glance back and sense Alkima thinking ahead—that it's all well and fine to start a revolution, but we will need a 'home' afterwards...

Abana, little Heaven and I look to each other and whisper, "What, tree houses?!" Giddily, we almost run over each other... haha!

CHAPTER THIRTY-SIX

Be Afraid, Be Very Afraid

Trix still shakes from the after-effects of all the conflicting experiences she's been through. In the morning, she calls in sick. She's never done that before. In fact, she's so tense she wants to puke her guts out.

At home in her private suite, instead of sleeping it off, she can't help herself. She has to touch the fresh, psychological wounds that have recently scarred her. For all of her young life, all she really wanted to be was a top scientist. Now, she was wondering, "Why am I fighting this? Simplicity and order has made me happy and given me freedom. No, hold on, be honest—all it's really done is to numb me into accepting a sort of somnolence. Asleep at the wheel."

But, she also fears and knows that a little self-awareness can be a really risky thing. And, this newfound self-awareness is already causing mini cataclysmic changes in her being. In effect, she senses she's being turned on. Onto what, she doesn't quite now. And, she doesn't know if she likes it, as it scares the hell out of her. But she doesn't know if she can stop it. She holds out her hand and it trembles.

Next, in her personal investigation, she turns on simultaneous feeds of the Flower-Power art performance and of the Thalandian savage wall painting in his cell. She adds in a feed of the Commander's last speech. She then puts the three feeds onto multiples screens on her wall. She wants to be almost bathed by the feeds.

Wrapped up in a warm blanket, she sips steaming hot liquid and lets herself be immersed in the conflicting images. As the images flash on her retinas, her ears fill with the sound of the young rebels shouting "Power to the People. Right on," of the tall Thalandian shouting in despair, and of the Commander chanting his mantra, "Be afraid. Be very afraid."

She grabs her shaved head and rubs her hands along her throbbing skull. Confused tears begin trickling from her eyes, adding more beauty to her seeming perfection. "Occulo, please, please help me!"

X-3 has had his way with the sex worker drone all night.

He growls as his insatiable appetite has been temporarily sated.

As she hurriedly gathers up her clothes and starts to leave, dressing as she makes her exit, there are no apparent marks on her body. But, as he rises from his very Spartan bed to put on a robe, his back is covered in the red stripes of a whipping. His body is strong and supple but the welts cause him to gently wince as he puts his robe on.

"Excellent work, cherie. A la prochaine, next time, eh!"

She doesn't turn around as she bolts out of his place with a look on her face perhaps showing that she wants to tear her hair out. Except, she has no hair, as she's shaved it off to look like One-6. She melts into the morning corridor of marching-to-work life that is Mainlandia's reason for being. A beehive of activity, of everyone knowing their job and just doing it. Like clockwork. With their "happy" heads bowed.

Inside his suite, X-3 takes a shower with specially filtered water that contains antiseptic and healing chemicals. He squirms as the antiseptics work their way into his wounds. All the while he keeps his face in the shadows. Soon, he feels healed, so he stretches his strong body until he finishes by kneeling with his arms spread out and chanting a brief mantra.

Standing up, he starts to dry off and is about to check his e-messages when he quickly swipes through images of himself in various cloaks and hoods. For some reason, an image of a young X-3 jumps out, of him as a kid, as a chubby, young kid. Shocked, he can't delete it quick enough, desperately trying to forget his own childhood bullying for being fat.

Luckily, he gets a new message from X-33. He calls his subordinate as he looks through a closet full of hoods. He sensuously runs his fingers over the materials and finally selects one and puts it on in a ritualistic manner like a religious man putting on his habit. His back and arms are covered in old scars, some probably came from some self-flagellation ritual.

On the speaker: "Sir, I took the initiative and sent some special-op guys to ambush the traitors. But they figured out our move and our mission failed. I'm sorry, the girl and the disc are gone. We're dealing with some clever warriors, sir, even though they look no older than teenagers." The Commander doesn't answer as his adept mind quickly considers his options. Trying to be proactive, X-33 adds, "We could go after them, shift some troops up there, sir. Sir?"

"I've always appreciated you taking the initiative, X-33. Fortune always favors the brave. Blah, blah, and all that. It's not good that we don't have the second disc and you know how much I hate losing anything. But, on a positive note, to access the embedded images, they'd need the code. No teenage rebel would have that knowledge."

"Who are these misfits, sir?"

"Hopefully, just a fly in the way of the irresistible force that our way of life will continue to be. Okay, X-33, see where we are with our new weapons production schedule. The Commander, out."

As he finishes dressing, he disconnects the link, sits in a swivel chair, dims the lights lower in his suite, then spins around to face the cryogenic tank that appears like a giant test tube, standing in the recesses of his private space.

He talks aloud. "My friend, we screwed the pooch uptop. We have some scattered oddballs resisting the Darkness. But, we are 'In the Right.' I know we are." Distracted, he now reaches over and removes the horsewhip with the dried blood on it from its bag. He inspects it closely. Sniffs it. "I smell animal... and blood, but something very different." He puts it under a DNA scanner and orders, "Scan now and report...let's see who or what you are, shall we?"

Turning back to the test tube tank. "Where was I, my friend? Exactly. We are, 'In the Right.' But, I have a sense some mini-rebellion is being attempted. That's fine. Happened before. But we stopped them. Although, we didn't eliminate them that time. This time, we will." The monstrosity in the tank floats up and down as the artery-like tubes connected to him keep pumping liquids into him. "But, I'm wondering, what is to happen to my people? Where are we going? Is it time to leave our Underground City and expand outward uptop? Should we crush the Thalandians and take advantage of a ready-made, slave labor force? We could then spread out and own the planet again. And then the sky could be the limit. And we could leave Occulo, maybe?"

In the tank, the body's closed eyes seem to flutter. And, his powerful torso briefly convulses...

CHAPTER THIRTY-SEVEN

Home

Nonamé and his men lead our excited group along a beaten-down path deep into the jungle to a knot of thick undergrowth that totally obscures the way ahead. Above us towers a wall of giant trees. There seems no way through or around this impenetrable, natural wall. And, anyone approaching it would normally turn around and head back the way they came.

Feeling alive again, Nonamé turns on his toes and smiles at Alkima, then looks to Abana, pointing at the wall and challenging him. "You up for it, Abana?"

"You're on!" Abana senses it and takes on the challenge, as we watch. Abana steps back to get a bigger picture of the wall. He then enthusiastically shimmies up a tree with ease and ventures out dangerously on a well-selected branch to look at the wall from a different perspective. He tests the wall with a few slingshot projectiles. None get through the wall.

For some reason, he peers back down, to Nonamé's still-challenging grin. He surveys the ground where we friends stand on the beaten path. He scans to both sides of the path. About 100 yards from the path, but not visible from down below, he sees a rushing waterfall.

After he slides back down the tree with a knowing smile, Alkima asks Abana, "You have it? No way?"

"Way!" Abana laughs then joyfully hollers, heading toward the hidden waterfall with us friends in tow. Arriving at the waterfall, which is blanketed on both banks by the thick undergrowth, he stares into the torrent of falling water. When he reloads his slingshot, Nonamé applauds in anticipation. Abana fires several projectiles through the waterfall and they

don't bounce back off any wall behind the torrent of water. He
yells a victory cry. Then spies a hidden, narrow ledge that looks
like it winds just behind the great crash of water.

"Your entrance must be behind the waterfall, right?"

"I'm impressed, Abana. Let's go inside."

I am so proud of him. I want to eat him up, the sheer magical
brave energy of him.

Nonamé signals the way as his men let our group head in
first. One of the Thals laughs and punches the shoulder of
Abana, shouting, "Abana, victor!"

After our group including Big Red, who has to be calmed down
by Heaven, passes through the tunnel behind the waterfall, we
arrive in a wide-open clearing. Nonamé holds out his hands face
up and gazes up to the treetops where tree houses have been
built. "Home!" he gestures. And, the scene is just amazing.

Wow! To me, it looks like there are several central tree houses
and each has half-a-dozen smaller houses surrounding it.

"Each 6-unit cluster has a central, common area, so everyone has access to it from their little home. They can use the
rope bridges or they can swing over by rope."

"How cool!"

"The basic design is mine. Something I'm very proud of."

"Can we see?" I can't contain myself. And when Nonamé
nods, Abana scoops up Heaven, puts her on his back, and he
and I scoot up the rope ladders that hang down to the ground.

Nonamé turns to Alkima. "Welcome, brother!"

Later, our group sits up in a common area for a big feast.
There are a couple of hundred people in the commune and
they've gathered to break bread with their four new friends
who share a common heritage with their teacher, who they
now all call Nonamé. Or, at least try to call him that, as it's
a bit of a tongue-twister for them.

Wide-eyed Heaven asks, "Aiya, can I wear my hair like Frizz?"

"Sure thing, little one. Here, I'll brush it out for you!" And,
I do so with great pleasure. And, very soon, Heaven begins
looking like a mini-Frizz.

Meanwhile, Alkima explains how he received telepathic
messages from his scientist brothers in Thalandia. How
our group had left the not-island of Geto and entered the

Underground City and how we now have a plan to ferment
rebellion and affect change through nonviolent disobedience.
He also tells them about the other Mainlandian Rejexes we've
stashed away from the authorities, near the northern frontier.
   "There are more of us?" Nonamé is enthralled. "Count us in
on your plan, and let us help in any way we can. We have a few
friends on our own northern frontier who we could get to meet up
with your hidden young Rejexes and bring them here safely." He
sees Heaven, and I glance down to Big Red who's happily eating
real grass down below, and he senses what we're thinking. "Also,
if you say that there are corrals where there are more horses like
your fine creature, then we can catch two birds with one net. Free
the horses while saving our little brothers and sisters."
   Heaven claps her hands! The Thal children, who've been
watching the little Rejex with fascination, see her do that and
they follow suit, clapping, although kind of awkwardly. It is
a funny sight. There is true joy and community in the air.
   Abana notices Nonamé's computer system and the older
man shrugs and smiles. "Yeah, it's solar powered and, even
though it's a little ancient, it works. From time to time, I've
been able to secretly scavenge some computer chips from
a Mainlandian trash dump." Nonamé affectionately dusts off
the old dinosaur.
   Abana dips into his shoulder bag, pulls out some new computer chips and holds them out to Nonamé. "Our friend Zen
gave me these, just in case we might need them. I'm betting
you could put them to good use."
   Nonamé's eyes open wide. "Could I ever!"
   "So, where's the dump?"
   "Yeah, maybe we could work a side visit to it on our mission,"
I suggest, thinking ahead.
   Nonamé is ecstatic. Then, he gets serious. "Hopefully, we
can also find out for sure what happened to the brothers I sent
in." Our group all agrees, it's a plan, and a good one.

Over the next two days, while Abana and Nonamé's best warriors map out the details of our mission, I start working with
others on creating a uniform for our new army, starting with
jacket-like shirts with epaulettes. They're a big hit. Unisex kilts

are next. And soon we head out. We move with purpose and stealth. First, we're able to sneak out the Rejex children and their families hidden near the northern frontier without any fuss.

Then I lead Big Red to the equine corral where he calls out to his herd. The horses react immediately to his call and they cause enough of a distraction for our group to creep up on the corral's guards and knock them out.

Big Red proudly leads his herd out of their corrals. As they've already been broken, they're willing partners in letting the Rejex children ride on their backs as we begin the trek back to Nonamé's camp.

On the way, Nonamé's warriors show Abana one of Mainlandia's trash dumps, which, being close to a domed portal on the northeastern frontier, is guarded closely. And, the drone soldiers carry new revolvers in holsters on their hips.

I glance to Abana who reads me. "Hold on, she always has a plan!"

We rebels wait till dusk but we still need a distraction.

I whisper into Big Red's ear and point. He seems to understand and stomps his hoof. I carefully put a leash around his neck, making sure it doesn't spook him into bad memories. "Easy, Big Red, easy." Luckily, my touch soothes him and he doesn't rear up as I let the leash trail on the ground.

"Go, my Fire Horse, go!" I urge him.

My magnificent creature races past the domed portal with the leash trailing—tap-tap, terap. The drone soldiers shout, "Catch him! Bring him down!" as they try to grab the leash of the freed creature. But he's too strong and fast. While the distraction continues, Abana and I and a couple of warriors wade into the electronic trash dump, grabbing up everything we can.

"Okay, let's bounce!" I say with my arms full.

Our triumphant group disappears into the jungle and waits. Uncaught and still free, Big Red comes galloping in, shortly after, leaving his pursuers floundering on the dusty ground behind him. Then, we make our way with all our "booty" back to Nonamé's hideaway without further incident. Now, they shout, "Aiya, victor!"

I see the fire of pride in Abana's eyes. But, I realize there's so much more to do. Especially, downunder. Tick, tick, tock.

CHAPTER THIRTY-EIGHT

Praise the Darkness

In the morning, back at the tree village, we've touched base with our co-conspirators in the Underground City. Our plan is getting better by the hour, even though the "Darkness" is fast coming.

Up in the trees, little Heaven wears a pair of my goggles and has her hair all frizzed out. She's also wearing a cool hat embedded with all sorts of bibs and bobs that someone from the village has made for her. The cross mingling of ideas and styles is alive and growing. And, Heaven is impressing with her ability to solve puzzles and complex mathematical equations.

"Okay, Heaven, try this one, you little smarty pants," challenges Nonamé who hands her some geometry to solve. "It's called pons asinorum—the bridge of asses."

Alkima sits nearby as he checks out the stolen Voyager disc. He listens as Heaven giggles. "Asses!"

"It's the name of Euclid's fifth proposition in Book 1 of his *Elements of Geometry*. It's kind of a bridge to the more difficult propositions that follow."

Alkima gently strokes Heaven's head. "It represents a real test of someone's ability and understanding." He can feel young, fiery energy just bursting from her skull.

Heaven takes the paper and proposition, looks at it quickly, then starts writing some things down on the diagram while she reaches for some fuzzy fruit in a basket with her other hand. She's never tasted such succulent treats, squishing the soft fruit in her lips and making them squirt their purple juices. "Yum!" She wipes her mouth with the back of her hand and grins at Alkima. Then, without looking at the proposition, she soon adds, "Done like dinner!"

"What?" Nonamé looks on amazed as he picks up the paper.

"Story goes, she was raised as a drone worker but she's so much more than that," explains Alkima as he uses a small, flat crystal to magnify and inspect the grooves on the innermost, concentric circle of the disc. "Hold on, it looks like something is kind of hidden here. Like some more grooves."

"I can run a laser scan over it. It's not so up-to-date but it should do the trick," says Nonamé, so Alkima hands the disc to him while the alchemist gently wipes Heaven's purple-juiced, smiling face. The older man places the disc under a laser scan, which acts like a needle on an old vinyl record.

The two men watch the images popping up on the computer screen.

"Wow!" they say together.

"What is it?" she asks, squeezing between them to view the screen. She focuses her eyes. Tilts her cute head to the side then to the other side. "Look, there are a bunch of numbers and cool symbols."

"Heaven's right," enthuses Nonamé who writes down the sequence of symbols. The two men look them over. "It looks like a combination of elements from both Roman and Greek symbology."

"I'm bored," says Heaven as she heads over to watch two tweens swinging from tree to tree via ropes. She giggles with them. "Can I try, oh please?" she asks open-eyed.

"It looks like it's, you know, encrypted," offers Nonamé.

"I wonder if Mainlandia's authorities even know about this."

"Wow, a secret message within a message from the Blue Planet."

Removing her hat, Heaven is helped onto the rope and shown how to put her foot into a safety loop, she glances back at the two men, shouting, "Like I think I saw some prime numbers in the sequence, I think. And don't those encrypted thingees, I mean, aren't they made from prime numbers? So, maybe I can work on it later, if you want me to. But, you'll have to feed me some more of those yummy, fruit thingees, Mr. Wizard." Referring to Alkima, she grips her hands on the rope and shouts, "Okay, catch you, later!" As she gets ready to be swung, her young unbridled exuberance echoes out. "Yahoo!!!"

"Out of the mouths of babes," notes Alkima.

With that, she adjusts her spiffy, new goggles and giggles as she gets a push from one of her new friends. Then, she goes swinging happily across to the adjoining tree platform.

In the Underground City, the guards and enforcement drones are carrying new revolvers in fancy open holsters. It's scary, at times, especially when a guard shows off and pulls out his loaded weapon and tries to spin it around, gunslinger style. There are reports of guns accidentally going off. No one has been shot yet—at least, that's what they report—but, it's only a matter of time. So, the citizens walk down the corridors quicker than usual, their heads still bowed, but glancing around to avoid being accidentally shot.

What a nightmare, bullies with loaded guns!

"I want posters plastered above the crawl screens, all along this corridor, both sides, people!" orders X-33 who unfurls a poster of the Commander who's posing in a stylish pastel hood and cloak against a dark background. His eyes still glow, however. At the bottom, the slogan "A Vote for Freedom & Safety" is splashed in a sort of bloody red. Perhaps a not-too-subtle but ironic reminder and warning.

The next morning, dozens of posters with the Commander's shrouded face, looking out with numbing, overwhelming repetition, are indeed plastered down that same corridor. It's like the torturous *drip, drip, drip* of a leaky tap.

The citizens on their way to work glance up, but continue on. They are very afraid.

Zen and Zine are back in the Central zone. They motor by the posters. Zen reaches out, tempted to rip one down until a threatening voice stops him. "What're you doing, One-10?"

Zen pushes his hand onto the poster and casually flattens out a little wrinkle. "Uh, just fixing it. But the likeness to him. The inherent power in his eyes, wow. Superb work, X-33! I mean, it is your work, right?"

"Why, yes, I designed it. You really do like it?"

Zen nods. "For someone so young, it is impressive."

Zine gets an e-message on his handheld and motors aside to view it.

Zen rolls on with his false praise. "How could we not vote for him? It's so seductive, so powerful. And, yet so simple."

"Yes, the freedom of continuity."

"Of more of the same, uninterrupted. Well done, X-33!"

"I'll take that as a compliment, One-10."

Glancing over to his compatriot who's replying to the message, Zen adds, "You're probably up for a big promotion, right X-33?!"

X-33 is gliding on but halts. "You think so? Well, I never thought about that. Personal ambition is so second class, so hostile to our happily uniform world, don't you think?"

Totally faking it, Zen gives him two thumbs up and chants, "In the Right!" And X-33, seduced by false praise, glides away down the corridor out of sight. Zen takes a deep breath, relieved. He then tears down the poster, anyway. Now, a rebel with a major cause.

Zine quietly gives Zen a couple of hand gestures. He flashes the fingers on both hands to indicate 30—level 30, the mining level. He puts two hands together to show the shadow of a Fire Horse on the wall—the time's been already pre-set for 9 bells. Then he finger-snaps—the game is afoot.

As they pass other citizens, they flash the same "fire horse" shadow and quietly finger snap. If they finger-snap back, the scientists give the other hand gestures. And, so, the message ripples out across the surface of the unstoppable undercurrent that is the Change.

The tall Thalandian has been moved to level 30, close to the mining portals. He's probably targeted to be disappeared, thinks Trix. Seductively drawn, like a moth to a flame, she stands again in the shadows watching the savage who's been stripped naked. And, there he sits like statue, *The Thinker*, one of the many images of art that had been inscribed into Voyager's second disc.

Her heart *thump-pumps*. Blood swooshes through her temples. Her forehead is damp with a sheen of sweat. Her mouth dries from the bad air. Her stomach aches but for other reasons.

He sniffs the air. Yes, he can smell her. He can taste her skin in the air between them. His animal instincts are alive and on edge, even down in the suffocating air of the mines. Without looking up, he growls, "I say there is no darkness but ignorance."

Trix sags backwards to the damp wall, trembling and disbelieving what she hears.

"No darkness but ignorance," he repeats.

The automatic sound of 9 bells clangs and reverberates through the tunnels. But, she surprisingly doesn't hear the expected pummel of pile drivers and drills. After the bells, there are still no working sounds. Something is different. Something has changed. Then, there are shouts and orders and whips slashing the air. But, still no drills.

Trix checks her handheld. The miners have gone on strike. They're all just sitting down on the ground. She sees a live feed on her handheld. No cracking whips or barks can make them move. Her mind races. She acts without thinking too much, using her keycard to open the door of the savage's cell.

"Come with me, now!" she holds out her hand.

When his cagey hand touches hers, she feels electrified and her breath catches in her throat. But, there's no time for the strange yet intoxicating cravings she feels for the savage. Now, they have to run, faster.

CHAPTER THIRTY-NINE

In the Right

"Hello?! Of course, I'm going down there, now!" barks the Commander when he sees the live feed of the miners' sit-down strike. He attaches a holster belt around his waist. Checks his new revolver, spins the chamber and slips the gun into the holster, like an expert. He puts on a dark velvet cloak and covers his head with a matching hood. "Cut the live feed, now!"

X-33 and a small team of bodyguards wait in the outer area and walk in boot-stomping sync, escorting the Commander to a private elevator. On the elevator, the Commander doesn't say a word, so the bodyguards chant, "In the Right. In the Right!"

"Yes, we are!" he growls.

Arriving at the mining level, the sounds of nothing, no drills pummeling the ground, smash into the Commander's ears. Ironically, he hisses, "I do not like the sound of that, those sounds of silence. And, there will be a price to be paid for this... this disobedience!"

A live camera crew is clamoring to get close to the strike zone but is being held back.

The Commander glides past them to the rows of miners who sit on the ground, heads bowed on the edge of a big hole. Some have blood on their heads from weapon blows.

"What do they want?"

"They haven't said a word, sir!"

The Commander leans in and opens the jacket of a striker. On his chest is scrawled a rudimentary "fire horse" symbol. The Commander wonders, 'What, in Darkness, is that?'

As adept at sensing people as he is, he looks over the uniform sea of strikers. His laser-like eyes scan them and when he senses one whose body is over-heating, he points. The striker

is yanked up and brought to the Commander. The striker keeps
his head bowed. But he also wears a fire horse emblem.

The Commander circles the striker. "So, what is this,
some sort of ridiculous resistance against the slings and
arrows of outrageous fortune? Someone has misled you,
my friend. You're being hoodwinked. You want to live uptop
like a savage, scrounging for scraps, watching your loved
ones freeze and starve in winter, and suffer and die from
disease?" He casually beckons the camera crew to come
closer, but not too close, as he rolls on. "Really, is that what
you want? You already have the comfort of having your own
home unit, food and drink on your table, a variety of holographic entertainments, I bet you love the new *Get Outta
Here* game. Come on, think about this. The grass is not always
greener," he adds ironically, considering there is no grass on
Mainlandia's Basin.

He signals for the camera crew to keep filming.

"The Change is coming, it's inevitable!" the striker
says firmly.

"I'm sorry, what's inevitable?" The Commander's surprised
at the assuredness in the striker's voice.

"The Change."

He begins steaming up, his eyes glow redder under his
hood. "The Change, what's that, some pie-in-the-sky pipe
dream? Someone's been selling you a bill of goods, my friend."
He produces a flask of liquor and opens it. The richly strong
and strange odor reaches the striker's nose. "A sip of fine grog,
my friend?" He seductively waves the grog under the striker's
nose. "In fact, let's forget all of this, shall we. We'll provide
a ration of grog after work for everyone here for a week. Bet
you haven't had an offer like that recently. What are the trou-
blemakers offering you? If they say freedom, well that's an
illusion. We all must serve somebody, all of us."

He takes a sip of the powerful liquor. Smiles in a friendly
way then whispers, "Truth be told, my friend, as someone
much smarter than me once wrote: Life's but a walking
shadow, a poor player/That struts and frets his hour upon the
stage/And then is heard no more: it is a tale/Told by an idiot,
full of sound and fury/Signifying nothing."

His words make the miner pause and lower his head. And, they seem to affect the Commander who appears to shiver, or is he just acting. "Woooo, gives me de freesôns, the shivers, no?" The miner agrees. The Commander then helps the miner to his feet and puts his arm on the miner's shoulder. He softens his tone and pushes the flask close again. "Come on, let's have a drink on the Central Council and let's forget all this silliness and get back to work, okay?"

The miner smells the strong liquor and is tempted to sip. But he blurts out. "The Change is coming!"

The Commander's body shakes under his cloak. He collects himself and gently dusts the miner off a little. "Nothing is inevitable, my dear friend...except, of course, death!" With that, the Commander nonchalantly elbows the striker over the edge into the black hole. "Now, he really is free," he smiles while dusting off his own hands from the soot. He gazes at the camera, "Did you get the beauty of that, citizens? He wanted inevitability. And, by Darkness, he got it."

He starts moving away from the strikers, dusting off more soot from his cloak and boots. He taunts back to his men. "Every 15 minutes, throw another one in." He glances to his right-hand man, "And, X-33, call an emergency meeting of the Central Council." But X-33 is distracted, checking his hand-held. "Did you hear me, X-33?"

He looks up. "Sir?"

"Problem?" X-33 can't get his words out. "What is it, Dar?"

X-33 gives a slash across his throat to tell the camera crew to stop filming. They immediately do, as the Commander and his man move aside.

"The miners on our southern frontier have also gone on strike. Do you want us to execute one of them every 15 minutes, too?"

The Commander throws both his hands up, wanting to strangle somebody. He takes a very deep, slow breath. "No, let's not create a whole army of martyrs. And, nix the Central Council meeting. Instead, call a session of Cluster X and enforcement leaders from all five regions. We don't need any of those namby-pamby representatives from the other cluster groups in on this. This is a time for elegantly created solutions and firm, brutal, action."

He pulls out his revolver and kisses the silvery barrel. And, he shoots a random striker dead.

The cry goes up, "We are, In the Right!"

Trix doesn't know where to go or who to talk to. She has taken the Thal to her suite, and lets him shower away the soot and grime.

He reappears all scrubbed up and glorious in his nakedness. "Thank you!" he says. But he doesn't bow down or shy away. He looks up and takes it all in.

She wants to say "thank you" back to him as she can't take her eyes off his glorious physique.

"This?" he points to a robe and when she nods, he puts it on. "I, Torix."

She wonders if Torix is a short form for the mythical warrior Vercingetorix. The name seems to fit him. "I am One-6 but you can call me Trix, Torix." She smiles when she realizes their names rhymed, as she pours some hot steaming liquid.

"Beautiful."

"I'm sorry?"

He points to her. "Beautiful." She almost drops the cup of steaming liquid but manages to steady herself and hand it over to him. He sips it. "Ahhhhhh!" His smiling eyes almost break her scientist's methodically cool heart.

They stand there, kind of awkwardly, drinking the liquid until he finishes his and puts the cup down. He gently reaches out his massive hands to her shaved head. "Please?" She gives in and he places his hands on her head. For such a huge man, he has a gentle, symphonic touch about him. And, once again, when their skins touch, she feels a surge of overwhelming sensations. She is an adult virgin, which is the norm on Mainlandia, but his touch seems to reignite the dormant sex drive in her, as she groans involuntarily.

Hearing her groan makes him back off a little. But, she places her hands on his hands and directs him to continue his discovery. His hands gently brush her face, her eyes, lips and throat. She drops her own robe and folds herself into his body, trembling and whispering, "Trix is for you!"

CHAPTER FORTY

The Change

Like a secret brotherhood of monks, the Cluster X regional heads conspire around a round table in a private hall. Their regional enforcement heads are seated just behind them. In their ceremonial robes, the X'ers are served dark liquors and special snacks from the Commander's private stash.

Their questions fly out fast and furious, but the Commander calmly throws his *I Ching* coins on the table in front of him.

"So, is this strike inspired by the Thalandian incursions?"

"But we thought the Thals had only rudimentary language skills, so how could they organize anything like this?"

"Are they really the virus that is infecting us?"

"Or are they just straw men, which of course would be brilliant?"

"What is this thing, this fire horse?"

"And, what does it have to do with The Change, what does it mean?"

"What do they want?"

"Excellent move to throw that miner striker into the hole. Decisive. Sets a standard. We should all do that in our regions."

"And, then, to shoot a random striker, in cold blood. Brilliant."

"But, do we then run the risk of creating martyrs?"

"That wouldn't be good."

"Not good at all."

"Commander?"

"Yes, Commander?"

He doesn't immediately respond as he nonchalantly checks a handwritten sheet of paper titled, Reading the *I Ching*. Under his breath, he whispers, "Time has come today."

"You don't seem too concerned?"

"You seem a little distracted?"

"You called the meeting, sir!"

"And, why are you now running unopposed for X-1?" interjects a high-ranking X'er, X-8, in a rust-colored robe.

That snaps X-3 to attention. He pockets the coins and the sheet of paper. Now, he picks up a nearby revolver, which he easily spins. He still doesn't say anything as he then removes all but one of the bullets in the revolver. He spins the chamber. Then, very calmly puts the barrel to his temple and presses the trigger. It doesn't go off. So, he then calmly slides the revolver across the shiny black table to X-8, his high-ranking questioner.

"You want to oppose me, X-8, we play roulette, winner takes all. In fact, anyone who wants to oppose me, just pick up the weapon and take your best shot. Or not?"

That shuts the room up.

X-8 gently slides the revolver back to the Commander, who puts it away under his robes. No one sees that he has palmed the one bullet, not actually putting it in the chamber. Inside, he cackles to himself. Fooled them. Then, he pivots direction.

"Alrighty then…what to do, what to do?" he wonders aloud, as he peers deep into the syrupy liquor swilling in the glass in his hand. "I suspect this is just some little ripple. But, a ripple can grow into something much bigger. And, every problem is just an opportunity to …change. So, we go proactive. We'll use enhanced interrogation techniques and find out who's trying to disrupt our happy way of life. We root it out and destroy it. And we give the strikers something. Make them feel they gained something. But, we'll give it to them in one hand, and sneak it out of their other hand, and they won't even know the difference. Uptop, we continue our incursions into Thalandia—we need the natural resources—and we meet their opposition with extreme prejudice." He gulps from his glass and drains it. "Death to the cannibals, right?"

They grumble back in the affirmative. "Death to the cannibals!"

He continues, "Some supposed wise person said that 'Life is about suffering, pain and misery.' I disagree. We are on the cusp of a new era, a new Change for Mainlandia, and Occulo.

And, it will lead us into our bold, new future." He throws his empty glass at the wall, smashing it.

X-33 speaks up. "We are, In the Right!"

They all take their glasses, drain them and also throw them at the wall. And, then they all chant, "In the Right!" Even X-8, who senses the Commander's deadly intent, throws his glass even harder at the wall. The Commander glides over to X-8 and rests his gloved hand on his shoulder. Then, he inconspicuously squeezes a neck muscle a little too tightly, causing a jolt of pain in the lesser one's body. Everyone averts their eyes, and no one says anything to the bully of all bullies.

Zen and Zine are the pivot point for the Change, as they're the channel between the strikers and our group. They watch a replay of an unofficial feed from the Central mining level and applaud the strikers until they see the Commander push the striker into the black hole.

"That's just so not right!"

"The ultimate bully."

Wearing a lab coat, Bonzo screeches and sticks his tongue out at the screen.

"It's the price we have to pay for freedom, Bonzo. But, they're going to glom onto us, Zine. You know that, right?"

"You think they'll torture the strikers?"

"Of course they will and they won't be using some innocent lie detector test. You saw what he did to the two Thals."

"And, ultimately, they'll find someone who knows someone who knows we're the connection."

"So, the best-case-scenario would be for us to bait and switch. Lead them a mad merry chase to us. But turn control over to someone else we can trust."

"First, that probably means curtains for us, Dar. Second, who can we trust?"

Bonzo lets out an expression that sounds like "Aiyaaa!"

"Good idea, let's ask Aiya and Alkima."

Screeching cries creep out then spread and ricochet through the Underground City's corridors, as the enhanced interrogation kicks off.

The Commander ensures that the victims' anguished screams are being played over the common speaker systems, so all the Underground City's denizens know exactly what's going on. The horrible howls echo around the stainless steel walls and make one's blood chill.

"Ohhhh, scary, scary!" he murmurs mischievously as he hears the cries. He sits in his private suite that adjoins the hall the Cluster X'ers met in. The hall's being set up as operations HQ with all sorts of gear being brought in. And, while it's being set up, the Commander swivels around and around in his chair, watching screens full of interrogation scenes. He also has scenes of his marching army in training uptop, thumping their jackboots onto the Basin's dry surface.

The combination is exquisite for him and he conducts the sounds with an invisible baton in his left hand. "This is war, X-33, and this war will provide the final solution!" He then pounds his right hand on the table for emphasis.

X-33, who stands nearby with a headset on, sees his Commander's left-handed baton conducting and, for a second, he glances at his boss and wonders. "Is he ambidextrous? Left-handed? He likes and listens to private music, so what else?"

"Don't go there, my young friend," the Commander intuits. "And, make sure we get what we want!"

And X-33, who's in communication with the hooded interrogators on the screens, likewise commands into his headset. "Do whatever it takes, we are, In the Right!"

Meanwhile, the victims valiantly blurt out through pain and blood, "The Change is coming" and "Kiss the sky!"

Temporarily insulated from the horrors outside, and still embraced in each other's arms, Trix and Torix awkwardly smile. Tension has drained from her body. She even giggles, for the first time in maybe forever.

"What now?" she asks.

"You with us, Trix?"

"Be part of a revolution? Absolutely, I am so in!"

"A comm device, please!"

She reaches for her handheld and gives it to him. As little as he seems to speak, like a child, he intuitively knows about digital devices. He plays with it a little, till he gets the knack, then sends a signal out, a sort of SOS. And, then they wait.

Not long after, a visual flashes on her handheld. Nonamé's face appears.

"Brother, you are alive! Are you safe?"

"With new friend One-6."

"Call me Trix!" she exclaims as she gets into frame and smiles for Nonamé and his new pal, Alkima.

"A scientist, even better. Because you can help us to kiss the sky, Trix!" The two Rejexes grin back.

CHAPTER FORTY-ONE

Kiss the Sky

While the Commander waits for the blood results, still listening and getting off on the cries and screams of his victims, he throws his *I Ching* coins again.

"Sir, how does that work, again, do you think of a question or something?"

The Commander chuckles as he "reads" the coins: "Yes, be very, very afraid!"

X-33 immediately chants back a soldier cadence. "I don't know but I've been told, being afraid is the way to go!" The Commander's bright teeth show as he seems to smile.

A computer beep tells him that the results on the scan of the blood on the horsewhip have been done. The results pulse with color.

"What does it report, sir?"

"The blood reveals DNA sequencing beyond anything we have ever seen, even from our eugenics experiments in the past."

"Whose DNA, sir?"

"Another Rejex, but with more complicated sequencing than the young Rejex called 777."

X-33 peers closely at the sequencing. "That's off the charts, sir!"

"If somehow it's a child of two Rejexes—and although we secretly hoped, we never thought it possible—and if this young person is developing more specialized skills, then think what a tool she could be to us." He rubs his gloved hands in glee, his mind plotting all sorts of tricks. And then the computer beeps again. Eyes wide open, the Commander hisses, "What in Darkness is this?"

"It looks like the DNA has some similar sequencing to someone in our cluster, sir!"

The Commander quickly switches off the screen. "Keep this strictly between us."

Back at Nonamé's camp, our guerilla army is training the horses. It's in the genes of the Thalandians and even in ours to be good riders, so we all take easily to the new horses, showing off the natural riding skills that Alkima says many ancient equine cultures have.

Everyone is joyfully and seriously at work. While some make weapons like bows, arrows, and spears, others continue to finish off our new uniforms, adding in cadet hats, each topped off with a dazzling peacock-like bird's feather.

While Abana shows our new friends how to use a slingshot, I practice firing a deadly crossbow that can be held in one hand while riding, which I'm also a natural at—being an Adept's daughter. I jump off Big Red, who rears up in fiery joy. I'm decked out in one of our new warrior kilts dappled in camouflage colors. I look up to the sky and treetops where I track down Heaven who's working on a computer alongside Nonamé. With her goggles cutely askew, the little girl waves and I blow our mini-Frizz a kiss.

Nonamé is productively putting to use all the trashed computer chips and other salvaged gear. He waves down to me, as well.

I stroke Big Red's massive neck and give him sweet water to drink. I then stride over to Alkima who's preparing various new powders with Mystikat watching, almost silently directing. "Can I whip up something, Alkima?"

"Grind up that black powder nice and fine, little lady!"

I kneel down and grab up a tool. "Explosive powder?"

He nods. "And the red powder is poison, so don't be sampling it! Because you know how you can't keep your hands off new things!"

I laugh. He knows me well. I notice a mound of already prepared 'purple haze' just as Abana comes over with a Thal, with serious intent on their faces that are painted in action black. Abana also considers the purple mound.

"My Pa-Tu, my father, studied many of the ancient teachings and lessons on warfare. Misdirection, the very essence of purple haze, is a key to defeating a force with superior numbers or weapons," demonstrates my co-rebel to his new Thal friend and sergeant.

He then bows to the Thal warrior, while others watch and learn. They square up for hand-to-hand combat. "For example, feints are maneuvers designed to distract or mislead an opponent. They're done by giving the impression that a certain attack is going to happen, when a completely other move, or even none, will happen."

He fakes to attack his opponent with one closed fist but doesn't engage him. But, as he retreats, with the opponent watching that fist, Abana feint attacks him with a kick to the head. He pulls his kick, coming within a sliver of doing some serious damage. The Thal is impressed and grins. "Abana, snakey!"

"Sneaky!" he corrects with his own grin.

"And snakey!" he laughs.

The two young men laugh but keep in their defensive stance and parry hand thrusts and attacks. Others square up, following their lead. I glance over, proud of Abana's leadership role. Seeing the power and smoothness of his moves makes my own tummy tremble. He's like function and poetry blended into blinding motion. And, through his teachings, I feel I'm becoming one with him. I wink at him, trying to distract him.

Abana catches my distracting gesture, but stays focused. "There's a martial arts term called 'seme.' Seme involves applying psychological pressure and disrupting an opponent's confidence prior to attack. Kizeme is an advanced form of seme that involves further distracting an opponent." Abana appears to turn his ankle, "Arrghhhh!" The opponent lets his guard down for a second and Abana keeps low and takes him down. Then, he gallantly helps up his opponent.

I laugh out loud. "So, you remembered what I taught you, Abana!"

He playfully moves over to me and sneakily picks me up off the ground over his back, as I now scream out loud.

Alkima grins, pleased with his students. In many ways, he's the father of all of this. He keeps check on incoming messages on the handheld Zen has given him, then says out loud, "Abana is right, misdirection will be the key to our success. It's been part of all of our moves so far. And, it'll be the most important part of us moving forward."

The lead Thal gets the meaning of what Alkima says and lets loose a blood-curdling cry as he gazes up to the skies. Several of his fellow warriors do likewise and, together, we all howl, "Kiss the sky!" or something close enough to it.

In disguise as drone workers, Trix and her Thal make their way to the southern frontier from where Zine and Zen are running the strike program. They both keep their heads bowed as they approach Zen's private suite. She's getting directions and following them exactly. She knocks at the door and glances up to the security cam. The door swooshes open and they enter into their future.

"Good day, One-6!"

"You can call me, Trix, One-10. I know you've always wanted to!"

He grins as he motors over to greet them. "And you can call us Zen and Zine. And, this is Bonzo." With glasses on but slightly askew, and his arms folded, the chimp cackles.

"So, this is that clever fellow nailing those memory tests?"

Bonzo gets up and moves toward her. He reaches his hand out, and off Zen's nod, she lets him gently touch her bald head. He likes her and grins to Zen and Zine.

"He trusts you. Just don't ever try to take his food, okay!"

Zine brings some refreshment over and motions for them to sit.

"You weren't followed, right?"

"We followed your directions, which really were misdirections, right?"

"That's what this is all about, Trix. But, at some point, the Commander's thugs will track back to us as the source of the strike action. For backup, we'll need to shift the focal point to someone else."

"Who do you have in mind, Zen?" Before she gets the words out, she gets his meaning. "Hold on, you can't be serious. Us, really?"

"Commander, we've found the artists' Cave. It appears the genesis of the strike action was started here," says an X'er on a vid-screen in the Commander's suite. "But, there's no one here, sir!"

"I want you turn that room inside out! Find something, anything! Look in the nearby trash. Get in there, and find me something." He turns to X-33. "And keep the 'torture' going on. We will find them!"

Just then, a set of warning lights go off on another screen that's focused on the northern fringe of the Underground City. X-33 picks up the direct line to their people there. After conversing quietly, he turns to the Commander, who asks, hopefully, "Success, did we find ourselves a nest of hornets?"

"No, but we have more strikers, sir!...This time, it's the engineers up in the north on strike."

The Commander slides out his revolver from his holster and starts firing randomly around the suite, shooting up some screens. X-33 hits the deck. When he finishes shooting off all six bullets, he holds up the smoking, warm gun as his eyes seem to smoke as well. But on the screen, back at the Cave, an X'er finds a tiny memory stick in some unburned trash. "Gotcha!"

CHAPTER FORTY-TWO

Night Descends

"Why were you rejected, Nonamé?" asks young Heaven in her ingenuous way. While she's snacking, she's inputting the numbers and symbols from the golden disc onto a rebooted computer, as she tries to solve the code to breaking the encryption.

"You don't beat around the bush, do you, Heaven?"

I appear up in the tree house. "My Ma-Tu says I was just like that. But, why were you considered a Rejex?"

"I was the first Mainlandian to be marginalized for coming out as gay. They tried to change me, gave me and my partner electroshock therapy." I see tears come to his eyes. "He couldn't stand the stress and died. They gave up on me and sent me here, all alone."

It's quiet for awhile. Then, Heaven wiggles the toes on each webbed foot and the veil of temporary sadness lifts from Nonamé as he hugs the little girl.

"But, you had the courage and will to survive, Nonamé!" I stress.

"Here's to all the misfits, magicians and oddballs like me and you, Nonamé!" Heaven blurts out.

"With a smarty pants like Heaven beside me, I can handle anything!" he says, still hugging her.

Abana and Alkima appear in a rush. "We have to speed up the plan, starting tonight!"

"Why?"

"They found one of our memory sticks."

An X'er rushes towards X-33 and hands him the found memory stick. He jams it into a module and film of the performance art plays.

"Who're these people?" the Commander asks when he sees the trio onstage.

"The frizzy haired one, 451, was killed uptop during the failed negotiation. The young male and female…"

"They're Geto exiles, I bet, children of the banished Rejexes."

"So they're breeding, sir?"

The Commander's distracted when he catches a glimpse of One-10 watching the performance. "Where's One-10? Find him and his traitorous associate now!"

X-33 orders his men to get going. "Go, go, go!"

"And gather all our soldiers in training uptop, recall them all to be down here, where we need them!" X-33 gave a questioning glance to his boss who hisses, "No questions. Just do it, now!"

When he's left alone again, the Commander swivels to face the cryo tank again. He glides over and runs his hand over some control switches connected to the tank's life support system. He flips on a switch and a burst of energy shoots through a cable to the creature's brain. His eyelids flutter again. The Commander gives another jolt. This time, its eyes open—stark, scary, milky white. And, it lets out a silent scream, as the Commander cries out. "Cry havoc, and let slip the dogs of war!"

"Alkima says they found a memory stick," reports Zen who's gotten a message from the Thal base camp. "I'm surprised it took them this long."

"One of us should go back and play the part, Zen!"

"You mean, make the sacrifice, Zine!"

"Well, that is a risk. But, all in a bigger cause if it comes to that. Hopefully, our plan will win out."

"No, I'll go back," Zen says firmly.

"No, Dar, if Trix is now our new focal point, then you'll be needed as a last ditch obstacle between them and her."

"You're right, I can be the last resort of misdirection."

"Besides, you're stronger than me if it comes down to you know what." Zine starts packing his things. "You should all move to a location that I don't know about."

"We will."

Awhile later, Zine's ready to go. The two scientists look at each other. Zen jokes, "Don't be a stranger."

"See you, two, on the other side!"

"Not if I see you first, Dar!" With Bonzo involved, they actually try to do an awkward group hug. It's hilarious and sweet. But, they quickly release.

"Then bring on the Change, right, boys?" Bonzo does a happy jig.

Night descends and our guerilla army, kitted out in our military unisex kilts and epaulettes, is loaded up. But, Nonamé raises a hand for them to pause, as he hands three coins to Heaven. "Aiya and Abana, what's the burning question on your minds?"

Alkima jumps in with an excited look, "Go ahead, my friends, Nonamé's going to use the *I Ching*, an ancient way to confirm our path."

I smile at Abana, who gestures that I ask away. "Is our timing right?"

Nonamé points Heaven to throw the coins, which she does. He and she lean over the coins and he whispers to her. Heaven says, "It doesn't matter how slowly you go as long as you do not stop!"

We yell and wave to our friends. Then, we ride out on several horses, led by myself, Abana and Nonamé's guards. From afar, we watch as the Mainlandian vehicles and troops are taken back down from the surface near the expanding mining fields.

"Nonamé says sandstorms can kick up at night and they tend to jam up their motors. So, they use the hydraulic lifts in the domes to take their vehicles down to safety after every shift."

"Lucky us!" I say mischievously.

When the last vehicle disappears, the remaining guards notice flames near a mining pit. One shouts, "Damn, another fire! Can't those engineers get anything right?"

They rush over to extinguish the flames. Abana and I, and our small team, all wearing camouflage black on our faces, approach the dome like felines on the prowl. We scoop up simple dust and go about our secret business, continuing to pin our hopes on playing the gambit of misdirection.

CHAPTER FORTY-THREE

I Rejex, I Reject You

Just before dawn, the Underground City goes into total lockdown.

The sounds of sirens whir and echo through the various workplaces.

Only the recalled soldiers and their jackboots patrol the empty steel corridors, chanting, "In the Right!"

But, X-33 has tracked down Zine, unfortunately.

He wheels the stone-faced scientist into the Commander's private suite.

"Welcome, again, One-9."

"No lie detector test, this time, Commander?"

"You got that right. Now, you get to graduate to the big boys' league." He opens a toolkit bag and pulls out a pair of pliers. "Had any toothaches recently?"

"Torture is really a very regressive strategy, Commander."

"Well, regressive is in today. Where's your associate?" When Zine doesn't answer, the interrogator speaks to X-33. "Activate the subdermal tracking system for One-10." When his subordinate takes a pause, he adds, "Yes, under normal circumstances, I know we're supposed to get an executive all-council order to activate the implant tracking systems for our higher ranked citizens."

"But, I understand, these are not normal circumstances. Right away, sir!"

"What subdermal implants are you talking about, Commander?"

"Oh, right, you don't know about that, do you? Well, as I often say, it's been on a need-to-know basis." He approaches Zine, who's being held down by two X'ers, with a pair of wicked pliers in hand. "So you can give up the information and save yourself a hell of a lot of pain or you can suffer and suffer some more, and then just die. But, we'll still track down your associate and stop this delusional Change thing you've been talking up."

He jams the pliers into Zine's mouth. But stops. "Hey, you're not Harlequin, are you?" Zine shakes his head. So, the brute yanks out a tooth. Tears stream down the poor scientist's face. "When will revolutionaries ever learn that nothing ever really changes. The more things change, the more they stay the same. Here on Occulo and everywhere throughout the galaxy! Meet the new boss, same as the old boss. Blah, blah...You are such fools!"

Zine bravely spits out some blood, saying, "Just a flesh wound." But, his face is streaming tears and red.

Uptop, our team works through the night.

I tap a guard on the back of his shoulder. As he whirls around surprised, I smile innocently—as if. "Sir, can I borrow your gun?"

"Excuse me?" he says as he turns around looking stunned by my appearance—in my kilt and blackened face. For sure, he's never seen anyone like me, like ever.

I knee him in the groin, hard. "You are so excused!"

We take him out along with the rest of his fellow guards, who're no longer protected by the soldiers who've all been recalled downunder. We take them out in different ways, but they're all taken out, then quietly and efficiently removed from the scene.

Our team scoops up the new weapons, increasing our bounty. And, we plant our own explosive devices, making a high-low five gesture as we complete each task.

Back at the treetop commune, Heaven can't sleep, worrying about her new pals who she saw take off into the night. Wearing a mini-kilt to feel part of our effort, she lights a candle, not to wake any others. She sees Mystikat, who's watching her, and puts her fingers to her lips to shush. He brushes up against her leg and purrs, as she begins working on the encrypted message again. She writes down the symbols and numbers, mixes them up. Suddenly, she giggles, her eyes open up even wider, because the little genius can see right through it.

Hardly containing her joy, she creeps to where Nonamé sleeps soundly. She tiptoes to his hammock that's several feet high. But, she doesn't want to shout and scare him. Mystikat reads her mind, figures it out, and easily jumps onto the high hammock. He gently begins purring in the old man's ear. It works. Nonamé is roused with a sleepy smile and sees Mystikat at his ear and Heaven down below his hammock. She looks up with a heavenly smile and reveals, "I cracked that code thingee, and I think I found something really cool."

When dawn breaks, and the hydraulic lifts attempt to work, the Mainlandian operators find that sand and dirt are clogging up their use. So, no vehicles and no soldiers can be brought up. They're jammed, solid.

When the cameras turn on and relay visuals down to the Underground City, X-33 has to wake up the Commander who has slept in his private office area.

"Sir, I'm sorry, but you asked me to wake you if there was any news."

"You found One-10 and his band of silly rebels?"

"Well, we found the rebels alright, sir."

"But what?"

X-33 motions to the visuals being relayed. The Commander adjusts his hood and gets up, then plops back into his swivel chair. "What am I looking at?"

"Sir, that's the eastern frontier where we've been pushing back the jungle to expand our pit mining."

"Why is it so quiet? Where are the vehicles and the guards who are supposed to be watching over such an essential resource?"

"Everything's been jammed up, sir, none of the supply lifts are working." The Commander stares more closely, as his subordinate continues. "And there was only a token security force left overnight, sir, as we'd brought all the training soldiers back down to quell the strikers here...As you'd ordered, sir."

The Commander's face drops, then his gaze starts to burn.

The early morning sun beats down on the expanding, but empty, pit mining area. All is deathly quiet. Until two "guerillas" on horses ride into view, now backed by an army of about 100 other guerillas in kilts—some on horses, the others on foot. Fully armed, there we stand as one major obstacle. Then, I on Big Red and Abana on a white horse nicknamed 'Hotspur,' gallop into view, side by side. Both horses have painted handprints on their flanks. With goggles around our necks, we two have blue war paint on our faces, like the rest of our army. With that and our cobbled together, but spiffy military outfits, we paint a formidable image. Throwing off my jacket, I reveal a sleeveless vest that exposes my developing arms that are marked up with henna tattoos of thorn bushes. I make Big Red rear up on his hind legs, all power and passion and free. I've woven my Ma-Tu's saffron sash into his flowing mane. While Big Red is my "fire horse" in the flesh, Abana's my mythical knight-prince Min. Ironically, now that I've left paradise, I finally feel one with my steed and with my fiery dream.

Shocked, the Commander murmurs at the screens down below. "This doesn't look good!"

Remembering Frizz's sacrifice, I scream at the cameras, holding my equine's reins in one hand and brandishing a rifle in my other. "Authorities of the Underground City, yeah that's you Commander. We've taken control of your energy supply. If you finally find a way to bring your troops up here, we will blow the explosives we've mined the whole field with."

Wearing a colorful feather in his mohawk hair, Abana skillfully jumps off his horse and gestures to an explosive device on the ground, then motions all around him.

I continue on with my very real threat. "We'll begin poisoning your water systems if you delay. And, we'll also start turning off your supply of oxygen unless you meet our demands. Simply, all those who want to leave the Underground City, all the strikers and those who are with them, including the horses, will be allowed to leave immediately. There will be no negotiation."

Abana, who has returned to my side, takes aim with his revolver and shoots out one camera, saying, "Anyone who tries to stop us will suffer the same fate. I repeat, all those who want to leave the Underground City will be allowed to leave immediately."

Flexing my muscled arms with their war-like henna tattoos, I shout, "One more thing: I am the fire horse, I will not back down. And, I, Rejex, I reject you."

Abana adds, "I, Rejex, I reject you, too. And, all your narrow-mindedness. And all your scientific gobbledygook and intolerance."

I continue, "For anyone who's ever felt different or unloved, who's felt like an alien or an outsider *or the target of bullies...* you are not alone."

Together: "We, Rejexes, we reject you, Big Bully Brother!"

I sense, somewhere deep in the bowels of his own darkness, that the Commander is shaking with fury. And, he should be!

"Sir, we can use the personnel lifts in the other domes to send our army up, one by one. It will take a long time but we can do it." Then, X-33 gets an urgent message that dings and flashes. He reads it and his head drops. "Uh, sir, some of our own soldiers have just gone on strike on the northern frontier."

The Commander growls with venom, "Now is the winter of our discontent..." He calms himself and turns to his subordinate. "They have us, X-33! And, if they destroy our new mining pits, it would take years to recover."

"So, what should we do, sir?"

The Commander grabs a microphone and turns on access to the whole of the Underground City. "Citizens of Mainlandia, greetings. We have found a happy solution to our present challenges. But, we must act quickly. All citizens who wish to leave our beloved City are free to do so. Use the emergency personnel lifts to the Basin uptop. After that, you are on your own to deal with the cold and harshness uptop. For those who wish to stay, trust me, we will keep Mainlandia secure and moving forward, always forward—for a better Mainlandia, for an endless enduring dream and a thousand points of light."

He flips the comm device off. X-33 motions to Zine, who's passed out and bloodied with his face hanging down. "What shall we do about him, Sir?"

"Wake him up, see what else you can get out of him, then get rid of him!" With that, he dismisses his subordinate and stews, eyes glowing fiery red under his hood, murmuring, "Who is SHE?"

Several hours later, Mainlandian citizens are emerging one-by-one from the emergency lifts. It's a slow process, but people keep appearing on the Basin's ground, looking up to the sky for the first time perhaps in their lives.

Abana and I await them, happily perched on our horses, shouting, "Kiss the Sky!"

And, the people respond in kind, even the rebellious soldiers who've decided to be part of the Change. They're all directed forward into the jungle by Nonamé's people, stepping into their new lives.

Down below, the Commander has removed the giant, milky-eyed being in the cryo tank.

He tries to massage life back into his body, as the titan sits propped up in the Commander's swivel chair. The revived creature tries to mumble something but his tongue isn't quite working.

"Shusssh, my son, don't push it. This will take some time. But, there is no rush."

Then, the titan backs off, scared by the solitary light that's shining on him. The Commander covers it. He gently presents, then puts a pair of special shades onto his new friend, shielding his eyes. "The future's so bright, you'd better wear shades, Dar!"

Then, he gestures to a nearby screen. The titan looks over and sees a lab, way down just below the mines, a lab full of many cryo tanks in a row. Inside each tank floats another being, connected to pipes and tubes. Tank upon tank. Row upon row.

"Yes, the Darkness may be temporarily here, but the future's so bright!" And, the Commander's half-hidden face now creases into a wicked smile. Oh, yeah!

Uptop, night is laying down its darkness, but citizens are still emerging, although in smaller numbers now.

Out of nowhere, Zen appears on his motorized vehicle that sputters in the blowing sands. Wrapped around his neck is Bonzo, the chimp, all dressed up in his Einstein get-up and goggles and cutelycarrying his own overnight bag. Abana and I dismount and run to them. But, before we reach them, Zen slowly gets up from his vehicle and takes a couple of steps. As if on cue, Bonzo cackles and points to Zen.

"You can walk?"

"I haven't walked much in a long while, but it was always an affect Zine and I put on. Something to make them think of us totally buying into their science is god premise—why look up to the sky or even walk when we have technology to do it for us!"

"Where is Zine—coming?"

"You haven't seen him?" Off our concerned shrugs. For a second, doubt crosses Zen's face. "No, no, we shouldn't worry, he'll be here." He tries to cover up his concern by motioning behind him. "But, I did bring some new friends."

Along with Bonzo, Trix and her Thal appear holding hands.

"Welcome to the Change, One-6," says Alkima as he approaches with his arms open.

"Zen now calls me Trix. Thank you for accepting me." She looks up to the strangely darkening sky, breathes in real air, and throws her arms skyward.

Mystikat appears and is insistent on having Alkima's attention. Our alchemist steps aside to listen to this furry friend—something's up, something always is with those two.

But tired and pleased, Abana and I hug each other and walk on, our horses in tow.

"You and I have to make up for some lost time, little lady," says a drained, but relieved, Abana.

I answer him by kissing him hard and long. Now, perhaps, he is mine.

But, a message on both our handhelds beeps and flashes the words: "Heaven cracked the code!"

"What a smarty pants," we react together almost in sync, then we both high-five.

But, something distracts Abana and catches his eye, something out of the corner of his view. He lets go of me. He looks like he's seen something, maybe something familiar or something dangerous.

"Abana, what is it?" I shout but he doesn't answer. So, I look to where he's gazing, at a frail creature with close-cropped hair and very pale skin, who walks almost ghost-like. But, the astonishment and then concern in Abana's eyes strikes me like a serrated arrow to the very center of my heart. But, it can't be her, she's been lost at sea.

In this, our time of triumph, in my own moment of exaltation when I've become one with the fire horse of my dreams, I feel my mouth go dry and my once flying spirit sag.

Abana shouts to the frail creature, "Azi? Is that you?" The haggard girl turns to him. And, I see his eyes brighten.

"This cannot be happening," I grumble, as I desperately want to put on darkened goggles to blind me from seeing what I think I'm seeing.

But, something else interrupts us. In fact, it stops us all in our tracks, and everyone else around us, and everyone still remaining in the Underground City.

A huge tremblor rumbles into our lives, not a little one, but maybe the "Big One" coming from the far West again.

I immediately squeeze the trinket that Ma-Tu had given me when we said our goodbyes. I immediately think of her now, and I'm sure she's thinking of me.

And sure enough, they also feel the tremblor coming over in Geto. They're prepared, but are still concerned, especially for their missing friends.

Ma-Tu and Aiya, she and I, that strongest of bonds, mother and daughter—our hearts connected and thumping in sync over the miles in between, as we both shout out: "Ma-Tu, momma!" and "M-petite!"

But, everyone and everything everywhere, including the shadow of "big bully brother" in the Underground City, comes to a standstill. Even Alkima stops. With Mystikat on his shoulder, they both turn and look far to the horizon. I don't hear Alkima whisper to his cohort, "Yes, my friend, the end is often just the beginning."

As for me, all I can sense is my own hurt feelings and the added thought, Be very afraid—because, sometimes, paradise and hell, hopes and fears all become one. And, I so want to scream, "Welcome to my living nightmare!"

Acknowledgments

For all the Davids who battle their Goliaths, like my Middle Kingdom legend of Min whose personal emblem was a fighting cock with "Spurs" on its feet. And, for echoes of glory and doing things in style.

Thanks to Pulp Hero Press publisher Bob McLain, and to Gary Burak for your visual covers and online brilliance and friendship. Thanks also to Armen Orujyan, Tanis Deuter, Adam Cude, Zane Levitt, Alex Volpi, April McGinnis and Lorelei Brewer for your support. To my loving famliy. And, to the genius that is *The Twilight Zone*'s Rod Scrling, for inviting us into the "dimension of imagination."

One more thing: We are all REJEX, and we are not alone!

About the Author

Ashley Jude Collie has written and lived in different continents and cities, so he's adapted to being an outsider in new environments. From *HuffPost*, *Playboy*, *Washington Post*, and *LA Times*, to *Sports Illustrated* and *Movie Entertainment*, he's an internationally published and award-winning journalist, and an avid blogger. He's appeared on CNN, and written for episodic television. And, to paraphrase the Bard, Ashley will undoubtedly "write till his ink be dry."

Reviews

I loved the gong-banging nut-crackers out of it! REJEX is right up there with the best of young adult novels today, The Hunger Games, Harry Potter. Why? REJEX is a delightful tale of page-turning heroism and adventure, where the forces of light that have been rejected crash up against the forces of darkness that have been accepted as the norm, and where the magical, raw, powerful strength of metaphysics and myth meet the technological, crushing, iron hand of science and logic. Ashley Jude Collie pulls you into his gorgeously drawn world slowly and smoothly, and then you find yourself flying through the pages as fast as possible, eager to know what happens next. With the humor of Tolkien, and Card's feeling of methodical, well-thought-out planning, REJEX has all the flavor and joviality of The Hobbit and the serious, surprisingly cunning twists of Ender's Game. As much as it is a comment on today's society and its pitfalls, Ashley's mental child also brings a message of hope: that nothing is impossible; there is good in everything, even that which may at first seem horrible! REJEX will be irresistible to those who love sci-fi and Ray Bradbury's works of mental playgrounds, as well as those previously mentioned. Could not put it down!

—Lorelei Brewer, young adult reader

Right from the Prolog, REJEX had me hooked! You paint such a beautiful setting which displays the polarized nature of this society, much like our own, right from the get-go. And, I'm entranced by the Great Darkness…such ominous foreshadowing! I think this series is going to have a very wide demographic appeal! There's something in it for everyone.

—Alana Smithy, adult reader

Made in the USA
San Bernardino, CA
27 May 2019